SAVING PARKER

A FOREVER HOME SERIES NOVEL - BOOK 3

DAN WALSH

BAINBRIDGE PRESS

Praise for Dan's Forever Home Series Novels

"*Anyone familiar with Walsh's books knows he writes great stories with memorable characters, and Rescuing Finley is no exception...* I've read several books recently that feature a dog as a main character, but this one is by far the most realistic I have come across." – **RT Reviews Magazine**

"*Walsh knows how to shred readers' heartstrings in a good way. In Walsh tradition–the ending of this book is multi-faceted. What appears as a relationship of forgone conclusion is ramped up to a nerve-tweaking, breath-catching, standing ovation ending this author has perfected. With my final gasp, I began ordering extra copies for family, friends, and veterans.*" – **Harold Wolf (Top 50 Amazon Reviewer)**

Saving Parker
Copyright © 2018 Dan Walsh
ISBN: 978-0-9979837-2-2

1

What was going on? All this yelling and banging. Strangers running across the yard. Cars making loud noises and lights flashing. Parker ran and hid as far back in the shed as he could. It was a dark crawl-space under a roof made of rusty sheet metal perched above a wall of old tires. He wanted no part of whatever was going on out there. He curled up in a tight ball and lay there, trembling.

Not all his tension came from the strange goings-on. Some came from restraining himself from doing the one thing he wanted to do most. To bark at the top of his lungs at these invaders who'd come onto their property. Four men all dressed alike. What were they doing here? They had no right. As soon as they'd arrived, he could tell they weren't here on friendly terms.

But Parker didn't bark. He didn't dare make a sound.

His mouth still stung from a kick he'd gotten that morning. The Man hated it whenever Parker barked. Felt like The Man hated everything Parker did. There was no pleasing him, no matter how hard Parker tried. Barking was clearly the worst thing. But how could Parker stop doing something so essential to his main purpose? He existed to serve and protect...this property...this owner. Even if the effort was unappreciated. The need to bark came from deep within, beyond his reach.

Another loud bang. More yelling.

"Come out, Alfredo. Do it, now. Hands over your head where we can see them."

Another voice. "If we have to come in there, we *will* shoot you."

"Don't shoot. I'm coming out. Geez, what's wrong with you people? I didn't do nothing. I don't even have a gun in here."

Parker didn't understand most of what was just said, but he understood *Alfredo*. That's what people called The Man. And he recognized The Man's voice. But this was the first time Parker had ever sensed fear in his voice. What was going on? Who were these people? Why were they yelling at The Man?

"That's right, Alfredo. Keep walking. Hands up. Walk straight to me. A few more steps. Stop right there. Now get on the ground, face first. Arms and legs spread out. That's right. Just like that."

"Calm down, Man. You don't need to point your gun at me. I'm cooperating."

More noises. Feet shuffling in the dirt. Clicking metal. Then The Man yelled out in pain. "C'mon, man. You're hurting me. Get your knee outta my back." Grunting and groaning. "Geez, would you get off me?"

"We're almost done. All right, on your feet. You got anything in your pockets? Any weapons? Anything sharp, like a knife or needle?"

"No, man. My pockets are empty. See for yourself."

"I will."

Parker was starting to cook in his stuffy hiding spot. It was hot everywhere in Florida these days, but back here it was stifling. No breeze. Just nonstop humidity and the glaring afternoon sun beating down on the metal roof. He started to pant. He had to get some water. But where? The metal bowl was empty. Had been all day. Yesterday, his last three gulps were disgusting. Warm, stale, debris floating on the surface, dirt on the bottom, almost undrinkable.

He hadn't eaten anything today, either. Or yesterday.

"You guys are making a mistake. I'm tellin' you. You got the wrong house."

"I don't think so. You sold two bottles of fentanyl to an undercover officer yesterday. I'm sure the guys searching the house will find plenty more."

"Where is this officer? I don't see him. I'm telling you, you picked the wrong house."

"Uh...no, we didn't. We got you on video doing the deal. Listen Alfredo, we read you your rights. I suggest you exercise your right to silence and shut up."

A car door opened.

"Get in."

The door closed. He listened some more. He didn't hear The Man anymore. Were they leaving? Were they taking him somewhere?

Officer Ned Barringer of the Summerville PD felt relieved, the suspect now safely situated in Jeb Hodgins patrol car. "That went way easier than I expected." During the briefing that morning, they'd been warned the suspect should be considered armed and dangerous.

"Yeah," Jeb said, "he didn't even try to put up a fight. I watched the video from yesterday, so I was expecting a very bad dude. This guy's a marshmallow. You see the fear in his eyes when you put those cuffs on? He's acting like he's never been arrested before."

"Maybe he hasn't," Ned said. "or maybe he's been watching the news and heard about the string of fentanyl ODs this past month. He knows those deaths can be tied to what he's selling in that house. You know of any other houses selling this stuff around here?"

Jeb shook his head.

"Me, either." Ned looked the house and property over, from one side to the other. It was an older neighborhood, many of the homes needed serious repair, but this one was in a league by itself. "What a dump. I can't understand how anyone can live like this."

"Yeah, I was glad to get out of there." Jeb pointed to the front door. "Smells like something died in there. You go into the kitchen?"

Ned nodded. "About gagged me. Alfredo's a pig."

"That's something I don't get. Doesn't his nose work? How's he put up with it every day? He's been making a fortune selling this stuff. Why doesn't he hire someone to keep the place up?"

"I know," Ned said. He looked at the front door. "You watch him a minute? I want to talk to the guys inside, see how they're making out."

"Sure," Jeb said. "It'll give me time for a smoke."

Ned headed across the weed-filled front yard. Just as he reached the cement slab by the doorway, the door opened. Out walked Detective Jason Strand, a big smile on his face, holding up a large baggie filled with bluish-gray pills. "Is that it?" Ned asked.

"The mother lode," Strand said. "And these are an exact match to the ones we nabbed yesterday in the undercover operation. I'm 99% sure they're going to match up with the overdoses we've been having lately." Strand put the bag of pills into a larger evidence bag.

"So, you guys done in here?"

"We are. For now." He started walking toward his car. "This should be enough to shut this guy down for good. He'll be going away for a long time."

"Good."

"My partner should be right behind me."

"I'll wait and lock up," Ned said. "Then we'll get this guy downtown and booked."

STILL TUCKED deep inside his cubbyhole, Parker sat up and listened. He could hear two men talking in the front, but neither was The Man. He hadn't heard his voice for several minutes. Was it safe to come out? How would these strangers treat him? He barely understood a single word, but their tones still didn't sound friendly. What if he came out and they treated him as badly as The Man did, or worse?

He was so hot and so thirsty, but an overpowering fear held him in place. He'd better just wait until he was absolutely sure the coast was clear.

Hopefully, it wouldn't be too much longer.

2

"Wait! Don't leave yet!"

Ned looked up, searching for the woman behind the screaming voice. He saw her trotting across the street, waving at him furiously. She looked to be in her fifties, way-too-bright red hair.

"You taking that man away? That drug dealer?"

"Yes, we are."

"Finally. But you gonna let him out again like last time?"

"Nope. Not this time. There's a good chance he won't ever be back."

"Good, I'm glad. But if that's the case, you can't leave yet."

"Why not?"

She looked over at Alfredo sitting in the backseat of Jeb's patrol car. "Can he hear me?"

Ned wanted to say the people three streets over could probably hear her. "I don't know. Why don't you come over here to my car and talk a little quieter, just to be safe?"

She did.

"So, why can't we leave just yet?"

"Because someone's got to do something about the dog."

"What dog?"

"The little dog." She looked toward the left side of the house. "See that old rickety shed in the back, surrounded by all that crap? I think he's in there. I haven't seen him all day, but that's usually where he hides."

"There's no fence back there," Ned said. "How do you know he hasn't run off?"

"I wish he could run away. He'd be better off anywhere else than here. The way that man treats him is a crime. But the poor thing's always chained up. If you go back there, you'll see what I mean."

Ned tried to see where she was pointing. The backyard looked more like a junkyard. No lawn at all. Trash and garbage everywhere. Besides that, this was the hottest part of the day and that shed had a metal roof. "I don't understand how an animal could even survive in there. It must be over a hundred degrees."

"I know. Isn't it awful? He never lets him inside, whether it's boiling out or freezing in the winter. You should see the poor thing. His hair's all full of mats. His coat's a mess. I'm sure he's probably got a ton of fleas, and who knows what else. I've wanted to say something a thousand times, but he's such an angry little man. And you know how drug dealers are. See 'em all the time on TV shows. I was afraid he might shoot me."

"Have you ever tried calling Animal Control? You can do it anonymously, I think."

"I've thought about doing that a thousand times, too. But I was afraid he'd still know it was me. He caught me one time trying to give the dog some water, and you should-a heard the tirade of profanities he threw at me. He ran at me and literally chased me off his lawn."

What a coward, Ned thought. "Well, he won't be bothering you anymore. Let me talk to my partner a sec, and I'll go take a look. Can you stay for a minute? It might go better if the dog sees someone he knows."

"I don't mind staying if you're here. But I'm not sure it's going to make a difference, me being here or not. It's not like he knows me. I'm not sure I've ever even got to pet the little guy."

"Well, wait here. I'll be right back." Ned headed over to Jeb's patrol car. He was leaning on the hood, writing something. "Hey Jeb, you think you can take Alfredo in without me? Looks like I've got another situation to handle here."

"Sure. What's up?"

Ned talked a little softer. "See that redhead over there? Looks like ole Alfredo here's a dog abuser, besides everything else. She said he keeps it locked up on a chain in a shed behind the house. I'm going to take a look, maybe get Animal Control involved."

"Sure thing, Ned. But don't get too close to it. A dog abuser's usually a dog neglecter, too. Probably hasn't had any shots in a while."

"I'll be careful." Ned headed back to the redhead, who was now walking toward the backyard.

She stopped to allow him to catch up. Ned reached out his hand. "I'm Officer Ned Barringer, by the way. What's your name?"

She shook it. "My name's Betty. Do I have to give you my full name?"

Ned laughed. Sometimes people were so overly cautious

with cops. "No, not if you don't want to. But I was hoping you might be willing to talk to the Animal Control Officer when she gets here. Since you've been observing the situation for some time. If things are as bad as you say, they might want to add animal cruelty to the list of Alfredo's crimes."

"Will I have to testify in court?"

"I don't know. Probably not. But really, you don't have to be afraid of this guy anymore. With the amount of drugs we just seized from that house, he's looking at least twenty-to-life. And we've had three overdose deaths in the last month. Pretty sure those deaths will connect back to this house."

"Oh, my. Well, thanks for explaining that, Officer. I feel better now. My name's Betty Crocker, by the way. And before you say another thing, I'm not joking. That's my real name. But I'm a terrible cook. That's another reason I didn't want to give it out. Once people hear it, they never forget it."

"Well, Betty, let's go take a look at this little dog. You know his name?"

They started walking toward the shed. "His name's Parker. I don't think he even had a name before the little boy came. Except maybe *stupid dog*. The little boy's the one called him Parker. Not sure why."

"Little boy?"

"Yeah. About six months ago, there was a young woman living here with Alfredo. She had a son. I forget his name, but he really loved that dog. You're not gonna believe what Parker looks like now, compared to what he looked like back then. Back when the little boy looked after him. He was the cutest thing."

"What happened to them?"

"Toward the end, I could hear yelling and screaming

almost every night. It went on for weeks. Then one night, I was looking out my window, and I watched Alfredo drive off. A few minutes later, I saw the woman hurrying her son into their car, carrying a suitcase. I opened my window a crack. He was begging her to let them take Parker with them. She said she wanted to, but he wasn't their dog, and she was afraid Alfredo would come after them if they took him. The boy started crying. They drove off, and I haven't seen them since."

PARKER'S EARS perked right up. Shortly after a car had driven off, two people started walking this way. He heard a man and a woman's voice. He didn't recognize either one, but their tone wasn't angry or unpleasant. The most surprising thing was, he was almost certain he heard the woman say his name. Only the boy ever called him that. It was the only thing the woman said that he did understand.

Slowly, he started to get up and crawl forward toward the opening. He wanted to see who they were, see if he could tell what kind of people they were. Maybe they were nice. Maybe they would get him something to drink. He felt so thirsty. He barely had the strength to keep moving forward, but he forced himself to keep going.

He had to see who they were.

3

Remembering Jeb's warning about the dog not being up on his shots, Ned approached the old shed with extreme caution.

"I don't think he bites," Betty said, coming up behind him. "He's mostly pretty skittish and shy. If he's out of that shed and people walk by, he doesn't bark or growl. Mostly, he runs and hides."

"That may be," Ned said. "But how many of them have gotten this close, and gotten in his space?"

"That's a good point. People mostly just keep walking on by. But still, I think he's harmless for the most part."

"Well, I saw a training video about what people go through if they've been bitten by a dog with rabies. I'm not taking any chances."

"Fine by me," Betty said.

Ned approached slowly, keeping his body sideways as he came closer. He'd been told this was less threatening body language for a dog. When he heard some movement, he stopped. But so did the dog. "Parker," he said in a calm voice. "Are you in there, boy?" He took a few more steps forward. "Parker? Here boy."

There was no response. Not even a sound. He saw the chain now, leading from a metal stake into this little dark hole behind some tires. When he got still closer, Ned noticed an empty, metal bowl off to the right. He got angry. It was the hottest part of the day. "Poor dog."

"It's so filthy," Betty said.

He also noticed the foul odor coming from the shed. The whole back area smelled bad, but it was especially strong here. "Let's try a different approach." He picked up the metal bowl and backed away from the opening. Looking toward Betty, he said, "How about I clean this up and fill it with fresh water? Would you have a snack of any kind?"

"You mean, like a dog biscuit?"

"Yeah, or anything would do. Especially if it had some meat or cheese. Like a hot dog. Have any hot dogs?"

"I think maybe I do. Want me to go cut up one?"

"That would be great. Do you mind?"

"Not at all. I'll be right back." Betty hurried across the yard toward her house.

Ned brought the metal bowl over to the front corner of the house where he'd seen a garden hose rolled up by some bushes. After turning the hose on, he let the water run a minute or two to let all the hot water out. Then, looking at the condition of the hose, he decided to turn it off and unscrew it from the faucet. It was probably filled with a thousand different kinds of bacteria. He rinsed the bowl out and cleaned it with his hand as best he could. Then carefully walked the bowl of fresh water back to the opening in the shed and set it down. Betty was heading back this way, smiling, holding a little baggie.

"I got them. All I had was chicken dogs, which taste terrible, you ask me."

"I don't think a dog'll mind," Ned said. "Can you hand me a few pieces?" She did.

"Parker? Hey, boy. Look what we've got here? Water? You thirsty? Here's some water?" Ned swished his fingers around in the bowl, making some noise. "And food. Are you hungry? Want something to eat?" He rolled a piece of hot dog into the dark opening. He had no idea how far back it went.

Betty crouched down beside him. "Here Parker. You can come out now, boy. It's totally safe. Come and get something to drink." She looked at Ned. "Try throwing in another piece."

He did. Then they waited, listening for any sounds.

Parker was torn.

This man and woman were talking so nice. Nicer than anyone had in such a long time. But how could he know for sure they were safe? They came closer, then went away, and now they were back. Then Parker heard a word he recognized.

Water.

Then the sound of water swishing around. A moment later, something came rolling toward him. What was it? He sniffed the air until he picked up its scent. He wasn't sure. Some kind of food. Was it meat? At this point, he would eat anything. But he was even more interested in the water. Then something else rolled toward him. Another piece of the same kind of food. They called his name several times and always sounded friendly.

He decided to take a chance. Crawling slowly forward, he gobbled up the two pieces of food. Meat. Or something close. They tasted *so* good. He continued a few more steps, now aware of the sharp pain in his back leg. A memory flash. The Man throwing a can at him, half-full, yelling for him to shut up.

"I HEAR MOVEMENT," Ned said. "Sounds like he's coming this way."

"Throw in another piece of hot dog," Betty said.

Ned did, only this time not as far. Then he tossed another one an even shorter distance. "Come on, boy. It's okay. We won't hurt you." He swished his fingers around in the water again. This time, he tossed some drops into the opening. That seemed to do the trick. The dog was coming closer, though they still couldn't see him yet. Ned tossed some more water drops in his direction.

Parker came close enough to see his front paws and head. Ned could hardly believe what he was seeing. You could make out his mouth and nose but the hair on the top of his head and around his ears was covered with mats. One eye was almost closed due to some infection. And the hair on the middle part of his left leg was almost completely gone.

He stopped moving. Ned could see, he was trembling.

"Look at the poor thing," Betty said. "I hardly recognize him. What has he done to you, boy?"

"Let's try this." Ned lifted the water bowl up and carefully placed it as far into the opening as he could. Immediately, Parker got up and began to drink.

And drink, and drink, and drink.

Parker coughed and choked a little and stopped. Sadly, now Ned could tell where the smell came from. It was the dog. Ned slowly reached for the bag of hot dog pieces. As soon as he put them down, Parker gobbled them up and backed away. "Did you see his back leg?" Ned asked. "He's limping." When he drank, they had been able to see one side of his coat. Like the front paw, much of the hair was missing. And he had little scabs all over his skin. "This dog's in bad shape."

"He really is," Betty said. "That Alfredo's a real devil. Why would anyone ever treat an innocent animal like this? I can't believe the condition Parker's in. You should've seen him back when the little boy was here. I'm telling you, he was a gorgeous little dog. And so happy. It's like I'm looking at a totally different dog now."

"Well, there's no doubt," Ned said. "This is one of the worst cases of animal cruelty I've seen. I'm definitely calling Animal Control."

Betty's expression changed. "What do you think they'll do to him? I mean, the dog."

"Do to him? I suppose they'll rescue him from this horrible life. Bring him to a shelter where they can fix him up, maybe get him adopted in a good home."

The look on Betty's face became more serious. "You don't how these things work, do you? I've done some volunteering down at the Humane Society. That's probably the shelter where they'd bring him. A dog like this, that looks like this? Don't get me wrong, there's some wonderful people down there working hard to try to find dogs new homes. But these situations don't always have happy endings."

"What do you mean?"

"For one thing, they can't find homes for all the dogs that

come in. There's just too many of them. And they don't have
unlimited space or resources. One of the staff people
explained it to me. They always do their best, but some of the
dogs don't make it."

"You mean they get put down?"

Betty nodded. "Sometimes. They do everything they can to
avoid it, but sometimes they have no choice. It breaks their
heart when it happens. The lady who explained it to me got all
teary as she talked. I did, too. But I'm telling you...they bring
Parker down there looking like this? There's a chance he won't
make it. A pretty good one, I'd say."

Ned was a cop. He knew how the world worked. Sometimes life wasn't fair. Sometimes it was even cruel. But he just
couldn't see this poor little dog—after all these months of
being bullied and abused by this jerk—being brought down to
a shelter all alone, just to be put to sleep. It struck a chord
deep inside. "We've got to do something. Because I'm not okay
with that."

"Me either," Betty said. "But what can we do?" The look on
her face changed again. She was smiling. "I just got an idea.
Don't call that Animal Control Officer yet. Wait here with
Parker. I'll be right back."

Ned watched as she all-but-ran across the street toward
her house.

4

As Ned waited for Betty to return, he got down a little lower on the ground, put several hot dog pieces in his hand and slowly extended it toward Parker. "Are you hungry, boy?" he said softly.

Still tucked far back in the cubbyhole, Parker lifted his head and looked at Ned, then at what was in his hand. He did this several times, his nose twitching all the while. But he didn't move.

"I'm not going to hurt you, buddy. I promise. We're here to make everything all better. We're going to get you out of here, get you all cleaned up and put back together." Parker just stared at him, cocked his head once as if trying to comprehend.

"I get why you're afraid of people. After what you've been through, I would be, too. I'll just leave these here. You can eat them when you're ready." He dumped the hot dog pieces on the pavement, pulled his arm back to give the dog some space.

Ned heard something over his shoulder and turned in time

to see Betty trotting across the street toward him. She held
something in her hand, looked like a postcard.

"It took me a few minutes to find it, but here it is." She held
the card up as she stepped onto the sidewalk, then headed
right toward him. "You're not going to believe this, when you
see it."

Ned quietly backed away from the opening. She handed
him what he clearly now saw to be a photograph. He instantly
recognized the place; very close to where they were standing.
In the center was a nice-looking, mixed-breed dog of medium-
size, standing on a concrete slab. He was chained and looked
forward with a concerned expression. His coat was brown and
tan. "Wait, is this—"

"Parker?" Betty said. "Yes. That's what he used to look like,
back when the little boy took care of him."

Ned looked back at the pitiful creature, as much as he
could see, then at the picture. Back and forth, several times. "I
would never have guessed this is the same dog."

"Makes a very good argument for animal cruelty, doesn't it?
All by itself."

"It certainly does. The dog in this picture, other than
looking a little worried, is really cute."

"Cute? He's adorable."

"Okay," Ned said, "adorable. The point is..." He held up the
picture. "I could easily see this dog being someone's best
friend." Ned bent down and looked at Parker again. "How
could someone treat this dog so bad that in a few months' time
he winds up looking like that? I definitely think we can use
this as evidence against Alfredo. It's even date-stamped. Do
you mind if I ask, why did you take this picture? It seems like

you were pretty nervous being anywhere near the dog, because of how Alfredo acted."

"Oh, I definitely was afraid. I took it one day after I'd seen him drive off. It was just after the mom and little boy left. My sister had been talking about wanting a dog, so I thought maybe she might like to adopt Parker. So, I ran over here and took this pic, so she could see what he looked like. I was thinking, if she wanted him, I'd work up the nerve to talk to Alfredo about it."

"I'm guessing she didn't want him, or did Alfredo turn you down?"

"She thought he was cute but, it turned out, I misunderstood her. She wasn't saying she was actively looking for a dog. Just that she wanted one. The apartment she was living at didn't even allow them. So, nothing came of it. But then, when you and I were talking about what might happen to Parker if he got taken to the shelter, I remembered it. I wasn't really thinking so much about it being evidence against Alfredo. I was thinking you could show it to that Animal Control Officer, so she'd be able to see the kind of dog he really is, underneath all that...mess."

"I think that's a good idea. I will show it to her. And maybe get it to the folks at the Humane Society, so they can see what kind of dog Parker really is, too. Or at least, could be. Maybe then, they'll be willing to invest the time to patch him up."

"That gives me an idea," Betty said. "I'll be right back."

"Where are you going?"

"To get my phone. We need to get some footage of Parker in this condition, and in this place. To help with the case against Alfredo. Once he gets all cleaned up at the shelter, who will believe he was as bad off as what we're seeing now?"

"Not a bad idea."

She came back with the phone and did her best to document the scene. Parker seemed alarmed at first when she bent down to film him, but she didn't get too close. After, she stood up. "There. That should be enough. I'll save this video. You let me know if you need it for the case."

THIRTY MINUTES HAD PASSED. Ned had said goodbye to Betty, thanked her for making him aware of Parker's situation. He checked in with Jeb at the station, filled him in and let him know he'd decided to wait for the Animal Control Officer. Then Ned called her.

The ACO was named Hannah Scanlon. Ned had worked with her on a few other cases that involved dogs. She seemed to really know her stuff. While he waited, he tried several more times to engage Parker, but it was pretty clear: Parker was fine keeping things as they were. He did find the courage to eat the rest of the hot dog bits. But that was the extent of their interaction. Ned felt so sorry for the little guy. He had never seen a dog this bad off and wondered if Hannah would find it shocking, too. Or maybe she saw things like this every day.

He heard her truck pull up and tucked the photo in his shirt pocket. "Here comes the cavalry, Parker. We're going to get you out of here." He stood to greet her. "Hi, Hannah. Don't know if you remember me. Ned Barringer, the officer who called this in."

"I do remember you, Ned. Nice to see you again. Sad it's always for something like this." She bent down to look at Parker. "So, what can you tell me about the situation?"

Ned took a few minutes to fill her in, then added, "He had

a nice long drink about thirty-five minutes ago. My guess is, it was the first time he drank anything in days. The neighbor across the street cut up a hotdog for him. I've been feeding it to him in pieces, talking real sweet and kind as I did, hoping he might trust me a little and come out of that hole. He hasn't come any further than what you see there, but he hasn't backed away from me, either."

"He's just scared, Ned. It isn't you. You can tell just by looking at the condition he's in, and this place...this is a seriously abused and neglected animal. I suspect it would take quite a bit of time and a lot of TLC for him to ever start trusting people again."

"Will the people at the shelter give a dog like this enough time? I've been told sometimes they put dogs to sleep, when they don't have any choice. What are the chances of that happening to a dog like Parker?"

She looked down at Parker again. "Hard to say. He's in pretty bad shape, but I've seen worse. But look, I'll take him in, see what they can do. They'll clean him up, probably shave off his coat, tend to his wounds. They'll even do a pretty thorough medical assessment. If he's not aggressive and none of his wounds are life threatening, and if he doesn't have any terminal disease, he could still make it." Ned hated hearing her talk like this. Way too many "ifs." He pulled Parker's picture out of his shirt pocket and handed it to her.

"Who's this?"

"That's Parker," Ned said. "That's him. Look at the date stamp. That's like, five months ago."

"Wow, what a difference. This is a beautiful dog."

"I know, right? That's what he could look like, should look like, if this drug-dealing jerk hadn't treated him so bad. Don't you think he could be fixed up? You know, maybe over time, little by little? Have you ever seen a dog in this condition ever bought back to the way he was before?"

Hannah looked at the picture again, then back at Parker. "It's possible. I've seen some tear-jerking videos on YouTube and some other dog sites where dogs who looked like this, some even worse, were brought back around to become someone's amazing companion. Like I said, it would take a lot of time and he'd have to pass those assessments I mentioned. Even with that, there still could be some challenges."

"Like what?" Ned said.

"I've just come from dropping another dog off at the shelter. They're completely full. No kennels left, for big or small dogs. When that happens, they have to prioritize the animals more."

"Prioritize?" Ned said. "What about foster care? Why do all the dogs have to be housed at the shelter? Don't they have volunteers who can take some of them home temporarily? Just till they heal up?"

"They do...have some. But not nearly enough to meet the demand. Especially in the summer. I don't know why, but a lot more people turn in their pets during the summer months. But even with that, if they had enough people doing foster care, it would change everything. It would certainly make a difference with a dog like Parker here." She looked at the picture again. "If he turns out *not* to have aggression issues, and if none of his medical problems are life threatening, a dog like this would be *extremely* adoptable. They'd go out of their way to save him. Especially if someone came forward and volunteered to provide foster care."

5

N o one said anything for a moment. Hannah got a little closer to Parker's little hideout. "Have you ever thought about doing something like that?" she asked.

"Being a foster parent? For a dog?" Ned thought about it a moment. "Can't say I have. I'm not even sure, with my schedule, if I'd qualify. But I know I don't want this dog to be put down."

"Then maybe you should look into it. Can't hurt to find out. I know they train folks who want to do this right there at the Humane Society. You should check it out. Doesn't cost anything."

Ned wanted to change the subject. "So, is that where you're bringing him now?"

"I will be very soon. Got one more stop to make after this."

"So how are you going to get him out? I notice you don't have that stick with the loop on the end."

"You mean my catch pole? I've got it in the truck, but I

don't think I'll need it here. For one thing, he's on a chain. For another, he doesn't seem even a little aggressive. If anything, he's just the opposite."

"So, how are you going to get him out?"

"With these, and my sweetest voice." She pulled out a little bag and reached inside. A moment later, she had several small, brown dog biscuits in her hand.

"Dog biscuits? I don't know what your biscuits are made of, but he didn't come out for hot dogs."

"Apparently, these..." She held one up. "...Are made from the finest food on earth."

Ned laughed.

"I'm not kidding. These aren't just any dog biscuits. I started using them a few months ago. Kim Harper, the Animal Behavior Manager down at the Humane Society recommended them. Dogs absolutely love them. They're soft and chewy. Here, feel it. Break it in half."

Ned did. Then he smelled it. "Doesn't do anything for me."

"But I guarantee you, Parker will want more of these the moment he tastes one. I'll probably still have to gently pull on his chain, but I'm not expecting any big deal here. Do you mind stepping back a little?"

"Sure." Ned gave her lots of room.

Hannah got even closer to the opening. "Hey Parker," she said in an almost cartoonish-sounding sweet voice. "You're such a good boy. Are you hungry? Want a treat? A treat? Here...try this." She broke the dog biscuit in half and tossed it to him.

Ned bent down to get a better look.

Parker's nose instantly reacted to the treat. Then he turned his head and began to crawl toward it. He quickly ate it then seemed to perk right up.

"Want another one? Here." She tossed the other half, but not as far, which required him to move closer to the opening. He did, eagerly.

"They're good, aren't they? Want more?" She broke another biscuit in half and tossed it a foot closer than the last one. This time he hesitated. She backed away to give him more space. "It's okay. Eat it. It's good."

Parker looked at the treat, then at Hannah, then up at Ned, then back at the treat. He crawled forward and gobbled it up.

"His tail wagged," Hannah said. "Did you see it?"

"No," Ned said. "But you're right about those biscuits. Whatever they're made of, he can't get enough of them. I wonder what they taste like on the grill."

Hannah laughed. Parker was within three feet of the opening now. She set a whole biscuit halfway between them. The dog hesitated a few moments but then quickly crawled toward the treat and ate it. "That's a good boy. Good boy, Parker. They're good, aren't they?"

"That's amazing," Ned said. "He's almost there."

"I'm going to try a little trick Kim taught me," Hannah said. She held the next biscuit out at arms' length but low to the ground and looked away. "This lets him know I mean him no harm." Parker looked at it then at her, as if sizing up the risks.

A few moments later, he moved forward slowly and took the treat, nibbling on the end of it at first, then biting bigger pieces. As he did, she whispered, "Good boy," in a soothing tone and actually scratched under his chin.

"I can't believe he's letting you touch him," Ned said.

She began gently stroking his back as he ate the rest of the biscuit. He didn't flinch or pull away. "This is a very sweet dog," she said. "You can tell. He doesn't have a mean bone in his body, which is amazing after how he's been treated."

She took out another biscuit. "You still hungry?" His tail wagged a little. "Okay, let's try something new." She let him nibble on one end while she held firmly to the other. With her other hand, she gently picked him up.

Ned was shocked. He just kept right on eating and actually tried holding the treat with his paws.

"Oh, my. The poor thing is skin and bones. He weighs about half of what he should."

"Can I try giving him one of those biscuits?" Ned said.

"Sure." She handed him the bag. "But remember, this dog's been abused by a man. So be calm and pleasant and speak to him in a whisper. And don't make any quick motions."

"Okay."

"No direct eye contact, either" she continued, "and bring your arm from below. Don't come over him. I'm pretty sure the jerk who did this slapped him around pretty good, so he'd be real skittish about a hand coming at him from above."

"Got it." Ned did exactly what she said. When he brought his hand close to Parker's mouth, he lifted his head a little but didn't pull away. He didn't eat the treat, either. He just looked up at Ned, as if trying to sort things out.

"He's not tensing up," Hannah said. "That's a good sign."

THIS MAN SEEMED SAFE, but how could Parker be sure? All the men he could remember had treated him badly. Not just the owner but all the men who had visited the house.

But this man seemed different. This nice woman who'd

just given him these amazing treats and was being so kind to him...clearly, she trusted him. But wasn't this the same man who—just a little while ago—was yelling angrily at The Man? Parker was sure it was. But then, he hadn't talked to Parker that way. Not even once. Even when the other woman was here. He always spoke in a nice voice.

Parker looked at his eyes again. He sensed the man's mood. There was no anger. And that treat in his hand was so delicious. Parker was still hungry, and he hadn't ever tasted anything as good as that treat in the man's hand.

"Go on, Parker," the man said. "You can have it." He was still smiling.

Parker reached for it and pulled it off the man's hand before chewing.

"Try scratching under his chin gently," Hannah said. "But if he growls, pull your hand back. Don't want to overdo it."

Parker continued munching on the soft biscuit. The man moved his hand. He was scratching under Parker's chin. A flash of fear surfaced but then faded. He was being very gentle.

Maybe some men could be nice.

"I THOUGHT that's how he'd react," Hannah said. "This is a really nice dog, Ned. You should really give that idea some thought."

"What? The foster parent thing?"

She nodded. "It doesn't obligate you to keep the dog. You're just taking care of him while he's on the mend. Maybe a few months. Until he gets in a condition that won't scare people off so easily. You obviously care about the dog already, even the way he looks right now. So, you're halfway there."

Ned sighed. "I hear what you're saying. I just don't see how it could work with my schedule. Seems like Parker's going to need a lot of time. I'm no party animal on my off-hours. I usually just stay home. But I work some pretty long shifts. It doesn't seem right to leave him by himself all that time."

"Well, here's another way to look at it. For the last several months he's been left alone pretty much all the time. Even if you're home half the time, that's twice as much care and attention as he's been getting. Besides, you don't have to decide anything now. He's going to be in the infirmary for several weeks at least. Maybe in the meantime, you could go down there and talk to Kim. She's a really nice lady. She won't paint any rose-colored picture. She'll give it to you straight. Do you mind if I take that picture? Certainly wouldn't hurt for them to see what Parker could look like."

"No, here you go." He gave her the pic then patted Parker gently on the head. "Oops, I forgot. Not to bring my hand up over him."

"Well, looks like no harm done. See? He's already warming up to you."

6

I t was the next morning.

Russell's mom came into his room and woke him up like she always did on school days, gently shaking his toes as she called out his name. She didn't stop until he responded in a way that convinced her he really would get out of bed once she left the room.

"I'm up. I'm up. You can let go of my toes."

"I really need you to focus this morning. I might have to drive you to school. Supposed to rain."

Russell liked the sound of that. Not the rain, but the idea being driven to school. If she drove him, he wouldn't have to face Edmund and Harley, two bigger kids who'd been making his life a nightmare the past two weeks.

Why did he always have to be the new kid at school? It happened every time they moved. Why couldn't they move over the summer? Just once. Why did they always move after the school year had begun? He was always the new kid, the unwanted center of attention. Guys like Edmund and Harley wouldn't even know he existed, except for that grand entrance into the classroom, where he'd been introduced to the whole class by the teacher, then everyone watched as she figured out where he should sit.

Why not just paint a big red bull's-eye on his forehead? Or hang a big Kick Me sign on his back?

And why did he have to be born to short parents? To a mom who was five-two and a dad who was five-eight? At least, that's what his mom told Russell. Russell had never actually met the man. But he'd inherited his short genes.

Why couldn't his dad have been six-four, or bigger? Russell would have been one of the bigger guys in class. Would that have been so bad? He wouldn't have used a gift like that to bully anyone, but it would've kept bullies from messing with him. But no, Russell had to be born a runt. Not the smallest kid in class, but definitely in the small-kid bracket. Just the right size for bullies to feel safe giving him a hard time.

The new kid and a runt.

Strike two on the bully checklist.

His bedroom door opened again. "I thought you were getting up."

"I am."

"You need your toes shaken some more?"

Russell laughed. "No." He sat up, stuck his feet on the rug. "I'm up, see?"

"Did you shower last night like I told you?"

"I did."

"Okay, keep moving, Buddy. Really. I can't be late today."

"All right. I will."

He grabbed the clothes he'd picked out last night and headed into the hallway bathroom. Turned on the light, closed the door. Staring back at him in the mirror was Bully Checklist Item Number Three. Why did his mom make him have such a short haircut? Now his stick-out ears were sticking straight out of his head for all to see. They weren't as bad as they used to be several years ago. He'd grown into them some. Enough to where--with a longer hairstyle--they hardly stuck out at all.

Russell wasn't just imagining his ears were part of the problem. Edmund and Harley had actually called him "Monkey Boy" several times already. As he washed the sleep out of his eyes and dried off his face, Russell thought about the boy who sat in front of him, Rick Henshaw. Proof positive that life was unfair. Rick was well on his way to male model good looks. Great hair. Great face. Great smile. Great ears. Perfect height. Everyone liked him, Russell included. What was not to like?

Edmund and Harley wouldn't even think of bothering Rick. He was born into the untouchable bracket. His whole life was already set. He probably had no idea what it was like to wake up dreading the day ahead. He awoke handsome and well-liked and went to bed the same way. Day in and day out.

As usual, Russell's daily dose of morning dread had already greeted him this morning, temporarily postponed by the news his mother was driving him to school. Thereby shooting right past the section of road where Edmund and Harley preferred to taunt him. Of course, they'd have no problem reconnecting with him at other parts of the school day.

A knock on the bathroom door. "I don't hear any noise in there. You fall asleep on the john?"

"No. I'm getting dressed. I come from a long line of quiet dressers."

Mom laughed. "Okay, just keep things moving."

Russell had to stop thinking about Edmund and Harley. That was the worst part of this bullying thing. Not the fear that happened in the moments surrounding the bullying situation. It was all the moments after, when you're trying to get over it, trying not to think about it anymore. And all the moments before the next event, worrying about that. What's gonna happen this time? Will it be worse than the others? How could he make it stop? Why wouldn't they leave him alone?

He wished there was some kind of switch in his head, some way to turn off all this thinking. It never made anything better, only worse. It took the suffering and multiplied it by a factor of ten. These jerks didn't deserve to spend all this time in his head.

He took one last look in the mirror, which did nothing to improve his mood. His ears were still there. It's like they grew bigger, the more he stared at them. Bringing his pajama bottoms out with him, he dropped them in the hamper just inside his bedroom doorway, then made his way into the kitchen.

"There you are," Mom said. "Handsome as ever."

He could always count on his mother's maternal delusions. "Did you buy any milk yesterday? Remember it went bad?"

"Check the fridge. Brand-new half-gallon in there. Guaranteed not to stink. You gonna have your Peanut Butter Cap'n Crunch?"

"As always," he said, carrying the milk to the dinette table.

"Then I want you to eat that banana. At least half. I already cut it. You need something real in your stomach."

His mom was eating some microwave breakfast sandwich. The box promised it was supposed to be healthy, made of egg whites, turkey sausage and a whole-wheat muffin. Last week, when she tried the first one, she went on and on about how good it was. Insisted he take a bite. She was sure he'd want to switch from his Cap'n Crunch. He could tell by the smell, it wasn't going to work out. But he took a bite.

It didn't even taste like food.

"Okay, Kiddo. You ready to get in the car?" She was halfway through her sandwich. Apparently, she wanted to finish it while they drove.

"No. I can bring the banana with me, but not this bowl."

"Okay, finish up. I'm going to check my hair and face one more time."

"You look fine, Mom." She headed down the hall toward her bedroom. Russell gulped down the last several spoonfuls of cereal then lifted the bowl to drink the amazing concoction created when little puffs of peanut butter-flavored cereal soaked in cold milk. When she came back, he stood, rinsed the bowl in the sink, grabbed his banana and backpack, then followed her out the door.

As they made it to the car, they saw a dark wedge of storm clouds rolling in from the west. "Guess the weatherman was right for a change," she said. "Hurry up and get in."

Russell wanted to, but his Mom had accidentally parked way too close to their neighbor's car when she came in from shopping last night. He wasn't about to smack his door into it trying to get in. It was a cop car. Their neighbor drove it home when off duty. Russell stood behind the car. "I can't get in. You parked too close. Why don't you back out and then I'll get in?"

"All right, but move further off to the side."

A bolt of lightning flashed nearby, followed by deep rolling thunder. "That's getting close." She backed out and Russell got in.

"How do you know he didn't park too close to me?"

"Mom, he's a cop. Pretty sure it was you. Must've happened when you came back from shopping last night. But I'm also pretty sure he never saw the infraction."

"Infraction? You and your big words."

"What's the guy's name again?" Russell said. "We met him last week when he was coming up the steps, but I forget."

"I think it's Ted. Or Ed," she said.

"No, I remember," Russell said. "It's Ned. I called him 'Officer' and he said when he's off duty, feel free to call him Ned."

"Seems like a nice guy," she said. "Makes me feels safe living next door to a cop." She started driving out of the apartment parking lot.

Safe, Russell thought. *Wish I felt safe.*

7

Russell made it through his first period at Summerville Middle School without harm. Fortunately, Edmund and Harley weren't in that class. Both attended the class just after lunch. But of course, that wasn't the greatest concern. They always behaved when adults were present. It was the time in between classes, or on the way to and from school that posed the greatest threat.

The storm did roll through the area throwing down lots of lightning and torrential rain. The thunder got so loud on a few occasions some of the girls in class screamed. The lights even flickered on and off a few times. But as quickly as it came, the storm left. By the end of the class, the sun was already making an appearance.

"Your name's Russell, right?"

Russell turned to find a kid about his same height coming up behind him. He recognized him as a boy who sat two rows over in the class they had just finished. "That's right, Russell. What's your name again?"

"Pete. Used to be Petey up till last year. Now that we're in middle school, I'm trying to get people to drop the Y. Pete sounds a little more mature, don't you think?"

"I guess so. Pete, Petey. Yeah, Pete's better." Russell quickly realized just by the nature of this conversation Pete was a nerd. Which was okay, since Russell also considered himself one.

"Made any friends yet?" Pete asked.

"Not too many." The correct answer would have been none.

"That's what I figured. I never see you walking with anyone between classes."

"Well, we just moved here a few weeks ago. Usually takes me a while to connect with people. Kind of a loner." Russell thought about asking Pete why he'd been watching him for a long enough time to be able to form that conclusion but decided against it. Why chase away the first and maybe only chance he'd have to make a friend?

"Is that your way of telling me to leave you alone?"

"What? No, not at all. Just explaining why I haven't connected with anyone else yet. Guess you could say, I am not the gregarious type."

"Gregarious. Fortunately, for you, I know what that means. But I'd say you, me and maybe two other people in that last class would get what you just said."

They walked down a crowded hallway leading toward Russell's locker. It was just up ahead. "I knew you'd know what it means. I could tell by the look in your eyes."

"What did you see in my eyes?"

"Intellect. Some people call it a knowing look. If I didn't see it, I would've used a simpler word or phrase. Like, I'm not much of a people person."

Pete laughed. "I like the way you think. And I'm glad you

think I've got that, what did you call it? *Knowing look.* I guess there's something to that. That's why I approached you. You've got that look, too."

"And the fact that you took the initiative to approach me reveals one way that we're not alike."

"Which is…"

"I may not be the gregarious type, but you are. Otherwise, you would've kept on watching me indefinitely, maybe formed a number of opinions about me, but never bothered to start a conversation."

When they had reached Russell's locker, he stopped walking and opened it. "Your locker near here?"

"Just down the next row." Pete looked at his watch. "I may be more gregarious than you but, let's say, I'm selectively so. I don't initiate conversations with everyone. Or really, anyone. Not unless they have that… knowing look. So let me guess, you like to read."

"I do."

"And you're not very good at sports."

Russell laughed. "I'm not. But I like to think I could be if life had been a little fairer to me."

"You think life is unfair?"

"I know it is."

"I'm not disagreeing with you, but why do you say it?"

"Well, for starters…I never had a Dad. Well, of course I did biologically speaking. But you know what I mean."

"I do."

"So, no male influence available to introduce me to sports and mentor me along the way. But I've got great eye/hand coordination and decent balance. I am pretty good on a skateboard, considering how little time I get to ride it. That makes me think I might have been good at something like baseball or soccer. How about you? You good at sports?"

"No, I'm not."

"No dad, either?"

"No, I do have a dad. But life can be unfair in a variety of ways. My dad is a brilliant computer engineer. But he was lousy at sports. Never played any growing up. And so, it never dawned on him that sports might be something I might like to pursue. Instead, I have a mom who stepped in to fill the gap with piano lessons. So, guess what? I'm already a pretty amazing piano player. I'm sure that's going to come into play with the girls several years from now. Right now? Not so much. Because as you can see, I'm all squishy around the middle, and I already have a double chin."

Russell laughed. "We make quite a pair. But hey, at least your ears don't stick out."

"No, they don't. But I think I'd rather have ears that stuck out and be fit and trim like you."

"Trust me," Russell said. "You wouldn't. Believe me, it's no fun being called Monkey Boy."

"Monkey Boy? Ouch. Who calls you that?"

"My good friends, Edmund and Harley. Don't know their last names yet."

"Ahh," Pete said. "Edmund Jones and Harley Bolger."

"You know them? They bully you, too?"

"No, but I'm sure they'd like to if they could."

"What's that mean?"

"I guess you might call it more evidence for your Life-isn't-Fair theory. For you, anyway. For me? It helps make up for the fact that my dad couldn't teach me sports."

"What are you talking about?"

"Here's what I mean. We're in sixth grade. Edmund and Harley are in seventh. Both of them have flunked a grade, so they should be in eighth. I have an older brother who is also in eighth grade, named Rob. He flunked a grade. He should be in ninth. And he's big for a ninth grader. And oddly enough, Rob is muscular and athletic. And he's good at sports. I'm pretty sure, he's either adopted and my parents won't admit it, or he got switched at birth with my real brother, who is now growing up with athletic parents who can't figure out where their brainiac son came from, and why he can't throw a ball to save his life."

Russell laughed.

"The first time Edmond and Harley bothered me at the beginning of the year, I helped them make the connection between me and Rob, and suggested they might want to look elsewhere for their bully fix. They haven't bothered me once ever since."

Russell sighed. The big brother option. Foolproof bully insurance.

Pete looked at his watch again. "Well, I better scoot. I've got two minutes to get to my next class."

Russell closed his locker. "Yeah, I better get going, too."

"Say, you want to sit together at lunch?"

"Sure."

"Let's eat at the far end, the one closest to the gym. Usually lots of empty tables back there."

Russell hesitated.

"What's the matter?"

"As a rule, I don't generally sit by myself. Too easy to be noticed and singled out. I kind of like to find a crowd and bury myself in the middle of it."

"I understand. But it'll be okay. They won't bother you when they see you with me. When they see me, they see Rob. If they forget about Rob, I'll remind them. So either way, you'll be fine. At least during lunch."

Yeah, Russell thought. Thirty minutes of fear-free dining. He wished there was a way he could rent Rob's big brother services on a permanent basis.

"So, see you at lunch?"

"Sure," Russell said. "See you then."

8

Summerville Humane Society

K im Harper was running a little late this morning. She had taken a sick day yesterday, still getting over a summer cold. Her assistant trainer, Amy Seger, formerly Amy Wallace until her wedding a few weeks ago, was already at her desk, hammering away at the computer. Kim set her purse in its place on the filing cabinet and her coffee thermos in its coaster next to the keyboard.

"There you are," Amy said, spinning in her chair. "How are you feeling?"

"Not great," Kim said. "I think well enough to come in. I don't have a fever anymore, not sneezing or coughing very much. Just feel a little run down."

"Maybe you should have taken one more day."

"Maybe. But I was so bored. I figured if I'm not contagious, might as well get back at it. Sorry I missed your first day back."

Amy and her new husband, Chris, had taken a two-week

honeymoon driving through the Rockies, Grand Canyon and several other beautiful places out West. "I loved seeing all your pics on Facebook. Looks like you guys were having a great time."

"It was wonderful, Kim. Best time I ever had. The only hard part was leaving Finley behind. I told Chris I'd be fine if we brought him, but he felt like he was doing well enough to leave him behind. He thought we'd be able to do a lot more things and be more spontaneous if it was just the two of us." Amy's husband had lost a leg in Afghanistan and still struggled with PTSD. Finley was more than just the couple's pet; he was Chris's service dog as well.

"How did Chris make out?" Kim sat in her chair, turned on her computer.

"Pretty well, for the most part. Had a few rough nights of sleeping, but the daytime hours were great. Of course, we were never in any crowds and constantly in big open spaces. But you should've seen Finley when we picked him up at the kennel. He went nuts. You would have thought we had gone away for a year. If we had videotaped it, we'd already have a million hits on YouTube."

"I wished I could've seen it. He's such a great dog. Is he with Chris now?"

"Yep. Already back in the old routine." Amy looked at her watch. "He's probably sitting next to Chris in the air-conditioned cab of that big mower." Chris maintained the grounds at a local golf course. "One of the girls told me you had a pretty big development happen while I was gone. She said you and Taylor are officially no longer a couple?"

"I wouldn't say it was a big development. With all his trips, we really hadn't seen each other for almost a month. We've only been seeing each other off and on this past year. But yes, I told him I really like him and have enjoyed our times together, but we just live in two different worlds and those worlds have very little in common. The problem is, we both like our worlds. Neither one of us really want to give ours up to be together."

"I kinda figured it was something like that," Amy said. "For one thing, I know you're not big on taking trips."

"I don't mind a nice vacation here and there. But being a mega-billionaire developer, Taylor has to travel all over the country, sometimes different parts of the world, several times a month. And he loves it."

"But I'm sure it wasn't too hard flying around in his own private airliner."

"No, it wasn't, I guess. But it was also kind of weird. Sometimes it was just us and his staff in this huge plane. I couldn't get used to it. I hadn't even flown in first class before. I would've been happy with a little extra legroom, maybe something better than a bag of peanuts. And the places we stayed at...these palatial suites. Most of them were twice the size of my apartment. I would have been much happier taking the kind of trip you and Chris just did. And then only once or twice a year."

"So, how did Taylor take it?" Amy asked.

"He was fine. A little disappointed. He could tell things were heading in that direction, too. So, he wasn't totally surprised. Neither one of us shed a tear, so what's that tell you?"

"That you weren't really in love. I'd be a basket case without Chris."

"See, that's how you should be when you meet *the one*."

Amy made a funny smile.

"What?"

"I was just thinking about what some of the girls in the kennel said when they heard you two weren't an item anymore."

"What? What did they say?"

"Let's just say, with a guy who looks like Taylor and has Taylor's money and super-nice personality, they were pretty much in agreement--they'd figure out a way to make him *the one*."

Kim smiled. "I can see them saying that. Believe me, I've had some of the same thoughts. They probably think I'm nuts to let him go, right?"

"Pretty much. But I totally get it. I'd be the same way. Let's face it, neither one of us play the lottery. I know most of the girls do."

Kim didn't follow.

"We're not in it for the money, or what the money buys."

"We're in it for love," Kim said. "Well, you are. We don't know about me yet."

"Yes, we do," Amy said. "If you weren't looking for true love, you definitely would have settled for someone like Taylor. But don't worry, Kim. You'll find the right one. It's just a matter of time."

"I know." Kim was glad she could honestly say she didn't feel even a hint of anxiety, or anything close to desperation about this. She had a good life. A job she loved. One where she knew she made a difference every day. And she had good friends. Well, a handful anyway. But who needed more?

"Say Kim, a dog came in at the end of the day yesterday. Hannah brought him. He's a little guy, about knee high. But he's in pretty bad shape. I got involved a little, but I was thinking you're going to want to look into this one yourself."

"Really? What's his name?"

"It's kind of different. Well, I guess it's not that different, considering our dog's name is Finley. The tag said *Parker*."

"Parker," Kim repeated. "Yeah, never heard of a dog named Parker. Wonder if there's a story behind that. So, what's his situation?"

"Is there anything you need to do right now?"

"I don't think so. Not in the next five minutes."

"Let's go check in on him, and I'll tell you what I know."

9

K im braced herself as she opened the shelter's infirmary door. Between her office and here, Amy had filled her in on what was known about Parker's situation.

She both loved and hated this part of the job.

She loved seeing dogs rescued from abusive situations and loved being a small part of their recovery story. She hated seeing the condition they were in when they first arrived. Especially knowing it was altogether unnecessary and avoidable. Dogs are such wonderful creatures, and they require so little care and attention to keep them physically healthy. There is no acceptable excuse for abusing and/or neglecting a dog.

And so often when they came in, they were like Parker's situation: not mistreated for a day or two, or even a week. But for many months. Why? Why be so deliberately cruel to such a loving, thoughtful and intelligent animal? Kim never understood it. If something happens in a person's life, and they can no longer take care of a dog, why make a choice to abuse or neglect it? To cause it to suffer needlessly for days, weeks, or months at a time? Run an ad for a week, *free to good home.* Bring it down to a shelter, where at least it has a chance of having a better life.

"Are you okay?" Amy asked.

She probably wondered why Kim hadn't opened the door yet. "Yeah, I'm fine." She opened it and walked in.

Under a bright light, she saw Dr. Angela Porter and her assistant working on a dog at a surgical table at the far end of the room. Clearly not Parker. It was some kind of Pit mix, and it was completely out of it.

"I think I know which cage they put Parker in," Amy said. She took the lead and Kim followed.

There was a row of dog cages on the left, each occupied by a different dog in need of some kind of medical attention. Something that required a veterinarian's skill. Kim had seen several veterinarians come and go at the shelter since she'd been there. Doctor Porter was certainly one of the best. Not just in terms of her skill, but in her obvious care for the animals. Kim didn't know how she functioned, day-to-day. There were just too many heartbreaking stories back here.

Amy walked to the last cage and stopped. She bent over. "There you are." She said a few more things to him, but the dog didn't respond. "Looks like he's asleep."

Kim peeked in the cage. Scrunched up way in the back was a bundle of brown and black fur. Kim looked at the plastic sleeve hanging from his cage that contained all his info. In it, she found a picture of a cute little dog chained up in some old shed. "Is this him?"

"Yes," Amy said. "The neighbor across the street took it five months ago, when he was being cared for by a little boy who lived at the house."

"Hard to believe it's the same dog," Kim said, putting the pic back in the sleeve.

Dr. Porter noticed them, stopped what she was doing and walked over. "He's a little sedated right now. Not completely knocked out but enough to let him get some rest. He'll be on the table next."

"Does he need surgery?" Kim asked.

"I don't think so. At least not yet. Still have some tests to run. But the first order of business is getting him shaved and cleaned up. I could tell, looking at how badly matted he is, he's in a lot of pain. Some of that hair is just pulling on his skin. We gave him a pill that killed all his fleas, but he's got a ton of infected flea bites. Not to mention, he's severely malnourished and dehydrated. But I didn't see any open wounds, so it doesn't look like he's been in any dogfights."

"No," Amy said, "when Hannah brought him in, she said he was all alone. The owner didn't have any other dogs."

"At least there's that," Dr. Porter said. "The poor dog I'm working on now has bite marks all over. I'm up to fifty stitches already. Apparently, he was a bait dog for some fighting ring."

"There's a dog fighting ring in Summerville?" Amy asked.

"There was," Dr. Porter said. "It got shut down this week."

"What was Parker like before you sedated him?" Kim asked. "Amy said he's extremely skittish around people."

"I'd agree with that," the doctor said. "I could tell he was very uncomfortable being handled. But he never growled or snapped, even when I was poking and prodding him, trying to make sense of the mess that his coat's become."

"What did he do?"

"Mainly, he just started shaking. But that's also because of the level of pain he's been in. Hopefully, after we get him all patched up, he'll begin to respond to people a lot better. I know that matters when you're trying to get these dogs adopted. Speaking of adoptions, I heard the shelter's full again."

"It is," Kim said. They all knew what that meant. Kim hated this part of the job the most. Putting dogs down. Sometimes it was unavoidable. Like when a dog was vicious or dangerous. Or if it was too sick or injured to be saved. But overcrowding was a different story.

"Know if there's been any improvement in the foster care program?" Dr. Porter asked.

"That's where I'm heading next," Kim said. "To talk with the new Foster Care Coordinator. He's only been on the job a few weeks, but he knows how desperately we need him to succeed drumming up new volunteers. The Director told me that's why he hired him. He's supposed to have some great ideas about getting the community more engaged in the program."

"Either that," the doctor said, "or we need a few millionaires to donate some community outreach money, so we can make some decent commercials. Have you ever seen some of these national commercials that talk about mistreated dogs? They break your heart. The last time I saw one, I thought, wouldn't it be nice if we could make something like that, but at the end talk about us, what we're doing here? Or even better, talk about how the people watching can make a difference by joining our foster care program?"

"TV commercials," Kim said. "We can't even afford radio spots. All we can pull off are the free public service announcements."

"Doc, you said we need a few more millionaires," Amy said. "That would be nice. Or maybe...just one billionaire?" She smiled and looked at Kim. "But where could we find a billionaire?"

Dr. Porter looked at Kim, too. "That's right, didn't I hear somewhere that you were dating one?"

"I *was* dating a billionaire, but we're not together anymore."

"Okay, so you're not together anymore. But did things end badly? Did you burn the bridge?"

"No, I didn't burn the bridge. But I'm not going to start dating him again just to hit him up for money."

"Who said anything about dating him again? Maybe you could go out with him again just as a friend. You know, just staying in touch. And then look for an opening to bring up a wonderful idea for a tax write-off. I've heard everyone say what a nice man he is."

"He is a nice man. But I'm not very good at manipulating people. That's one of the reasons I like working with dogs. No games or schemes."

"I'm not suggesting you lead him on or anything," the Doc said. "You can even be right up front with him when you call. See what he says. Let's face it, it would be for a very good cause. I hate the thought of spending all this time patching up these dogs, only to have some of them put down because we have no place to keep them once they leave the infirmary."

"I know. I hate it as much as you do," Kim said.

"Amen," Amy added.

"I'm not saying no," Kim said. "I will think about it, and even pray about it."

"Great," the Doc said. "That's all I can ask."

10

K im walked through several hallways and greeted several coworkers on her way to meet with the Foster Care Coordinator. Thankfully, no one stopped her for very long. The Coordinator's door was open. Sitting at the desk inside was a heavy-set man in his thirties, with auburn hair and a round, jovial face. The sign on his door said: *Alvin Connors*.

"Mr. Connors, hi. My name is Kim Harper. I work on the other side of the shelter. I'm the Animal Behavior Manager." She held out her hand.

He half-stood and shook it. "I know who you are, Kim. Your reputation precedes you. May I call you Kim?"

"Yes, you may."

"And you can call me Al. You know, like the song. *And Betty when you call me, you can call...me...Al.*"

Kim didn't follow.

"You know. Paul Simon? That African-sounding song with

the great beat." He started humming it and tapping his fingers on his desk.

"Oh yeah, I remember it...Al." So, Al was quite the character. But that's great, she thought. We need a people-person in this job. She instantly liked him.

"So, what can I do for you, Kim?"

"I'm not sure you can do anything for me, Al. I just wanted to chat with you a few minutes. I was talking with your boss, and he told me you had some new ideas to help increase the number of people volunteering for our foster care program. I'm especially interested in this, because you've probably heard, the shelter is full. We have zero kennels left for adding any new dogs."

"But new dogs keep coming in," Al said. "I did hear this unfortunate news. And I also understand the implication, which is why I'm putting all my attention on this very thing right now."

"I'd love to hear some of your new ideas."

"One of them doesn't really involve foster care so much. It's the idea of getting other shelters to take some of our dogs. I made a few preliminary calls to some of the smaller towns with animal shelters. Turns out, quite a few of them don't have our problem. And they do have some empty kennels. Some quite a few. We have that big van outside. We just don't have any extra workers on staff who can take the time to make this happen."

"So, you need more volunteers?"

"That's it. Just some folks with some time on their hands and a valid driver's license. Another campaign I'm working on is the idea of Adopt-a-Pet-For-the-Weekend. The thrust of it is to lower the sense of commitment people have to make to get involved. It's not for weeks or months, just the weekend. Of course, the hope will be that a whole lot of these folks--after the weekend's up--will be so bonded to their new houseguest they may want to adopt them, or at the very least become a foster parent."

"I love that idea. Very clever."

"Thanks. But it's not mine. Just borrowing it."

"How are you getting the word out?" Kim asked.

His happy expression changed. "That's the challenge, isn't it? Right now, just through our normal channels. I posted to various social media outlets like Facebook, Twitter and Instagram. But we don't have any advertising budget, so the reach isn't anything like it could be. And I'm writing up some PSA's for the local radio stations. Another freebie avenue. Who knows if anyone hears 'em? And, of course, I'm sending out an email blast to our mailing list. See if anyone bites there."

Al's phone rang. "Excuse me." He picked it up. "Yes, this is Alvin Connors, but you can call me Al." He didn't go into the Paul Simon ditty this time. "Yes, Amy, Kim is still here. Want to talk to her or want me to just send her back your way?" He handed the phone to Kim. "It's Amy."

"Hey Amy, what's up?"

"There's a very nice looking fellow here who's asking to see you."

"I'm guessing he's not standing there by the phone."

"No, he asked for directions to the rest room. But he'll be right back. His name is Ned something. He's out of uniform, because it's his day off. But he's the policeman who helped Hannah rescue Parker yesterday. And I'm guessing, this guy doesn't eat too many donuts, if you get my meaning."

Kim laughed.

"He wants to talk to you. Hannah gave him your name and suggested he chat with you. And get this, he wants to talk about the possibility of being trained for the foster dog program."

"Really?"

"Yes. So, can you head back over here? Or do you want me to send him to Alvin's office? Since he's asking about foster care."

"No, I'll chat with him first. Don't want to jump too fast on this. I'd like to hear what he's thinking. If he's a good fit, then we'll definitely get him back here with Al."

"Great. I'll tell him you're on your way."

11

N ed walked down the hallway on his way back to Kim Harper's office. He didn't really need to use the restroom. He needed a few quiet moments to think and pray about what he was about to do. Ned wasn't a quitter. Once he signed on to something, he saw it through to the end.

Yesterday, when he drove up to the drug bust at Alfredo's house, he had no thought of getting a dog. It wasn't anywhere on his radar screen. He'd had one as a kid but none since. That experience had certainly created a soft spot for dogs somewhere in his heart, but he'd never describe himself as a dog lover. Seems like you'd have to be one to take on a project like this.

But something real did happen in his heart yesterday during that hour with this little dog. Hannah, the ACO, had challenged him to think about becoming a foster parent for Parker (or whatever the correct term was for fostering a dog). He'd thought about it often the rest of the day. He woke up still thinking about it.

And here he was, at the Humane Society about to make his interest official. Was he really ready for such a commitment?

He walked through the doorway and smiled at Amy, Kim's assistant. The room was big enough for two sets of desks, one on each wall, divided by a worktable covered with dog things.

"Kim should be here any second," Amy said.

"Okay if I sit here?" He pointed toward a straight-backed chair next to Kim's desk.

"Sure. So, how long have you been with the police?"

"Almost five years."

"Are you thinking of making a career out of it?"

"Right now, I am. Eventually, I'd like to become a detective."

A petite, attractive woman suddenly appeared in the doorway.

"There you are, Kim. I was just chatting with Officer... Barring...I'm sorry, I forgot your last name."

"No problem. It's Barringer. But please, just call me Ned." He got up to shake Kim's hand.

"Hi, Ned. Sorry, to keep you waiting." She walked over and sat in her office chair. "Amy said you were interested in finding out a little more about our foster care program. She also said you helped Hannah with the rescue of that abused dog she brought in yesterday."

"Parker," Ned said.

"That's right, Parker. That's an interesting name for a dog."

"I know, isn't it? Have you seen Parker yet?"

"I just did a few minutes ago, but he was asleep all scrunched up in the back of his cage. So, I didn't get a good look at him. I did see the picture of what he looked like several months ago. He was really a beautiful dog."

"I saw him before they sedated him," Ned said. "Abuse charges are definitely called for."

"And I know our veterinarian would agree with that assessment."

"Would you guys be able to get any pics or video of Parker with the vet?" Ned asked. "You know, before and after kind of stuff. Maybe have the vet talk about his condition a little."

"I'm sure we can do that," Kim said. "There was some talk about you possibly joining our foster program to look after Parker once he leaves here? Could we talk about that?"

"Would you be the one training me?" Ned said. He certainly hoped so.

"Not in the details of what's involved with foster care. We have a special coordinator who runs that program. I was just there at his office before coming here. His name's Al. But I do get involved in other ways. For example, it's my job to, sort of, qualify you to be a volunteer. To make sure you're really ready to do something like this, especially with a special-needs situation like Parker."

"I'm actually relieved to hear you say that. That's the kind of help I need. I've got my own doubts about doing this. I'm definitely open to the idea. In some ways, I feel almost compelled to get involved. But on the practical side, I'd love someone who's not emotionally attached to evaluate this, help me see if this is the right thing or if I'm about to make a huge mistake."

"Good," Kim said. "Shows me you're making this decision with the kind of seriousness it deserves. Maybe we should take a little walk so we can chat without interrupting Amy any further." She stood.

Ned stood also.

"I appreciate that guys," Amy said. "I do have a bunch of phone calls to return."

Kim headed out into the hall, so Ned followed her. He enjoyed the idea of spending more time with her. "Where are we going?"

"Outside. That last doorway on the left leads to a little covered pavilion. There's a picnic table out there. We can be alone and, hopefully, not sweat to death."

12

Once outside, Kim headed over to the shaded pavilion just to the left of the door. Ned continued to follow until they sat on opposite sides of the table.

"Before I say anything else," Kim said, "I want you to know I'm not trying to scare you away or talk you out of this idea. I just want to make sure, if you do this, you're doing it with your eyes wide open."

"I appreciate that. Fire away. Ask me anything you want."

"Have you been thinking about getting a dog lately?"

"No. Not even a little bit."

"Have you ever had a dog before?"

"Just when I was a kid."

"How come you've never gotten one as an adult?"

"I guess it's been just the way my life has gone. Especially since joining the police force. I've never had a roommate, so there's no one in my apartment when I'm not there. I don't go out much when I am off duty, but I've wondered about whether it's right to leave a dog alone for that long."

"How many hours are you gone at a time?"

"Our shifts are usually ten hours. But we never patrol outside the city limits and, as you know, this isn't a very big town. So, it's possible I could stop by for a few minutes in the middle of the day to let him out. How long can a dog Parker's age hold it?"

"He might be able to wait that long. But if you could visit him in the middle of the day, that would certainly help."

"I'm pretty sure I can. At least on most days. But the other thing for me with Parker isn't just the bathroom thing. It's about leaving him alone for so many hours. Hannah didn't seem to think that would be such a problem, considering what he's been experiencing at Alfredo's place."

"You mean having zero interaction with people 24/7?"

Ned nodded. "I would certainly be able to pay attention to him whenever I'm off duty."

"You don't go out with friends, or have a...girlfriend?"

"Nope. On the first one, I'm usually too tired. And on the second?" What should he say? *Haven't met the right girl*, which was true.

"You don't have to give me any details on that," she said. "I don't mean to pry. I'm just wondering how much time you could be with Parker. It sounds like, other than work, he'd be getting way more attention than he's used to. There's another side to this, though, that you need to be prepared for."

"What's that?"

"We're not even sure how Parker will react to a new human in his life, one who is attentive. He might respond very well to someone treating him kindly and gently. Could come totally out of his shell. Or, with some dogs who've gone through what he has, they have some...emotional damage. You might need to be very patient with him. Parker might not be the kind of dog who throws a party every time you come home, or the kind who sits on your lap while you watch TV."

Ned laughed. "I get that. I'm glad you said that, in case that happens. But I think I'd be okay with that. I'm not doing this to satisfy some deep need for companionship."

"Do you know why you are doing this? What's motivating you to get involved here?"

Ned thought a moment. "Not totally sure, Kim. Something just happened to me yesterday, being with him. Something on the inside. I've been thinking a lot about it, as I've wrestled with whether or not to pursue this. It may have something to do with being bullied."

"Being bullied?"

"Yeah. I used to be pretty scrawny as a kid, and I got bullied something awful. For a bunch of years. About ruined my childhood. It's why I decided to become a policeman. To help people who are being picked on by others. There was a moment yesterday when I was looking at Parker, after he finally started coming closer. We were looking right at each other and, I don't know, something clicked inside. I felt so bad for him, for how he'd been treated. And I decided then, I had to do something about it. I couldn't stand the idea that we'd finally rescue him from this horrible existence and then he gets put to sleep, without ever knowing what it felt like to be loved."

KIM WAS STARTING to really like this guy, the more he talked.

These were not the kind of things she'd expect to hear from a tough-looking police officer. "You said you used to be a scrawny kid? I find that hard to believe, looking at you now." Did she really just say that? That came out sounding wrong. Hopefully, he wouldn't take it as a flirty comment.

He smiled. "I was. And back then, I thought I was doomed to be a runt forever. My mom was only five-three and my dad five-ten."

"You've got to be over six feet," she said.

"Six-one. But the growth didn't come until the eleventh grade. I was, like, five-six before then and didn't weigh more than a hundred-and-twenty pounds. Then in the summer between eleventh grade and my senior year, I grew almost five inches. Felt like someone was putting me on a rack. My joints ached all the time. I couldn't stop eating, too, but I hardly gained any weight. Then in my senior year, I grew some more but finally started filling out. Started working out at a gym, eating right. But the best part was, no more bullying."

"I wonder what happened? Where the growth came from."

"Oh, that mystery got solved pretty quick. My mom's youngest brother is six-three. And her dad, my grandfather, was six-feet even. Thankfully, their genes came to my rescue."

"And now you want to come to the rescue of little Parker." Oh my, that sounded way too corny. For some reason, being around him made her a little nervous.

"I guess. If you think I could do some good. But if someone comes along while he's recovering and you think they'd be a better fit, I'm fine if you want to let him go with them. I just want to make sure he's got somewhere to go after his time here."

"That's really great, Ned. So, do you think you'd like to take the next step?"

"Which is..."

"Getting with Al, our Foster Care Coordinator. He'll give you some training about what's involved, all the practical stuff."

"So, I passed? I'm in?"

Kim laughed. "This wasn't a test, Ned. I just wanted to make sure you knew what to expect and had a home situation that could work for Parker, once he's ready to leave this place. But yeah, I think Parker would be lucky to have someone like you looking after him."

Ned smiled. "Thanks. But seriously, I'm open to all the training I can get. So, can I get with him now? I've got the day off."

"I'm not sure. I'll have to call him, see what he says. But if he can't do it today, it's no big deal. My guess is, Parker's going to be in our infirmary for at least a week, maybe more."

"Oh."

"But you can start coming in to see him before then. We'll set up the training with Al, and you can check in on Parker. And I'm going to stay involved, too. We offer free dog training for our foster care volunteers. I'm almost certain Parker has received zero training, so I'll help you teach him all the basics. Then, whether you decide to adopt him or someone else does, he'll have a much better chance of finding a forever home."

"A forever home," Ned said. "I like the sound of that. And I like the idea of you staying involved. I mean, you know, to help me out with Parker."

"Right," Kim said. But the look in his eyes seemed to suggest that wasn't all he meant.

13

———

A few hours later, Kim received a phone call from Dr. Porter, saying she had finished working on Parker for the day, and that she expected him to begin waking up in about ten minutes or so. Kim was on her way there now but decided to stop in and chat with Al. Earlier, he'd been able to make some time with Ned, so Ned wouldn't have to come back another day before signing up for the Foster Care Program.

Kim turned left down one hallway then opened the door to the Intake area. She could see Al sitting at his desk through his open doorway. She rapped gently on the door twice. "Hey, Al, how did it go with Ned? Do you think it's gonna work out with him and Parker?"

"I do. He's a great guy. Real easy to work with, and he's already got a pretty strong connection to the dog, which counts for a lot. I think between what you said and what I said, his eyes are wide open going in. He knows this isn't like bringing home a cute puppy. Truth is, we don't know what Parker's gonna be like. I shared with him several possible situations, ranging from easy-peasy to worst-case scenario. He didn't flinch. I think there's a better than 50-50 chance he might wind up adopting Parker before this is through. But don't quote me on that."

"That was my sense too."

"He gave me some time slots we could get together over the next week. I'm sure we'll get things sorted out."

"Great," she said. "I'm heading to the infirmary. Doc's all done with Parker. For now, anyway. He should be coming out of it any minute. Want him to see my smiling face when he wakes up. We'll be in touch." Kim headed back to the main hallway then made a right toward the infirmary. When she walked in, Doc Porter was already working on another dog.

She noticed Kim. "He's back in the same cage he was in a few hours ago." She glanced in that direction. "You're just in time. He just lifted his head."

Kim walked quietly up to the cage and looked in.

"Don't be shocked at his appearance. As our volunteer groomer worked through the mats, she had to go pretty deep into his coat. He's close to a doggy crew cut right now. The upside is, she got them all off. Then I was able to work on cleaning up his infected flea and tick bites. He's nothing but skin and bones, the poor thing. But you did say he was eating, right? Before he was brought in?"

"That's what I was told. He was loving those soft and chewy treats I use in training."

"We'll give him some soft food to eat once he's fully awake."

Kim looked back at Parker. He was still lying down but his

head was up and looking slowly around. He still looked woozy. The Doc was right about his appearance. Hardly looked like the same dog. But she was used to this, seeing dogs shaved for health reasons. Most of them looked awful afterward. But his coat would come back and with proper care, he'd be looking like that picture in the sleeve in a couple of months. "Hey Parker," she said softly. "How you doing, little buddy?"

PARKER HEARD his name spoken by a pleasant-sounding woman's voice. He could see her beyond the bars of his cage, though his eyes were having a hard time focusing on her face. He didn't recognize the voice or the surroundings beyond this cage.

He didn't even remember how he'd gotten here, but it was clear this place wasn't where he usually lived. For one thing, he wasn't hot or thirsty or hungry. And he was lying on something soft. That was new.

"You feeling any better? You should be, with all those mats taken off."

He didn't know what she was saying but, after several more blinks, he could see her face more clearly. She was smiling and had kind eyes.

The woman turned and said something to another woman across the room. "Would it be okay if I opened his cage? Maybe gave him a treat? Or is it too soon?"

"It couldn't hurt to try connecting with him a little. He'll let you know if he doesn't want to be touched. But I'd hold off on the treat till he's fully awake and alert."

The woman looked at him again, still smiling. Eyes still

kind. A clicking noise inside his cage. What was it? The door started to open. He tensed up but only a little. Inside, he felt different. Calmer somehow. Then he realized something else. Something very nice. He wasn't in any pain. For the first time in a long time, he wasn't in any pain. Now the woman's hand was opening the cage. He moved to the back.

"Hey, Parker? How are you feeling, boy?" The woman reached her hand inside the cage but stopped halfway.

He looked at her hand as he sniffed the air. Nothing in it. He remembered those delicious, meaty treats he'd had yesterday. The best thing he'd ever eaten. He looked up at her eyes and her mouth. As nice as she seemed, this place was so unfamiliar. He pulled back as far into the cage as he could and looked away.

"How's it going?"

"Not great Doc. He seemed interested for a moment, but then he pulled away."

"He's probably just confused. And the anesthesia might be messing with his mind a little."

"You're probably right." She pulled her hand out and closed the cage.

"But my guess is, physically speaking, he's probably feeling pretty good right now from the leftover effects of the sedation. Even when it wears off, I think he's going to feel a lot better in general, with those mats not pinching his skin all the time."

"When do you think he'll be completely alert again?"

"Maybe in another hour or two. Why don't you try again then?"

"I will," Kim said. "But I think I'm going to call that police officer, Ned. Since he really wants to take care of Parker, and he's already been approved to foster, I'm going to see if he'd like to come back here when I try and connect with Parker again. Parker might recognize him, and I think his memory of Ned is a good one. He might respond better to Ned than me."

And Kim realized but didn't say...she wouldn't mind seeing Ned again, either.

14

J ust after 4PM, Ned pulled into the Humane Society parking lot for the second time today. A few hours ago, Kim had called him with an update about Parker's condition and invited him to join her when she checked on him again. He'd spent the time between then and now at the pet store knocking off a shopping list of things he'd need when Parker was released.

His misgivings had evaporated. Now that Ned had set his mind on it, he was all in. And really, there weren't any significant risks involved, considering all the help he'd get from Al and Kim at the shelter. He walked through the glass front doors and signed in at the reception desk.

"Is Kim expecting you?" the receptionist asked.

"I am," Kim said loudly, entering from a door at the back of the lobby. She closed the distance. "Hi Ned, good to see you. Glad you could make it." She extended her hand, and he shook it.

It was soft but, oddly, a little wet.

"I'm sorry. I was just working with a dog and washed my hands. The restroom was out of paper towels."

"I'll tell the maintenance guy," the receptionist said.

"Thanks. So how has your day gone, Ned?"

"Pretty good. Just spent a bunch of money at the pet store to get my apartment ready for Parker."

"Did Al give you a checklist?"

Ned nodded. "Plus, I got him a separate doggy bed for the living room, and a few dog toys."

"Parker's going to think he died and went to doggy heaven. And you just gave me an idea." She started walking back toward the door she'd come out of. "Follow me." They meandered through some hallways. "Are any of the dog toys stuffed, or made with any kind of cloth?"

"One of them is."

"This may sound like an odd request, but could you start putting that one in the bed beside you for a couple of nights, then bring it back here?"

"Uh...yeah. Definitely qualifies as an odd request."

She laughed. "I know, right? But there's a meaning behind the madness. If you do this, the stuffed dog toy will pick up your scent. He can sleep with it while he's here. Then when the time comes for him to go home with you, he'll already be familiar with your scent."

"That makes sense," Ned said.

Finally, they reached Al's office. Familiar territory. Al was at his desk talking with a couple. They continued walking a little further toward a door at the end of the hall marked *Infirmary*. She opened it and went in, Ned right behind her.

She stopped. "I need to warn you. He looks pretty bad right

now. We had to shave off much of his hair. That highlights all the infected bites on his skin. Add to that, he's half-starved. It's not a pretty sight."

"Thanks for the warning."

"He's in the last cage on the left. When I saw him a few hours ago, he was still woozy, but the Doc said he's supposed to be wide awake now."

They were almost there. "How did he respond to you?" Ned asked.

"Well, he didn't growl, but he wasn't exactly eager to see me, either. I gently put my hand in his cage as I said nice things to him. He sniffed at it but then backed away, as far back as he could get. It'll be interesting to see what he's like now."

They reached his cage. "Why don't you stay out of sight for a minute? Let's see how he responds to me now. I'll do the same thing I did last time, only this time, I'll include one of those treats he loves." She took one out of a pouch and with the other hand gently opened the crate door. All the while, saying nice things in a pleasant voice.

"What's he doing?" Ned whispered.

"I can see he's curious. His eyes are much more clear and focused. They're darting back between my face and the treat. It's okay, Parker. You can have it. It's a treat, remember? You like these treats." She waited a few moments more. "Nope. He's not budging. Why don't you take a shot at it?" Kim handed him the treat.

She stepped to the side to let Ned take the center spot. But she could still easily see what went on in the cage. Instantly, Parker's head reacted to Ned's presence. He held it straighter and it cocked slightly. "Hey, Parker. Remember me? From

yesterday? I'm the one who got you out of that horrible place."
Ned remembered something and laughed.

"What are you laughing at?"

"I just remembered a Far Side cartoon. Know what those are?"

"By Gary Larson? I love them."

"Remember the one where the guy is talking to his dog, saying all these specific things, and above it, it says: *What We Say to Dogs*. In the bottom half, it's the same picture, but it says: *What They Hear*. All the dog hears the man say is *Blah blah blah blah, Ginger. Blah blah blah, Ginger*. I'm doing the same thing. Telling Parker all these things, as if he understands it. But it's all just, blah blah blah to him."

"It probably is. No, it definitely is. But for now, he can certainly read your tone of voice. No one has ever worked with the poor thing. You'll be amazed at how many words he can learn, once we begin training him. He reacted way more positively to you than he did to me."

"Should I go a little further?"

"I think so. Why don't you put a treat in your hand, see if he'll take it?"

Ned opened the door and slowly moved his hand inside, saying pleasant things to Parker all the while, and looking at his face. He didn't seem to be alarmed. Ned took hold of the treat and put it in his open palm. "You want this, Parker? You want this treat?"

His eyebrows arched.

"I think he already knows the word *treat*," Kim said. "That one doesn't seem like blah blah. Go on, Parker. You can take it."

Parker leaned his head forward and sniffed, but he still didn't make any attempt to eat it.

"Maybe he's just not hungry," Ned said. "If he was, wouldn't he have eaten the treat you left in the cage after you left?"

"You might be right," Kim said. "Maybe the shock of what he's been through in the last twenty-four hours has thrown off his system. But I hope he does start eating soon. As you can see with his hair shaved off, that guy was starving him."

"I know. He almost looks like a completely different dog without his hair. How long will it take to grow back or, should I ask, will it grow back?"

"It'll definitely grow back. And with proper care, all those wounds on his skin will heal up. In fact, they should heal up well enough for him to leave here in a week or two. I have to confirm that with Dr. Porter to be sure, but judging from what I've seen through the years, that seems about right for what we're looking at. Now his coat, that could take a couple of months. But I'd be surprised if he doesn't look almost exactly like that picture of him in the sleeve."

"Yeah, when Betty showed me that yesterday, I couldn't believe that's what he looked like a few months ago."

"Well, that's what he can look like again. With your help. In two months from now, when he looks like he's supposed to, he'll also be almost fully trained. The perfect pet for someone."

"Or maybe for me," Ned said. He couldn't imagine after putting in all that time with Parker, he'd want to give him to someone else. "But is that okay? If I keep him? Is that something you guys frown on?"

"Not at all. Al might try to talk you out of it. He'd hate to lose a good foster parent for other dogs. But I wouldn't worry about that. Either way, it will be your choice. And you certainly don't have to decide anything now."

"Should I leave the treat in his crate?"

"I think so. At some point, his appetite will kick in."

"Can I ask you something?" Ned said, still looking at Parker's eyes. "He seems really calm to me. Do you sense him tensing up at all?"

"No, his body language is very calm."

"I'd like to try something before pulling my hand out, if you're okay with it."

"Like what?"

"I'm going to try and scratch under his chin, see if he'll let me. He did yesterday when we brought him out of that cubby hole. Think it would be okay?"

She looked more intensely at Parker. "I think so. If he stiffens up, just gently pull it back."

PARKER NOTICED SOMETHING. The nice man's hand was moving closer. He was reaching toward him. What was he doing? Parker tensed up. What was happening?

"That's a good boy, Parker. You're such a good boy."

The way he said these words put Parker at ease. And besides his name, there was a phrase Parker recognized. The one he repeated twice. *Good boy*. He hadn't heard that phrase in such a long time. The Man never said it. Who was it? He remembered. It was the little boy, the one who used to care for him a long time ago.

Now the nice man was touching him. Under the jaw. But it didn't hurt. He was scratching him softly. It actually felt good. Slowly, Parker moved his head around so he could scratch more places.

"Look at this, Kim. Look what he's doing."

"Well, I'll be. I'll bet in no time at all, you'll have him eating out of your hand. I knew he was a sweet dog."

Ned moved his hand and scratched gently behind Parker's ears. First one, then the other.

"WELL NED, it's pretty easy to see, Parker is willing to let at least one person into his world right now. And that person is you."

Ned smiled. "Good boy, Parker. We'll just leave that treat in there for later. You can eat it whenever you're ready. Okay, buddy?"

"Or," Kim said, "as Parker understood it: *Blah blah blah, blah blah blah blah.*"

Ned laughed as he slipped his hand out of the cage and gently latched the door. He looked at his watch. An idea just popped into his head. He decided to go for it. "I'm kinda hungry, and I'm actually in the mood to celebrate a little. What time do you get off?"

"What?" Kim said. "Uh...five o'clock usually."

"That's only thirty minutes from now. How about I come back then and take you out to dinner. You can jump start my first training lesson."

"Well, I usually do those with the dog present."

"Okay, then we won't call it a training lesson."

"Then what do we call it?"

She was still smiling. She seemed very open to what he was suggesting. This was good. The word "date" seemed a little too forward. "How about a get-to-know-you-better session?"

She hesitated. But her eyes were still bright. She was still smiling. Maybe even a little wider.

"I guess we could do that. But nothing fancy. I'm not dressed for anywhere fancy."

"I don't even know any fancy places to eat," Ned said. "I'm a beat cop. I won't be able to afford fancy until I make detective."

"Okay then, Ned," she said. "You come back and get me around five."

15

F or the last two hours, Russell had been at Pete's house, playing video games on his PlayStation. After school, Pete had invited him over. Russell instantly said yes. Not just because he thought it would be fun, but it gave him the opportunity to foil any plans Edmund and Harley had to ambush him on the way home.

As soon as Russell arrived at Pete's house, he'd been confronted with another reality about life's unfairness. Pete's house was huge. Not only did he have a live-in bully-proof big brother, he lived in a subdivision of single-family homes with a big, green lawn, front and back. After Pete met him at the door and led him through the maze of rooms back to his bedroom, Russell decided this house was as big as three apartments put together.

This unfairness was offset, however, by how nice Pete was and how easy he was to be with. For the first thirty minutes, they'd played games that pitted them against each other. Pete had become frustrated at how consistently Russell beat him.

"How is this possible?" Pete had said. "You don't even own a PlayStation." Russell said he'd always possessed superior eye-hand coordination. As soon as Pete showed him how each button and trigger worked, Russell began to dominate the game.

From then on, Pete decided they should play in co-op mode, which put them on the same team fighting imaginary villains and monsters together.

After completing yet another successful level, Russell looked at his watch. "This has to be the last one for me. My mom gets home from work in thirty minutes. I should be there when she gets home."

"Where does she work?" Pete said.

"She's a department manager at Hobby Lobby. I heard your mom come in about an hour ago. Where does she work?"

"She doesn't. I mean, she does work, she just doesn't have a job. Well, she does have a job, sort of. She's a stay-at-home mom. Like the moms in those old black-and-white sitcoms. You know, they clean the house, do all the shopping, cook all the meals."

"Must be nice. So, I'm guessing that means your mom and dad are still together, and he must have a pretty good job."

Pete nodded. He already knew about Russell's situation. It was nice that he never tried to gloat. "He's a software engineer."

Russell stood. "Well, I better get going."

"You live far away?"

"Not really. About a fifteen-minute walk from here. The Bent Oak Apartments. Know where they are?"

"I think so. The ones not far from the Walmart?"

Russell nodded.

"A shame you didn't bring your bike."

Russell decided not to mention he didn't own one. "It's not that far." He started walking toward the front door.

"So, did you have fun?" Pete asked.

"What? Yeah, it was great."

"You want to do this again sometime?"

"Definitely," Russell said.

"I never do anything after school. So, you can pretty much come over any time you want."

"Great." Russell opened the door. "See you at school tomorrow."

The first ten minutes of Russell's walk home were smooth and uneventful. He didn't even struggle with fearful thoughts. Why should he? Things at school had gone fine. No Edmund and Harley incidents. And now he'd just spent two full hours playing video games with his new friend.

He turned a corner two streets away from their apartment complex. Across the street was a large park. The sidewalk was on the same side of the street, so he crossed and walked along a waist-high hedgerow that bordered the park. Lots of smaller kids played on the playground equipment. Lots of moms sat on benches nearby, some with strollers.

On the big grassy field, a group of older kids were playing soccer. He was tempted to stand there and watch, but he really needed to get home. With less than fifty yards before he'd reach the end of the playground and the last intersection before home, he heard someone yelling behind him.

"Hey, Monkey Boy. Where you going? Missed getting with you today at school."

Fear seized Russell's heart. He didn't even want to turn around, but knew he must. If only to size up the situation before deciding his next move. There stood Edmund and Harley, not fifteen feet away on the sidewalk.

"I was just saying to Harley here, how did Monkey Boy get by us on the walk home from school? We were standing right there for over twenty minutes."

"I told Edmund, I think he's trying to avoid us. He must-a went home some other way."

"And then look, here you are almost two hours later, walking right by us. What happened? You start taking ballet lessons?"

Harley laughed at his friend's remark. "That's a good one. Now I'm seeing him in a pink tutu."

Now Edmund was laughing, too. "No really, where'd you go?"

One thing was certain, Russell was faster than both these guys. He could run. But then, he couldn't get far enough away from them before reaching his apartment complex. Then they'd know where he lived. He couldn't have that. "I was just visiting a friend," he finally said.

"A friend?" Edmund said. "Since when do you have any friends? We've never seen you with any friends."

"Since today. We just met at school."

"What's his name? Maybe we know him."

For a moment, Russell thought about telling them Pete's name. Maybe they'd remember his big brother, Rob, and decide to leave him alone. No, he couldn't do that. He'd talked about this with Pete while they played video games, about his big brother and his current bully dilemma. Pete didn't think it was a good idea. Not unless Russell got to know Rob and Rob thought of him as a friend on his own.

"I asked you what's his name," Edmund repeated.

"It's Harry," Russell blurted out, though he didn't know why. "Harry Roberts."

"Never heard of him."

"I didn't think you had. Hey look, I've got to go."

"But you aren't dismissed yet."

Russell hated this. These stupid games. Why not just hit him and get it over with? The two boys started closing the distance. Russell backed up enough to keep them apart.

"Where you going? Stand still."

"Why should I?"

"Because I said so," Edmund said. "We're just trying to collect the money you owe us."

"What money?"

"It's like a tax," Harley said. "A new kid tax."

"I don't have any money."

"Then we have to hurt you," Edmund said. "Because you gotta pay the tax, one way or the other."

That was it. It was time. Russell turned to run, but he hesitated a few seconds too long. He got three or four steps in before one of them stuck his foot out, tripping him up. He fell straight down but managed to get his palms out before hitting the sidewalk.

"Where do you think you're going?" Harley grabbed him, picked him up and spun him around in one motion. Then he socked Russell in the stomach.

Russell doubled over in pain. Then Edmund yanked him back up by his hair and punched him in the face. Russell fell back a few steps but didn't fall to the ground. It hurt like crazy. Without thinking it through, he kicked Edmund in the shin with all his might then, with the other foot, kicked Harley in the groin.

Both boys screamed out in pain. Harley fell to the ground. Edmund moved toward Russell, as he cocked his arm back and made a fist. Russell didn't stand there long enough for him to connect. He turned and ran as fast as he could. Edmund gave chase, but he couldn't run well on the leg Russell kicked.

In no time at all, Russell reached the edge of the park then crossed the intersection. Edmund was yelling something behind him, but he didn't hear clearly. He kept running until he reached the entrance to the Bent Oak Apartments, then crossed the street in the opposite direction, just in case either of the boys were still following him.

He looked back for a moment. The coast was clear, for now. Still just to be safe, he ran past the apartment complex, then turned left to go around the buildings and come in the back way.

By the time, he reached the stairway leading up to their apartment, he was totally exhausted. As he cleared the last step, he bumped into a big man. He looked up. One of Russell's eyes was already closing but through the other he saw it was Ned, their next-door neighbor.

The cop.

16

"Excuse me, Sir. I didn't see you." Russell hurried past him and quickly brought his hand to his face, pretending to scratch his head.

"That's all right. No problem." The man stopped and turned. "What's the hurry? Your name's Russell, right? Live next door to me?"

"Yeah, but I'm kinda in a hurry to get home." That wasn't a lie. Russell wished he was there right now.

"And you don't have to call me, sir. Don't you remember when we met last week? I said feel free to call me Ned."

"I forgot." Russell kept walking toward his front door. His hand still up by the swollen side of his face.

"Say, are you all right Russell?"

"Yeah, I'm okay." Russell wasn't sure why he didn't want Ned to see. It's not like he could do anything about it. Kids got bullied all the time at school. He never saw anyone arrested over it. Besides, these guys were always careful to harass him either outside of school or when no adults were around.

"You don't seem, okay. Why are you holding your hand over your face? Can I see it?"

Russell gave up. There was no use fighting this anymore. He stopped and let his hand down and looked up at Ned.

"Oh, man. That looks pretty painful. What happened? Guess that's a stupid question. Obviously, someone hit you." Ned walked closer.

"I got in a fight. If you could call it that."

Ned stood right in front of him now. "Mind if I take a look?"

"No." What else could he say? He looked up at Ned.

"How did the other guy make out?"

"You mean, the other *two* guys."

"Two guys? This was two against one?"

Russell nodded. "Two older and bigger guys. They've been after me almost since my first day at school."

"Bullies?"

"A classic case," Russell said. "Almost a cliché for bullying. Two knuckle-draggers without a brain to split between them, pick on a kid half their size, just for kicks."

Ned laughed. "That's a good way of putting it. But I know this isn't a funny thing. These guys have been making your life a nightmare, haven't they?"

"That's a good way of putting it," Russell said.

"Is this the first time things got physical?"

"Yeah, but it wasn't for a lack of trying on their part. I was just able to get away before, or else some adult would walk by, and I'd latch onto them."

"What was different this time?"

"Just bad luck, I guess. I was coming back from a friend's

house and walked past that park around the corner. They saw me, but I didn't see them until it was too late."

Ned shook his head and sighed. "I hate bullies. You shouldn't have to be afraid walking home. Ever. This is just wrong."

"Tell me about it. But I know this isn't over. If anything, I just made them madder than before."

"What'd you do?"

Russell explained what happened.

THE MORE RUSSELL TALKED, the angrier Ned got. It was shades of his childhood all over again. "So, you're what, in seventh grade?"

"Sixth."

"And these two kids were, what?"

"Seventh grade, but they both flunked a grade I'm told."

"So, they should be in eighth?"

Russell nodded.

"Two years can make a huge difference at that age," Ned said, "in terms of physical development."

"I'd have to agree with that assessment," Russell said.

Ned laughed. "You've got a good sense of humor, at least."

"At least," Russell said. "Right now, I'd trade that for about four inches and thirty pounds of muscle."

This kid's a scream, Ned thought. "So it's two against one, and both these guys are two years older than you. You've got nothing to be ashamed of, kid. I'll tell you what these guys are. They're cowards. Insecure, little cowards. I know that doesn't help too much right now, but it's the truth. I was bullied something awful when I was your age. And I'm guessing I was about the same size as you in sixth grade."

"What? You, same size as me? That's impossible."

"I'm not making this up, Russell. It's true."

"But you're like this big, strong cop now. How could you be as small as me?"

"I don't know, but that's what happened. Bullies made my life a nightmare, all through the middle school years. Even through my first year at high school."

"Then what happened?"

"Then? Then I grew like five inches over one summer, and I started working out. I actually got bigger than my bullies."

"Then what happened?" Russell said. "Did you get revenge?"

"On two of them, I did. But it wasn't really revenge, not the way it went down. On two different times, I caught them bullying some younger kids, and I was able to step in and take them out. So in a way, I was just protecting someone, not getting revenge."

"But that's still way cool, that you got to do that."

"It felt pretty good. I'm not gonna lie. It's what made me decide to become a cop. I decided I wanted to feel that kind of good more often. I wanted to protect people who were being hurt by others. Like right now, that's why I didn't just say hey to you, and keep walking down the steps."

"Well, I'm glad you decided to talk to me. I didn't want to say anything at first. But I'm glad I did. I don't know what you can do for me, though. It's not like you can walk me to and from school every day."

"No, but there might be something else I could do to help. But let me ask you, have you told anyone else about this?"

"No, just my new friend at school. His name's Pete."

"Not your mom? None of your teachers or administrators at the school?"

He shook his head no. "It would just get my mom upset, and I don't need that. She couldn't do a thing except feel guilty about not being able to help me, and worry herself sick every time I left the house. And what could the people at school do? It never happens while actually at school. They'll say things and shoot me mean looks, but they haven't done anything during school hours or on school property."

"I'd still talk to them, just so they know. Maybe there's more they can do than you realize. And I'd definitely tell your mom. In fact, I want you to promise me, you're going to tell her. Tonight, or at least before I see you again."

"I'll talk to someone at school tomorrow, Ned. But don't make me tell my mom."

"Russell, she's going to see your eye. You can't hide something like that. So when she does, just tell her what happened. You don't have to give her the play-by-play, but she needs to know what you're going through. Would you say it's helped you, even a little, with me talking to you about this?"

Russell nodded. "It has, I guess. Like I said, I don't know how, but I do feel a little better than I felt before."

"Well, the same thing's going to happen when you tell your mom. At the very least, she can help you sort out how you're feeling and what you're thinking about. Believe me, that matters a lot. I remember, for me, most of the battle was dealing with the stuff going on in my head." Russell nodded. Ned could see, some of this was getting through. "And I've got an idea, about a way to help you deal with this that's even more effective. But to do it, your mom will have to be okay with it."

"What is it?"

"I'm not gonna say right now. But you tell me after you've talked to your mom and told someone official at the school, and then I'll tell you some more."

"Okay." A slight smile appeared on Russell's face.

Ned recognized the look in his eyes.

Hope.

He looked at his watch. "I've got to go and meet someone. But promise me you'll talk to your mom, and to someone at school."

"Okay, I will."

"And Russell, no matter what, you can always talk to me about this. All right? I'm right next door. My two parking spaces are right next to yours in the parking lot. If you see my patrol car in one of them, I'm definitely home."

Russell nodded. "Okay, thanks. I better go."

17

Twenty minutes later, Ned had picked Kim up at the Humane Society for their little dinner out together. Unfortunately, she had to follow him to the restaurant. She'd forgotten they closed the shelter gates at 6PM. If she had ridden in his car, hers would have been stuck behind the gate all night.

After learning she loved Italian, Ned had said, "Just follow me. I know just the place." Ten minutes later, they pulled into the parking lot of Sorrento's. They met on the sidewalk and started walking toward the front door. "This isn't the best place for atmosphere," he said. "Unless you like the atmosphere of a New York diner. But the food here is the best. It's a Ma-Pa place. Everything comes from their family recipes. And the prices are reasonable, too."

"I'm surprised I've never heard of it."

"Well, now you have." He opened the front door. "If I've oversold the place, let me know after. But I'll be surprised if you don't love it."

She walked in, faced a little sign that said: "Please Seat Yourselves." The place was half-filled.

"It's still early for dinner," Ned whispered. "But you watch, it'll be completely filled by the time we're done. Let's sit over here." He led her toward the back.

"We heading to your favorite spot?"

"Not really. It's actually on the opposite end of where I usually sit. But if we sat there, we'd get too much company."

"Company?"

"A lot of the guys I work with like this place, too. I didn't want to take the chance they'd come in and then we'd get sucked into spending our time with them. This way, they might come over and say Hi, but then head back over to their usual tables."

He led her to a table by the far wall. The bottom half of the wall was trimmed in dark wood paneling, the top half a mural of an Italian hillside village. The tablecloths were the obligatory red and white checkerboard you see in all the Ma-Pa Italian places.

"Dinner's on me," Ned said with a playful smile. "No arguments. Order anything you want." He leaned over and said quietly, "That's not as generous as it sounds when you look at the prices. Like I said earlier, I only go to places that are easy on the wallet."

"Well, thank you anyway, Ned. But you should know, I've already glanced at the prices. And this place is in the same price range as the places I usually go." Which would be at the exact opposite end of the spectrum from the restaurants she'd been eating at until recently on her dates with Taylor Saunders, her billionaire friend.

He picked up the menu and began to read, so she did the same. "Is there something you usually get here?"

"Yeah, there is." He set the menu down. "I don't even know why I read this. I always get the same thing, baked ziti with a side order of meatballs. It's what I come here for. I'm kind of weird that way. Every restaurant in town I go to, I go there for the one thing they make that I like the best. And I always pick up the menu and pretend like I might order something else. Then I put it down, like I just did, and get the very same thing I had the last time."

Kim smiled.

"Kind of weird, huh?"

"Maybe. But if it is, I'm the same kind of weird."

"You do that, too?"

"Pretty much. At some restaurants, there may be one or two things, but never three. I draw the line at two."

He laughed. "Well, you don't have to pick my favorite here. They're all good. My friends aren't afflicted with my limited culinary vision. They say you can't go wrong here no matter what you pick."

She began reading it over. "Oh my, they have linguine with white clam sauce. Ever had that here?"

"From what I've seen, it's loaded with clams. More than you'd put in if you made it yourself. You'll love it."

"Then that's what I'll get." She closed the menu. "Guess I'll have to find other Italian restaurants in town if I want something else."

He laughed. "You joke, but I actually go to two other places. One for lasagna, and another for chicken piccata."

She looked at him. He had to be kidding. A moment later he admitted he was. The waiter came, took their drink order, dropped off their water and silverware. He greeted Ned by name. But he called him *Officer Ned* with a pleasant Italian accent. "And who's your lovely friend," the man asked. Ned introduced her, told him what she did at the Humane Society.

"And what are you doing at the Humane Society?" the waiter asked Ned.

"Believe it or not, we rescued an abused dog yesterday during a drug bust and, wouldn't you know, the little guy stole my heart."

"So, you're getting a dog?"

"Pretty soon. He's still in pretty bad shape. But the folks where Kim works are going to get him all fixed up. And Kim is going to teach me how to train him."

"That's wonderful." He looked at Kim. "Officer Ned may look big and tough, but he's got an even bigger heart." He looked around the restaurant then leaned over toward Kim and said quietly, "He's-a my favorite police officer that comes in here. And I'm not just-a saying that. It's a-true."

"That's very kind of you," Ned said.

The waiter took their orders and headed back for the kitchen.

"He'll be right back out with our sodas and the most amazing Italian bread."

Kim was glad. She was actually thirsty and hungry. And she was really looking forward to this dinner. She hadn't found any place in town that made linguine with white clam sauce. And she was also enjoying this time with Ned. She could already tell, he was very easy to be with.

But when she looked up at Ned just now, she caught him releasing a sigh before he smiled again. She looked into his eyes and saw signs of stress there. "Is everything okay?"

"What? Yeah, couldn't be better. I'm here with you. I've had the whole day off. I'm about to become the proud parent of a special needs dog. I'm getting all kinds of help. And I'm about to have one of my favorite Italian dishes, perfectly prepared."

"I'm glad," she said. "I just thought I detected a little bit of strain in your eyes."

"An eye-reader, eh?"

She smiled. "Guilty as charged. Occupational hazard, I guess. I'm always reading dog's eyes. They say a lot with them. But people do, too. Even Jesus said that, *The lamp of the body is the eye*. Without even thinking, I often look at people's eyes."

"Well, guess I have to come clean then. There is something bothering me. It's not you, or even anything happening with Parker. It's just something that happened as I was leaving my apartment a little while ago."

"What was it?"

He sighed again, an even bigger one. "I bumped into this kid on the stairs. He lives next door. He and his mom just moved in a few weeks ago. Think we only met once, so I don't really know him. But after we bump into each other, I notice he's walking away holding his hand up by his face. Like he doesn't want me to see. Turns out, just a few minutes before that he'd got ambushed by two big bullies who've been bothering him at school ever since he moved in. His eye was almost swollen shut."

Kim gasped. "That's awful."

"Yeah, it really is."

"Can't you arrest them? That's, like, an assault, isn't it? Two big kids attack a smaller kid and punch him in the face like that? If two adults did that, you'd arrest them, right?"

"Yeah, we would. And it seems like we should apply the

same standard to bullies, too. But for some reason, we don't. Well, that's not exactly the case. We've been taught what the reasons are. I'm just not sure I agree with them. The thinking is, school-age kids have been getting in fights since the dawn of time. If we treated them all like crimes, it would overwhelm the justice system and give thousands of kids a criminal record that would follow them the rest of their lives. I get that. But I think school-age bullies need to experience a whole lot more consequences than they typically do. Most of the time, they simply get away with it. Meanwhile, they make their victims' lives a nightmare. It just isn't right."

"No, it isn't."

"Every now and then," Ned said, "bullies do face criminal charges, but it usually only happens if their victim winds up committing suicide or gets put in the hospital. But that's just crazy to me. If we'd punish these kids properly early on, things would never get that far." He sighed again. "I'm sorry, I didn't mean to get into all this."

"No, don't apologize. That's the reason you became a cop, right? To protect and serve? You even said earlier when you were talking about Parker, that you were bullied as a kid, and that's why you joined the force. I don't think you bumping into that little boy was a coincidence. Seems kind of like a God thing to me."

"You really think so?"

"I really do. I know this was supposed to be a get-to-know-you-better dinner. Guess that's what it's turning out to be. So, I should probably mention...I'm a Christian, and I read the Bible every day. I try real hard not to be pushy. I hope I'm not coming off that way. But the Book of Proverbs is full of verses that make it pretty clear, God hates it when people hurt or oppress others, especially people weaker than they are. So, I wouldn't be surprised if he didn't set up this accidental meeting with that little boy."

A big smile came over Ned's face. "I really like what you're saying, Kim. Looks like we have something else in common besides the weird way we pick restaurants. I read my Bible every morning before I leave for work."

"Really?"

"Yeah. With this job, I need a daily refresher. And I've probably read all those Proverbs you're talking about. And... I've actually got an idea about how to help Russell with this bully situation. That's the boy's name, Russell."

"I'd like to hear it," she said.

18

Russell's mom didn't get home from work for nearly an hour. During that time, he sat on the couch watching TV, holding an ice pack over his eye in hopes the swelling would shrink a lot before she got home.

It didn't. If anything, it looked a little worse.

He actually tried putting on some of her makeup but then washed it off. There was just no covering this up. She was in something of a hurry when she first got in and didn't notice his face. Scurrying about in the kitchen, doing this and that, she didn't really look at him for at least ten minutes. Then she asked him to join her at the dinette table. She'd brought home burgers and fries from McDonald's.

He sat down, began unwrapping his hamburger while she talked about how crazy things had gotten at Hobby Lobby, and how she had to fill in up front because one of the cashiers had gotten sick. Russell started eating, looking down as much as possible, hoping his baseball cap would shield his swollen eye.

She asked him a question. He didn't hear it. She asked it

again. "How did your visit go with your new friend? Russell, look at me when I talk to you."

He looked up.

She gasped.

"It went fine."

"What happened to your eye? Who did that to you? Did you and your friend get in a fight?"

"My friend, his name's Pete, didn't do this to me. Actually, I had a great time at Pete's house. This happened on the way home."

"Then who? Who did this to you?"

"Two big kids from school. They've been wanting to do this ever since my first day. Today, they finally got their wish." He picked up a french fry, dipped it in ketchup and took a bite.

"You're being bullied by two kids at school? And it's been going on for weeks? Why didn't you tell me?"

"Because there's nothing you can do. And I knew it would just worry you. And I was hoping I could keep avoiding them long enough until they finally gave up and started bothering someone else."

She got up, came over and stood behind him, wrapped her arms around him. "I'm so sorry, Russell. I still wish you would've told me. I'm not sure what I can do, but we have to do something. People can't go around hitting other people like this and get away with it. Does it hurt very much?"

"Some. But it's mostly just annoying, trying to see things out of that eye. And it stings a little. The ice helped some."

"I'm so sorry. Why did they do this? Did they tell you why?"

"Apparently, there's a new kid tax in this area that we knew nothing about before moving here. I didn't have the money, so they said they would have to hurt me instead."

"That is ridiculous. That sounds like something the Mafia would do. And you said there were two of them?" He nodded. "And you know who they are?"

"Yeah, I know their first and last names. They go to my school. But I don't know if the school can do anything. They hassle me at school, every day. But they did this on the sidewalk by the park just around the corner. Not on school property."

"We still need to talk to someone at your school. They need to know what's going on, especially if they're bothering you at school. What are they doing, saying intimidating things? Do they ever threaten you?"

He finished chewing a bite of hamburger. "That happens every day."

"Then see, we do have something to tell the school. That's not right for them to say those kinds of things to you. It's called verbal abuse."

He ate a couple more fries.

"And we should do more than that," she said. "We should call the police. That's a city park and a city sidewalk. You have the right to walk down it without being physically assaulted."

"Well, in a way, I've already talked to the police."

"You did?"

He told her about bumping into Ned, their next-door neighbor, and some of the things he had said.

"That was nice of him to say those things."

"Actually, he said he had a plan to help me with this bully situation, but he was in too much of a hurry to go into it. But he made me promise that I would tell you and the school before he could do whatever this thing is he wants to do."

"That settles it," she said. "I don't go into work until the afternoon tomorrow. I'm going down to the school and talk to someone in charge." She put her hamburger down and stood.

"Where are you going?"

She walked over to her purse on the kitchen counter. "To get my phone. I'm going to take pictures of your eye. Hopefully, that way they won't have to pull you out of class when I meet with them." She pulled off his hat. "Hold your head up into the light."

"Aww, Mom. Just take it."

"I want them to see what they did to you."

"But I told you, this didn't happen at school."

"No, but it was done by kids who go to your school, and who've been bullying you at school. This will help them see and believe we're not making this up or exaggerating."

"But what if...what if..."

"What if, what?"

"What if you do this, and the school does nothing about it? And then things get ten times worse for me?"

"They will do something about it. If they don't, I will."

"Mom, what can you do about it? You're a Mom."

"I don't know. But something. I can't let this go on. I can't let you keep getting treated like this. Now hold your head up into the light."

He did.

After she took five or six pics, she put the camera back and rejoined him at the table. "Now you'd never do something like this, would you? To smaller kids than you?"

"Mom, are you serious? There aren't any kids smaller than me. And even if there were, I wouldn't bother them. Why would I do something like that when I know how horrible it makes you feel?"

"Do you feel horrible...inside?"

He looked away, sighed. "Yeah, sometimes."

"How horrible?"

"How horrible? Horrible enough, I guess. I don't know what you're looking for here. Are there degrees of horribleness?"

"Yes, there are, in a way."

Then he figured out what she was getting at. "Are you worrying about...whether I'd ever do anything to hurt myself, because of being bullied?"

Tears filled her eyes. She nodded. "You wouldn't, would you? You'd come to me first, and let me help you, right? No matter how bad it got?"

"Mom, I'm fine. I'm not suicidal here."

"But you said you feel horrible inside. Maybe you're not that bad yet, but what about later? If this doesn't get fixed right away. Promise me, you'd never think of doing that, of taking your life."

"I won't, Mom."

"Promise me."

"All right. I promise."

"You'll come to me first. If it ever gets that bad. If you're ever even thinking thoughts like that, even for a minute. You'll come to me."

"I will. I will come to you."

"Because I will do anything humanly possible to protect you. You know that, right? I'll work two jobs if I have to, to get you into a private school."

"Mom, really. I'm okay. We'll find a way through this. Let's see what Ned has in mind. Maybe he's got an idea that'll work."

"Ned?"

"The cop next door."

"Oh, yes. I wonder what he's thinking."

"Me, too. But he said he'll tell me, after I tell you. Check that box off right now. *And* we talk to the school, which you're going to do tomorrow."

"I will. I'll drive right down there as soon as they open."

"Mom, sleep in a little. It can wait till ten." He thought about asking her something else.

"What?" she said. "You want to say something? What is it?"

"Would you mind if I don't go to school tomorrow? I really don't want to face those boys after the way things ended. You know, with me kicking them before I took off. And tomorrow's Friday. If I don't go in tomorrow, I'll have two more days to heal up. Maybe my eye won't look so bad by Monday."

"You can stay home tomorrow. But I'm still going down there. What did you do to those boys?"

He told her.

"Good," she said. "They had it coming."

19

Ned and Kim had finished their meal about twenty minutes ago. Neither had room for dessert. Ned was taking home about a third of his dinner in a doggy bag; Kim almost half. They had spent the rest of the time chatting and enjoying each other's company over coffee.

Ned kept looking for any telltale signs that Kim wanted to wrap things up but didn't see any. They really hadn't talked about dog training at all. Instead, they'd exchanged a hodge-podge of miscellaneous life stories that wandered back and forth over the timeline of their lives.

The most recent one Kim shared had, in some ways, impressed Ned the most. Off and on over the past six months she'd been dating billionaire real estate developer Taylor Saunders. They had recently broken it off but remained on friendly terms. Ned had seen pictures of Taylor in online news stories and magazine articles. He was a pretty handsome guy. That she had walked away from a relationship like that without any hesitation said a lot about her character.

He was about to say Taylor would be a hard act to follow but decided that would be pushing it, since they weren't really even on a date yet. Although this visit was starting to feel more and more like one, at least for him.

She looked at her watch for the first time. "Well, I guess I better get going. I was enjoying this so much, I forgot all about something I'm supposed to do."

That sounded sincere. "Like, washing your hair?"

"What?" She laughed. She'd gotten the joke. "No, I don't have to go home and wash my hair. Actually, I'm not even going home. I'm supposed to meet my mom in about twenty minutes. She's picking out a dress to wear for a big social event, and she always wants my input with fashion decisions."

"That's great you guys are good friends." He had already shared with her over dinner that, sadly, both his parents had passed away a few years ago.

"We do get along great. We didn't always, though. In fact, in my teen years we weren't close at all. But I think a lot of that was me. Like that old saying about how ignorant you thought your parents were when you were a teen and couldn't believe how smart they'd become by the time you reached your twenties. Something like that, anyway." She stood up. "Can I at least get the tip?"

"Nope." He stood, too. "You can go ahead and go if you need to, since I'm taking care of this." He picked up the check.

She glanced at her watch again. "I better if I want to meet her on time. But I really had fun, Ned. Now, I'm really looking forward to working with you and Parker."

"You weren't before?"

"No, I was. But a lot more now."

"I'm glad."

"Well, I better go." She took a few steps toward the door.

"Any chance you'd be open to getting together again, even if we're not training Parker?"

She turned, took a few more steps then looked back over her shoulder. "I believe I am." She smiled, waved and kept walking.

NED WAS in a great mood as he pulled into one of his two parking spaces at the apartment complex. He'd really enjoyed his dinner with Kim. Especially knowing that, at the end, it was clear she had enjoyed it too. On the way home, he'd stopped at the store to pick up a few things, grabbed a DVD from Red Box. When he reached the top of the stairs and turned down the walkway, he saw Russell carrying an empty trashcan coming from the other direction. He waved.

Russell set the trashcan down by his front door and ran up to Ned. "I did it, Ned."

"Did what?" He tried not to focus on Russell's swollen eye.

"Told my mom about the bullying. Told her everything. Well, everything except them calling me Monkey Boy."

"That's great, Russell. Let me guess, she yelled at you for it?"

"No."

"She grounded you for three weeks?"

He laughed. "No."

"She made fun of you, called you a weakling?"

"No, she was just like you said she'd be."

"So, it was a good thing to tell her."

"Yeah, it was. I'm glad I told her. But that's not all, she's going down to the school tomorrow to tell them what's been happening to me. I'm not so sure about that part."

"What do you mean?"

"Whether it will do any good. Or maybe even make things worse for me."

"I have a feeling," Ned said, "that it'll be just fine. They won't fix the problem, but it might be better if they're at least aware of what's going on. I'm sure they already have some anti-bullying programs. Most schools do now."

"And I'm sure, they're *so* effective," Russell said.

"Okay, they haven't stopped all the bullying. I get that. And I think they could do a lot more, should do a lot more. But believe me, it's better that they know. These guys need to feel some consequences, or they'll never stop."

"Speaking of consequences," Russell said, "before you said if I talked to my mom and the school, you'd tell me some idea you had that you thought would help me. Can you tell me now?"

Ned thought a moment. "I guess so. But first, I need to talk to your mom about it, make sure she's okay with the idea. No sense in getting you all lathered up about it, if she hates it."

"Can I go get her now?"

"I suppose so."

"Great. I'll put the trash can back and send her right out." He turned and hurried to his task.

Less than two minutes later, his mom came out and closed the door behind her. "Hi, Officer. Russell said you wanted to see me."

"Did he tell you why?"

She walked toward him and held out her hand. He shook it. "Just that you have some idea about how to help Russell with this bully thing he's going through. Before you tell me what it is, I really want to thank you, just for talking to him at all. I was horrified when I saw his eye, but even more so when I heard how it happened and what he's been going through."

"Yeah, bullies are the worst. I went through the same thing as a kid. Almost ruined my childhood."

"You read about it in the news and sometimes see stories about it on TV," she said. "But it never dawned on me that it would happen to my own kid."

"Sadly, the stories you hear about are only a fraction of the incidents going on. Usually, the worst ones. Like when someone commits suicide after being bullied. But there are hundreds more, like what happened to Russell today, that no one ever hears about. Except the victim, whose life gets turned into a nightmare. I used to wake up every school day gripped with fear. My experience is really why I became a cop."

"So, you really do get what Russell's going through?"

"I really do, Ma'am. That's why I want to help, so he doesn't have to go through what I did. There's no reason for him to live in fear, even if the school does nothing about it. I'm not saying they won't but, let's face it, they've been trying different programs for years, but it still goes on every day."

"So, what's your idea? How can you help him with this? Oh, and by the way, let's drop the Ma'am. I'm guessing I'm only about ten years older than you. Call me Marilyn."

"All right, I will. And you can stop calling me Officer. It's Ned."

"Okay Ned, what's your idea?"

20

N ed thought a moment. How should he explain this, exactly? Standing here, facing Russell's mother, he suddenly felt a little nervous about just saying it. It wasn't a bad thing. Really, it was a good thing, a needful thing considering the situation.

But she was a mom.

"What's the matter, Ned?" Marilyn said.

"Nothing's the matter. I just...hadn't thought through how to explain it."

"Is it a complicated thing? If it is, keep in mind, I'm very low-tech."

"No, it's not complicated. Controversial maybe, but not complicated."

"Well just spit it out. I'm a big girl. Even if I hate it, I promise, I won't bite your head off."

"Okay, maybe I'll start with this...do you have a problem with the idea of Russell defending himself? I mean versus the idea of always running away when confronted by a bully?"

"Not really. I guess he kind of did both things in this situation. Did he tell you what he did to the guys after they hit him?"

"Yeah, but I wouldn't exactly call that a solid self-defense. It was more about buying him time to get away. I'm not saying that's wrong. Considering the way things are now, it was a pretty smart thing to do. But it sounds like he just made the bullies madder. My guess is, they're pretty highly motivated to want to get him back versus deciding it would be in their best interest to leave him alone altogether."

"That's probably true. Which is why I said he could stay home tomorrow. Between that and the weekend, I'm hoping maybe things will calm down."

"They may, some. But the situation's not over. I'm afraid they'll still be looking for payback."

A look of dread came over her face. She sighed. "Why are boys so mean now? I don't understand. Russell is such a fun kid. So easy to be around. He can get along with anybody."

"I think that's probably true, just from the little time I've spent with him. And what's happening to him is not his fault. Not even a little bit. But I'm not so sure boys are meaner now than they used to be. Maybe they are, but they were plenty mean to me growing up. And in some ways, girls are just as mean as boys now. That seems like something new. I mean, there's a type of girl that has always been mean and cruel, but now it seems like they're getting as physically abusive as the boys."

"Then you throw in smart phones and YouTube," Marilyn said.

"Right," Ned said. "Everyone wants their fifteen minutes of fame. Whatever the case, the bottom line is, all we've got now is a band aid on this situation with Russell. I'm talking about an idea that might be closer to a real solution."

"Whatever it is, I'm for it. I don't want him to have to live his life in fear, always worrying when the next ambush might happen."

Good, Ned thought. Now he felt better about his plan. "The basic idea is for Russell to start taking self-defense classes. He needs to learn how to defend himself properly, so that he can stop being the victim in these kinds of situations."

"You mean, teach him to fight back? I'm not so sure that's a good idea. You heard there were two kids attacking him here, right? Both of them older and bigger than he is."

"I know, but—"

"If he started fighting back, he might get in a few punches, but I'm afraid after that, he'd be done for. He's not a big kid, Ned, and he doesn't really have the instincts to be a fighter. I'm afraid these guys would've beat him to a pulp if he hadn't run away."

"I see your point, Marilyn. But you're evaluating him based on where he's at now. The self-defense classes I'm talking about are intended to change the equation completely. I've taken them myself, even beyond the regular training we get as cops. Essentially, I'm talking about MMA classes. Mixed martial arts."

"You mean like karate and kung fu?"

Ned laughed. "Kind of. But more like Muay Thai and kick-boxing. Might be a little karate in there, too. The place I have in mind kind of repackages these skills in a way that can be taught to kids Russell's age. I've gone there several times to watch and met with the two guys heading it up. Both of them are great with kids. Did you ever see the Karate Kid movie?"

"Yeah. Actually, I was thinking about that while you were talking."

"Well, these instructors are nothing like the sensei in the movie. That's what they call coaches. He was a total jerk, and so were his students. These guys are just the opposite of that. In fact, they spend as much time, maybe more, on kids having the right attitude toward others than on MMA skills."

"Kind of like Mr. Miyagi?" she said.

"In a way, yeah. Maybe not so philosophical, and they definitely don't get kids to wax their cars or paint their fence. But they really drill them on character issues like self-discipline, sacrifice, and hard work. And really, they stress the idea of how to talk down a potentially tense situation. How to de-escalate the tension. My guess is, Russell's already pretty good at that."

"He definitely has the gift of gab," Marilyn said.

"And see, even with that, sometimes you just can't talk yourself out of a bad situation. Taking these classes would give Russell the confidence to know how to handle what came next, if bullies don't back down."

An incredulous look appeared on her face.

"What's the matter?"

"You're telling me, if Russell took these classes he could have defended himself against two bigger and older guys, like the ones who came after him today?"

Ned nodded. "Not right off the bat, but eventually yes. He would learn how to put such a hurt on those two kids that he could walk away, not run, from the situation. And they would likely think twice before they'd ever bother him again." Ned couldn't read her face for a few moments, but then she smiled.

"It almost sounds too good to be true. You really think that's possible?"

"Definitely. Like I said, not after one or two lessons, but probably by the time he finished the first series of classes. That is, if he faithfully attends them all and practiced a lot in between."

She bit her lip and muttered, "Seems hard to believe."

"I know, but I've seen it with my own eyes. And even though he wouldn't know enough to totally defend himself after those first few classes, you would already see a change in his attitude."

"Like what?"

"Hope, for one. A greater sense of confidence, for another. Because he'll see kids his own age, some no bigger than he is, who've been at this for a while doing things that he would never have imagined he could do."

Marilyn seemed to be thinking about it. But as she did, the look on her face changed. Like she was discouraged.

"Is there a problem?"

"Well, I did say I'd work two jobs, if I needed to, to put him in a private school. I guess I could do it for something like this. Do you know much it costs?"

"I do. But it won't cost you a cent. I've thought of a way this could work."

"What? I can't let you pay for it."

"You're not. Not exactly. I've thought of something that would allow Russell to actually pay for it himself."

"How? Russell doesn't earn any money."

"But what if he could?"

"Like how, doing what?"

"In a little while, I'm going to be fostering a little dog from the Humane Society. I rescued him from a drug dealer we arrested, but he was in pretty bad shape. The Humane Society is getting him fixed up. As soon as he's well enough, he'll be staying with me. But I don't like the idea of him being shut up in my apartment for the entire length of my shift. The poor dog's been neglected enough. I was thinking we could work something out, so that Russell could look after Parker when I'm at work. Not the whole time, obviously. Just visit him a few times, maybe change his water, take him out to go the bathroom."

"Parker?" she said.

"That's his name. So, what do you think? Could Russell handle something like that?"

"He definitely could. He's very responsible, and I know he loves dogs. He's always wanted one, but we could never get one. You know, because of how often we moved."

"Then that settles it. Russell can watch Parker for me, and I'll cover the cost of his classes."

"That hardly seems like a fair trade. I'm sure these classes cost more than the little bit of work Russell will be doing with your dog."

"I think it's a fair trade."

Tears welled up in Marilyn's eyes. "I can't believe you would do this for him, for us. She gave Ned a hug. "Can I go tell him? Is this really going to happen?"

"It's really going to happen, so yeah, go ahead and tell him. I'll find out more details tomorrow and let you know."

21

The next morning, Parker opened his eyes and surveyed his surroundings. Still here. Still in this same place, whatever it was. But he was no longer in a cage. At some point while he slept, he had been moved to a much larger space. The side walls were solid and rose high above his head. Same thing with the wall behind him. But in the front was a metal gate just as tall as the walls. Through it, he saw three identical pens across from him. In them were three different dogs, all still asleep.

As he lifted his head, he was suddenly aware of an almost insatiable thirst. Thankfully, a little water bowl sat in the corner. He stood and stretched and noticed how different his front legs looked. The hair was almost gone. He turned his head around and checked himself out, as much as he could see. Same thing. Most of his hair was gone. But so was most of the pain he usually felt every day moments after he awoke.

He stepped off a blanket that covered the padded cushion

he'd been lying on and headed for the water bowl. He drank until he could drink no more. So good to drink fresh water.

Where was The Man? He sniffed the air around him. Nothing. Only the smell of other dogs. Was The Man finally gone for good? Who should he look to now? Several different people had interacted with him in this place. All of them much nicer.

Like this, getting fresh water. Again.

He walked toward the gate and looked to the left, down the aisle in front of him, as far as he could see. No humans in sight, though he could hear some talking not far away. He walked back and lay down on the blanket. That's when he noticed a small doorway on the back wall. It was open enough for him to get through. Was that where he was supposed to go the bathroom?

He got up to explore. It was a closed fenced-in area about the same size as the space inside. The same type of smooth floor but perfectly clean. No blankets or beds or bowls. He had to go so bad. Would he be punished if he went out here? He sniffed the air. Other dogs had gone nearby. Really, he had no choice. He quickly did what he needed to do and scurried back inside and lay on the blanket. Hopefully, no one would hurt him for messing up the floor.

Suddenly, most of the dogs inside began to bark. He stood and cautiously approached the gate. People were coming. The dogs barked louder. Way too loud for him. He wasn't used to so much noise. He ran back to the blanket and curled up in a ball. He wished he had a smaller place to crawl into.

Someone was coming. She was calling out different names and saying pleasant things in a nice voice. She kept stopping and interacting with different dogs, who were clearly happy to see her. Her voice was definitely familiar. Another woman spoke, too. Her voice, also familiar.

Now she stood right in front of him. "And how's Parker doing this morning? There he is. I see you've been drinking your water. That's a good sign. Has he eaten anything yet?"

"Not yet, but none of them have. They'll be feeding them all in just a few minutes."

"Hopefully, his appetite will start kicking in. Look at the poor thing. You can see all his ribs."

"Especially now, with all his hair clipped off."

The first woman who spoke bent down and put her fingers through the gate. "Hey Parker, remember me? It's Kim. And this is Amy. Remember her?"

Parker looked up at them, both smiling, both wearing happy faces. They did look familiar, but he wasn't sure why. When he last saw them, his mind was so fuzzy. But now it was clear. Whoever they were, he liked the way they spoke, even if he didn't understand a single word they said. Then the woman took something out of her pocket. Instantly, he recognized the smell.

"Remember this? Look at his tail wagging, Amy. That's the first time I've seen that. You do remember this, don't you Parker? Yummy treats. You want one? You can have it." She stuck the treat between her fingers and poked it forward through the opening in the gate. "Come and get it. Do you want it?"

He sat up. He desperately wanted that treat, but an overwhelming fear pinned him to the blanket. Why couldn't he just step forward and get the treat? He looked at her face and her eyes, still so pleasant and nice. She didn't seem like someone who would ever hurt him. But how could he tell? How could he be sure?

"YOU CAN SEE HE WANTS IT," Amy said. "He's just afraid."

"I'm not surprised he's holding back," Kim said. "It's been a long time since he's been treated well by a human. I just want to keep reinforcing the message that people can be good, and that we're not going to hurt him. So, I'm going to keep stopping by several times a day, just being really nice and giving him a treat. Eventually, he'll start to recognize me, and maybe one of these times he'll actually take the treat from my hand."

"Is it okay if I do the same thing, if I'm back in this part of the shelter?"

"Sure, that would be great. Let's talk with the Doc first before we head back to the office, make sure we don't wind up overfeeding him. I'm sure she's going to have him on some special diet since he's so malnourished." Kim stood slowly and opened his gate door, enough to slip her hand through. She tossed the treat to the floor just in front of his blanket. "There you go, Parker. You eat that when you're ready."

Parker quickly stretched his head forward and grabbed the treat.

"Look at that," Amy said. "He really did want it."

"That's a good boy, Parker," Kim said. "You just rest and I'll be back to see you later."

She and Amy headed back toward the door that led to the Infirmary, stopping along the way to greet several of the dogs.

Just before they reached the door, Amy gently grabbed Kim's wrist. "Before we go back out there into the world of humans, tell me how it went last night?"

"With my mom? We had to go to four places and try on ten outfits, but we finally found the perfect dress."

"I don't mean with your mom. Although I'm glad that worked out, too. I'm talking about your dinner with Ned. How did it go?"

"It went fine. But it wasn't really a date, not officially."

"Then what was it, officially? Were you just talking about training Parker?"

"No. As a matter fact, we hardly talked about dog training at all."

"Then what?"

"It was more of, you know, this or that."

"Was he easy to talk to, or was it more like pulling teeth?"

"Ned was really easy to talk to. I enjoyed being with him."

"Where did he take you?"

"To a Ma and Pa Italian place I'd never heard of before. I guess a lot of police officers go there. It wasn't anything fancy, but the food was delicious. Got something I never get to have any more, linguine with white clam sauce."

"So, what did you guys talk about?"

"Things. All kinds of things. We talked about our backgrounds, different things about our childhood growing up. Talked about how he became a cop. Really, more about why he did."

"And why did he?"

Kim took a few minutes to recap what Ned had said about his experiences being bullied as a kid and the effect that had on him. Then she shared the story about the little boy he'd bumped into at his apartment complex, just before he'd left for the restaurant. "Then that got into an interesting chat about bullying in schools and how bad it's gotten lately. It's way worse than it was when we were young. Besides all the normal stuff, you've got cyber-bullying going on, too."

"And all these kids trying to get everything on YouTube," Amy added. "I'd hate to be a kid going through school now."

"Yeah, we talked about all that. But then he shared something that was pretty cool, about this kid being bullied who lives next door. Ned said he was going to talk to his mom about paying for him to take self-defense classes. He's already looked into it. There's some kind of place in town that specializes in teaching kids how to do properly deal with being bullied, so they don't have to live in fear anymore."

"Really? He's going to do that for a kid he barely knows?"

Kim nodded. "Isn't that sweet?"

"So, he's going to help out this neighbor kid in distress, he's going to foster an abused little dog? And he's really nice, and really easy to be with? And he takes you to a place that has great food, but you don't have to fly there in a plane. Does that about size things up?"

Kim smiled. "I guess it does."

"I don't know, Kim. Sounds like a keeper to me."

22

Ned's shift today didn't start until three. He had just finished eating lunch and decided to check in with Marilyn, Russell's mom, to see how her time had gone at the school that morning. A few minutes ago, he'd texted her. His phone chimed indicating a text. He picked it up and read it. It was from Marilyn.

Are you home? If so, can we speak outside?

He texted back. *I am. Door's open. Why don't you come on in?* As he put his phone away, he heard her front door open and close. He wondered what she wanted to say. Maybe things didn't go so well at the school.

His front door opened, and she slipped in. "I wanted to talk somewhere Russell couldn't hear."

The look on her face confirmed, she wasn't happy with the school visit. "That's probably a good idea. So how did it go?"

"Well, the upside was, they did listen, and they took some notes while I spoke. Asked me a bunch of questions, even looked at the pics on my phone."

"I'm sensing a *But* here..."

"Oh, there's definitely a *But* here. The man I spoke with-- guess he's the official designee for handling bullying complaints--seemed very polished and practiced. But it all felt very routine to me, like he was just going through the motions, following some set of rules and policies he'd been trained in at a seminar. It didn't feel like I was talking to a real person at all. Not someone who cared. And based on some of the things he said, I'm not sure they're really going to do anything about it. Not yet anyway."

"What were some of the things he said that bothered you?"

"Well, he made a big deal of the point that this incident didn't happen on school grounds, and that they didn't have any other reports on file involving these two young men. Not for bullying anyone anyway. I'm sorry, but I kinda lost it a little on that one. I asked him did he think I was making this up? Or that maybe my son was?"

"What did he say to that?"

"He apologized, very officially, for giving me that impression. That was not what he meant by what he said. That's when I showed him the pictures of Russell's eye. Just to prove to him, I'm not just some overreacting, irate mom."

"Let me guess," Ned said, "the pictures definitely registered on his face, but you wouldn't know it by what he said next."

"Exactly," Marilyn said. "How would you know that?"

"I didn't want to say anything to discourage you from doing it, you know, reporting what happened to the school. They really should be informed. There's always the hope they might make a difference."

"Sounds like you didn't have high expectations."

"Sadly, I didn't. I'm pretty aware of the anti-bullying policies and procedures being followed at public schools. And I've dealt with several other bullying situations involving kids in public schools. That's why I started looking into more effective alternatives. They know how bad the bullying has become, but just like any bureaucratic organization, they try to fix the problem by putting together all kinds of programs filled with legal jargon and protocols that end up not connecting to anything even close to a real solution. The bullying just goes on and on, the kids being victimized still keep hating life, and many wind up regretting they ever even reported it in the first place. Did they say they would do anything?"

Marilyn paused to think a moment. "I'm not even sure he did. Oh wait, he did say if these boys did anything to Russell during school hours or on school property, even if they just used words versus getting physical, he should come back and report it."

"Then what?"

"Then, I guess, that would start a process where someone would go to the boys and then talk to Russell, and then there would be all these steps that would be followed that would, hopefully, resolve the situation peacefully. After he got finished explaining, I didn't say what I was thinking."

Ned laughed. "What were you thinking?"

"Maybe he could then get them to hold hands and teach them the chorus to Kumbaya."

Ned laughed even harder. But it was such a shame to put all that time and energy into fixing a problem, a big problem, without even coming close to reaching the goal.

"I got the feeling," she continued, "that their whole approach to this issue is just CYA, you know? Have something in place, so they can say they do when people ask, but everyone who has to actually interact with it can tell right off the bat...they really aren't going to fix this."

"Sadly, that's the same impression I got the last time I dealt with this issue, though it's been a little while. I was hoping it might have changed. But in a way, it mirrors the kind of problems we run into in the criminal justice arena. The whole process has become so bogged down with laws and policies and regulations that seem to favor the bad guys. At least ones that give them the impression, they have very little to fear if they break the law and wind up getting caught."

Marilyn sighed. "That's the way things look to me when I watch the news. Which is why I don't watch it that much. Too discouraging. But I can see if a kid is wired to become a bully, and he has no internal compass telling him how wrong it is to treat people that way, and then he experiences almost no significant consequences when he gets caught...I can see a kid thinking that committing big people crimes might not be such a bad way to go."

"I think," Ned said, "what you just said happens all the time."

"Which is why," Marilyn said, "I wanted to talk to you. I didn't want Russell to get discouraged about how things really went at school, so I was totally vague with him when I got home. I quickly changed the subject to the self-defense classes you mentioned yesterday. Have you had a chance to look into the details yet?"

"I did. And I think it will work out just fine. The best class for him to start meets on Tuesdays and Thursdays after school, from five to six-thirty. The way my schedule works, I can probably take him to about half of them myself."

"My schedule's always changing, too. You know, retail. Hopefully, I'll be able take him to the other half."

"And for the ones you can't, and I can't, he could ride a bike. It's not that far away."

Her face looked sad. "Russell doesn't have a bike. Not anymore. His last one got stolen, and I haven't had the money to replace it yet."

"Well," Ned said. "We'll have to do something about that. I've got an idea that might just work."

23

Ned pulled into the Humane Society parking lot. After chatting with Russell's mom, he'd decided to stop in and see Parker a few minutes, so he texted Kim to see if she thought it'd be a good idea. She did and told him about her brief visit with him a little while ago. Sounded like Parker was still acting pretty skittish, but at least he was much more alert.

The vet had approved moving him into a regular kennel in the infirmary. Kim had explained that was sort of like being allowed to leave the intensive care unit and put in a regular bed. This was good news.

Before getting out of his car, per her instructions, he sent her a brief text saying, "I'm here." He walked into the lobby and greeted the volunteer receptionist.

"Hello, Officer. How can I help you?"

"Kim Harper is meeting me here to help with a visit to the infirmary. I'm going to be fostering a dog in there when he's well enough to leave. Do you know Kim?"

"Everyone knows Kim." A door in the back of the lobby opened. "There she is now."

Ned smiled in Kim's direction and waved then signed his name on the clipboard. "Glad you could make it."

"Me, too."

"I don't really have an agenda. Just thought it would be good for the little guy to keep seeing me, so he could get used to being around me."

"I think that's a great idea. Follow me."

They walked through a now familiar set of hallways and doorways.

"When do you go in?" she asked.

"My shift starts at three today."

"Do you see a lot more action when you work at night?"

"Usually more than in the day. Like that Bible verse in John's Gospel, *Men loved darkness rather than light, because their deeds are evil.* Of course, living in a town like Summerville the evil is nowhere near as bad as in a big city."

"Do you ever have to use your gun?"

"I've had to take it out several times but, thankfully, I've never had to shoot anyone." She looked like she wanted to ask him something else. "What?" She shook her head as if talking herself out of it. "You wondering if I've ever been shot at?"

She nodded. "Really, it's none of my business."

But Ned got why she was wondering. It was actually an encouraging sign, showed a level of interest in him. The danger issue was always there when people considered getting into a closer relationship with a cop. "I don't mind you asking. Again, thankfully, I've never been shot at, either. Had some drug busts where it was clear the dealers had weapons, but we always got the jump on them before any shooting started."

"That's good."

"Summerville hasn't had an officer die in the line of duty for over ten years. And the last one wasn't a shooting. It was a car accident during a chase situation."

"So, you feel pretty safe most of the time when you head out?"

"I do. Of course, we don't play it safe in training. We always train for the worst-case scenario, even though we hope we're never in one. But if something like a big-city situation occurred, we'd be ready. It wouldn't freak us out. For example, I've become a marksman with this pistol. I'm in the top three in the department. And I keep training, so I don't get rusty. But all the while, I hope I never use it."

"I bought a pistol last year. Someone broke into several apartments at our complex, and I hated feeling so helpless."

"Nothing wrong with that," Ned said. "Did you take any lessons on how to use it properly?"

"I did, right after I bought it. But then the burglar got caught, and we haven't had any trouble since. So, I've never used it again. You know, at a gun range. I'm not even sure I remember half of what the instructor told me."

"I'm actually a certified instructor. Maybe we could book some time at a gun range soon."

"I think I might actually like doing that."

"Good. Then I'll set it up."

They had reached the door to the infirmary, but Kim walked past it. "The kennel for the dogs under medical care is through this door at the end of the hall." Ned followed her through the doorway. Instantly, a number of dogs began barking as they entered their space. Ned hoped their little talk about how relatively safe he was being a cop in Summerville had done some good. If not, he'd know it if she started to back away.

He thought about one thing to add. "Kim, about this thing we've been talking about...thought I should mention...I'm not like any of the cops you see in movies or TV shows."

"What do you mean?"

"You know, the gung ho, macho kind of adrenaline-junkies always living on the edge. We actually have a few guys in the department like that. But that's not me. You already know why I became a cop. And it's not for stuff like that."

"Good. I'm glad." She turned her attention now to the dogs in the kennels, who were all clearly trying to get her attention.

He realized, he didn't need to say that last part. He was trying too hard. Time to refocus on the main reason he had come. "Which one is Parker in? Wow, feels like a lot more dogs here today."

"Yeah, they've all been neutered or spayed. Most will be going home today. Parker's just a few more doors down on the right."

PARKER WAS HALF-ASLEEP. The barking dogs instantly awoke him. Then he heard a familiar woman's voice interacting with the dogs. The same nice voice from a little while ago. Then a man's voice. He spoke his name. He recognized it, too. The nice man who had taken him away from the horrible place he'd been living in.

Parker sat up. There they were, coming from the left. Now they were standing right in front of him.

"Look at that," the woman said. "He's sitting up, and his tail's wagging."

The man was smiling. He bent down. "Hey, Parker. How you doing, boy? Looks like you're doing a little better." He turned toward the woman. "Boy, he looks so different without his hair."

"Doesn't he? But it should all grow back."

"Those reddish areas are a little better, don't you think?"

"Yeah, a little. The Doc cleaned them all up. We need to keep putting ointment on them, but they should heal up completely, too."

Parker didn't understand a word either of them had said, which made him a little nervous. Their voices seemed a little more serious.

"Oh look," the woman said. "His tail stopped wagging. Hey Parker, you're a good boy."

"Yeah," Ned said. "Let's talk about the medical stuff later." He reached his fingers through one of the openings in the gate, and his face got all bright again. "Parker, remember me? He's a good boy, aren't you? Such a good boy." He looked toward the woman. "Have any of those treats?"

Treats? Parker's tail began to wag again.

"I sure do." She handed him a couple.

Parker's eyes latched onto the treat now dangling between the man's two fingers, sticking through the gate.

"You want this, Parker? Sure you do. Come on, you can have it. Come on, just take it."

"I don't think he'll do that," Kim said. "You can see he wants it, but I think he's still got way too much fear to overcome."

"He's still looking right at it," Ned said. "And his tail's still wagging. You want this, Parker? Here you go. Come on, you can do it."

"Try this, Ned. Don't talk to him or look at him. Just keep

the treat in your hand and wait. Let's give him time to make a choice without any pressure."

"Okay. Guess we need to be patient."

Parker decided he really wanted that treat. He wanted it bad. And the man holding it out to him had only ever been so nice and kind to him. Even this new place, as strange as it was, it was so much nicer than anywhere he had ever been. And it was because of this man. He decided to take a chance.

"My gosh," Ned said. "He's getting up."

Parker walked to within a couple of inches of the treat and the man's fingers still holding it. The smell of the thing was overwhelming. And there was no way the man could touch him. Parker could get the treat safely, and be back to his blanket with it in a flash.

So, that's what he did.

"He did it!" Kim said excitedly. "I can't believe it."

"Yes, he did. I think he's warming up to me."

"I'd say he definitely is."

Parker lay there chewing the treat. He wanted to chew it slowly, but it was too good. He downed it in three more bites.

Standing, Ned turned and looked at Kim. "That was amazing advice, Kim. I can't wait to learn more about training Parker from you."

As they held eye contact, Kim realized, she was already starting to fall for Officer Ned Barringer.

24

I t was a little after 3:15 as Russell stood before Pete's front door. He hoped he timed it right. Pete should be home from school by now.

Russell had checked his eye out in the mirror before leaving. The swelling was down a little, at least it seemed like it to him. Even so, he felt better going outside wearing an old pair of sunglasses, although it had been cloudy all afternoon. And he had taken an extra fifteen minutes to walk here, to make sure there was no chance he'd bump into Edmund and Harley. He took a deep breath and was just about to knock on the front door when it suddenly opened.

"Oh, you scared me." It was Pete's mom, holding her purse and keys.

"I'm sorry. I just came over to see Pete. We met yesterday when I came over, remember?"

"I do. Russell, right? I forget your last name."

"Russell's fine."

"I like your sunglasses." She looked up at the sky.

"Although it doesn't seem too sunny out right now. I was even wondering if I needed my umbrella."

Change the subject, he thought. "Is Pete here?"

She stepped aside to let him in. "He's in his bedroom playing a video game. You remember where that is, don't you?"

"Yep, I do." Russell walked past her quickly, hoping to avoid any more conversation. "See ya."

She said bye and closed the door behind her. Pete's bedroom door was closed except for a few inches. Russell knocked, walked in and closed it behind him.

Pete turned around then paused his game. "You came. I was wondering if you were going to. Are those shades because..."

Russell took them off and set them on top of his head.

"Oh man, that looks painful." He got up and came closer.

"It was a lot worse yesterday evening. Now it just hurts if you touch it." He walked over and sat on the edge of Pete's bed. "Why were you wondering if I was still coming over?"

"Well, I didn't see you at school today, but then I heard some people talking about you getting in a fight with Dumb and Dumber." Russell laughed. "Then I saw them at the cafeteria and neither one of them looked like they'd been in a fight, so I put two and two together."

"So, is everybody talking about it, like it's a big deal?"

"Not everybody, but some folks were. It's not like you're a household name. So, you have that going for you. But I did hear Edmund say it wasn't finished yet, then Harley added you got away before the fight was over."

"So that's how they described it, a fight? It wasn't a fight. It was an ambush. Didn't anyone bring up the fact that it was two against one? Or that both of these guys have twenty to thirty pounds on me?"

"No, I don't recall anyone challenging or correcting Edmund and Harley's recollection of the event. That was probably because no one wanted to look like you."

"It's just so ridiculous that these guys would act like we had a legitimate fight. We've never even had a conversation before, let alone an argument." He pointed to his eye. "You know why I got this? Want to know what they said?"

Pete nodded.

"They decided there should be some kind of new kid tax, and I didn't have any money on me to pay it."

Pete shook his head. "Yeah, they neglected to tell that part of the story."

"And I guess they didn't share about how I got away?"

"They didn't. But I was wondering about that."

Russell shared what he did.

Pete laughed. "I would have loved to see that. Now I understand why they left that part of the story out. So, did your mom find out? Well, obviously she did. No hiding that. What did she say?"

Russell told him, then said, "But something pretty cool actually happened before my mom came home."

"Yeah, what?"

Russell told him about bumping into Ned and who Ned was.

"So, a cop knows about this?" Pete said. "What's he going to do, arrest them?"

"No, for some reason, they don't arrest bullies. I think if they killed me, they might."

"So, why's it good that your cop neighbor knows about this then?"

"He's going to sign me up to take MMA classes. He knows this place that does it for kids."

"MMA?" Pete said. "Should I know what that is?"

"MMA, Mixed Martial Arts. You know, like the UFC. Kickboxing, Mui Thai, and other stuff, I guess. It's some special program that teaches kids our age how to defend ourselves against bullies. Kids who don't have the big brother option like you."

"Really? Martial arts lessons," Pete repeated. "That really is pretty cool. And this cop's gonna pay for this?"

Russell nodded and explained the deal about how he's supposed to watch Ned's new dog after school.

"That doesn't sound so bad. So when do these classes start?"

"Next week, I think," Russell said.

Just then, Pete's expression soured, and he released a sigh.

"What's the matter?"

"Nothing. I just was thinking...it's probably going to be several weeks into these classes before they teach you anything you can use in a street fight. Probably spend the first few weeks covering the basics, don't you think? What are you going to do about Edmund and Harley between now and then? I get the impression they aren't planning on waiting several weeks before they..."

Why did Pete have to bring that up? Russell hadn't really thought about that yet. He sighed. "I don't know. Guess I'll have to just keep running faster than they can. I'm pretty sure they won't try anything at school. Other than make fun and try to intimidate me. But even then, my Mom did tell the school what happened."

"Oh, yeah? What did they say?"

"She didn't tell me much. I got the impression she wasn't too impressed with their ideas. She was really emphasizing these MMA classes after talking to them. But she did say, if they did ever bother me at school, even if it was just words, I should tell them and they'd make a report."

"A report?" Pete said. "Yeah, something like that'll really scare off Dumb and Dumber."

25

It was just a little after 5PM. Ned decided to take a short break from giving tickets and the occasional warning to speeders and stop by and see a good friend of the department. Jim Blakeman fixed and recycled bicycles for a living, mostly for kids.

He didn't make much doing it, but Jim said he was amply rewarded in other ways. He'd started doing this seven years ago, mainly as part of a volunteer outreach at Christmastime, to help underprivileged kids get a nice, refurbished bike under the tree. Over the next few years, it grew into a full-time operation, run as a non-profit. Jim got lots of volunteer help from the community. It had become one of the favorite places for people who'd been assigned community service by a judge, to fulfill their sentence obligation.

That's how Ned first became aware of Jim. Soon, the Police Department had begun donating bikes they'd confiscated to Jim, knowing he'd find them a worthy home.

Jim's bike shop was just ahead on the right. Ned pulled his

patrol car into one of the handful of parking spaces to the right of the building. He glanced at the clock on his dashboard. Jim would be closing soon. Ned walked around the back and came in through the open garage door. He nodded to a few of the volunteers he recognized working on the bikes. "Jim around?"

One of them said, "He's in the front room talking to someone at the counter."

"Thanks." Ned sidestepped around a number of bicycle projects in various stages of repair, tried not to knock any of them over. He opened the door into the front room, where most people came into the place. It was set up like a small store with bicycle gear and supplies stacked neatly on shelves or hanging on hooks. Then across the front all the bikes that were ready to go were lined up in two rows. Jim was talking to a woman who looked to be in her thirties. "That's right," he said. "All you have to do is sign here, and the bike is yours. There is no cost to you."

"But how is that possible? How can you do this?"

"Because all the bikes are donated and most of the work is done by volunteers. A lot of them go to my church, some are sent to us by the judge. I just supervise the thing now, make sure all the bikes are safe and ready to ride. And this one you picked out for your little girl is all set to go."

"I don't know what to say." The woman was getting teary-eyed. "A friend told me about this place, but I could hardly believe it was for real. My daughter's turning six tomorrow, and all she's been talking about is how much she wants a bike. I can't believe she's going to get one."

"Well here's one way you can thank me...take a picture of her smiling face when she sees the bike and post it to our Facebook page, so I can see it myself. That's all the thanks I need. You need help getting it into your car?"

"No, I think I can manage." She gave Jim a hug then started wheeling the little girl's bike toward the front door.

Jim held it open for her. He turned and noticed Ned. "Ned, good to see you again, my friend. How's the protect and serve business these days?"

"Plenty busy," Ned said. "Staying safe, as usual."

"Heard about that big drug bust on TV a few days ago, the one in the south end of town. Were you involved in that?"

"Right in the middle. Glad we got that guy off the streets."

"Yeah, that fentanyl is nasty stuff," Jim said. "The story I saw said they suspect some of those deadly overdoses last month came out of this guy's operation."

"We're almost certain it did. But something good came out of it, at least for me." Ned filled him in about meeting Parker and the likelihood of him becoming Parker's new owner, if this foster thing worked out.

"I can just see you doing that," Jim said, "taking in an abused dog."

"Well I'd never feel up to such a thing except for all the help I'm getting from the Humane Society." He told Jim about meeting Kim but didn't go into the part about his growing romantic interest. "But the real reason I'm here is for another situation I came across yesterday. There's this little boy lives next door to me. Doesn't have a dad, at least one that's in the picture, and he's fairly new to the area."

He explained the bullying situation Russell was dealing with, and the idea of helping to sign him up for some mixed martial arts classes. "The problem is, I can only get to about half the classes because of my schedule, and his mom works retail."

"Ahhh, the picture is becoming clear," Jim said. "The lad needs a means of transportation to and from the class, at least some of the time."

"Yes, his old bike got stolen."

"Say no more. Just pick out whatever bike you want him to have, sign a little form on my clipboard here, to help me keep things straight, and take it away."

"That's great, Jim. I was hoping this could work out." Ned turned around and glanced at the selection of ready-to-go bikes. "Looks like you have at least four or five that he should like." Ned's guess came from knowing which bikes were reported stolen the most.

"At least," Jim said.

Ned picked out a fiery blue one. "I'm thinking this is the one. But is it okay if I tell him, if he doesn't like it we can come back and switch it out for another?"

"Of course. You know my hours."

Ned thanked him, signed the necessary forms, then walked the bike back through the door into the garage area. He was just about to walk it out to the car when he heard Jim yelling from the front room.

"Sir, you can't take that!"

Ned turned and looked through the window in the top half of the door, in time to see Jim running toward the front of the store.

"Come back here with that bike!" Jim yelled.

Ned reached the door and saw Jim standing through the front door looking down the sidewalk. A scraggly, bearded young man had just hopped on a bike and was riding away.

Ned ran back through the garage and out to his patrol car. He turned it on and immediately turned on the lights and siren. After making sure the coast was clear, he flew out of the parking spot in reverse, changed gears and tore off in the direction of the bearded guy on the bike.

He reached him in seconds. The guy looked at him, shock on his face. Ned matched his speed, rolled down his window and yelled, "Pull the bike over now," and pointed his finger right at his face.

The man was so scared he almost fell over on the sidewalk after hitting the brakes. Ned pulled his car over, called it in and got out to confront the thief. "Stay right where you are. If I have to chase you, I will not be happy, and you will not win the race."

"I ain't going anywhere, Officer."

Ned reached the guy. Without being told, he held his wrists out ready to be handcuffed. Ned obliged him. "What in the world are you doing stealing a bike from a place like that?"

"I need one, bad. And I got no money."

Ned noticed Jim jogging up the sidewalk toward them. The thief had only gotten about a block away from the shop. "Here's the owner coming now."

"You can have the bike back, Sir. I didn't hurt it none. It's not like I stole any money."

"The point is," Ned said, "you didn't need to steal this bike either. This man coming up the sidewalk here? He'd have given it to you, and you wouldn't have to pay a dime."

"What are you talking about?" the man said.

"I'll let him tell you," Ned said. "His name is Jim."

"Looks like you stopped by at just the right time, Ned," Jim said.

"I'll let this guy tell you his story, and you tell me what you want to do with him."

"Okay." Jim looked at the bike thief. "What do you have to say?"

"You can have your bike back, Sir. I didn't mean any harm. I just don't have the money, but I need a bike in the worst way. I got a construction job a few miles from here, starts tomorrow. But the man said if I'm late, even one day, I'm gone. I haven't got twenty bucks left in my wallet, and I know a bike, even a used one like this, costs way more than that. I'm sorry. I shouldn't have stole it. I was just desperate. That construction supervisor, he's the first guy that's given me a chance for a job in weeks."

Hearing this, Ned couldn't help but smile. He already knew how this thing was going to go down.

"What's your name, friend?"

"John. John Henry."

"Well, John. I think God caused our paths to cross just now."

"God?" The look on John's face was priceless. This was about the last thing he probably expected Jim to say.

Jim looked at Ned. "Officer, I don't think I'll be pressing charges here today."

"You're not?" John Henry said.

"No, I don't think I will. That is, if you're willing to do just a little bit of honest work for this here bike."

"Honest work? I can do honest work. I'll do anything."

"Well Jim," Ned said, "looks like you got this thing well in hand."

"I think we'll be fine, Ned."

"Give me your hands," Ned said to John. He took off the

handcuffs, shook Jim's hand and headed back to his patrol car. He knew what Jim would do. He always gave his bikes away free to kids, but if any adults needed one, all he asked them to do was volunteer to work five hours in his bike shop.

Ned wouldn't be at all surprised if Jim offered to feed poor John Henry tonight and invited him to his church this Sunday. So Ned headed back to Jim's shop, grabbed the bike he'd picked out for Russell and tucked it into his trunk.

26

Ned had worked through the weekend. It was now midmorning on Monday. Fortunately, and as usual, the bad guys had either stayed out of Summerville, been on their best behavior, or had gotten away with any crimes they had committed. Both weekend shifts had been filled with mostly traffic stops and supervising fender benders.

He had stopped at the Humane Society once each day during his lunch break to visit Parker, but had only actually seen him on Saturday. He didn't know the infirmary was closed on Sundays. But the Saturday visit had gone much like the day before. Parker wagged his tail as Ned bent down in front of his kennel with a treat. Of course, he didn't run up to greet Ned, but he did eventually work up the nerve to come take the treat from between Ned's fingers.

Kim had worked on Saturday, but she was out doing a private lesson when Ned arrived. He was sad he missed her but encouraged that Parker's response to him had nothing to do with Kim standing nearby. Parker was getting at least a little more comfortable being around Ned.

Ned was back at the shelter again, since he had Monday off. At the moment, he was waiting at a picnic table under a shady tree, situated just outside the infirmary kennel. When he arrived, Parker's kennel was empty. A worker said he'd be back in a few minutes. The Doc was checking him over.

The side door opened. Ned looked up, happy to see Kim's smiling face. She waved and headed toward him.

"Doc's assistant called and said you were here."

"Thought I'd come over in the morning, since I have the day off. I didn't call, because I thought you'd probably be busy." It was also something of a little test Ned did, hoping for this very result...that Kim would seek him out on her own.

"I am, but it's not too bad." She came up and sat across from him at the picnic table. "Have you seen him yet?"

"No, he's in with the Doc getting a checkup. His assistant should be here any minute. She said she'd come get me when she put him back in his kennel. I thought when the door opened it was going to be her."

"My guess is, nothing will come of it. Unless the blood tests showed something, you can tell he's making progress. I checked on him late Saturday afternoon before I left for the day. It was obvious he had eaten about half the food in his bowl. So, his appetite's starting to return. And you should see how he reacts when you put down a fresh bowl of water. He really goes after it."

"Guess he knows what it feels like to literally be dying of thirst. So, how did you spend your day off yesterday? And before you answer that, they only give you one day off a week here?"

"No, I get two. Sunday's always one, but the other one kind of floats depending on my schedule."

"Yeah, that's one thing I miss," Ned said, "being kind of low on the totem pole in terms of seniority. I don't get two days off in a row. But that'll change eventually. So, what did you do yesterday?"

"Went to church in the morning. Well, slept in a little, then went to church. Then just hung out with my parents all afternoon. I usually do that on Sundays, just to make sure we stay connected. But I did something different last night when I got home."

"What's that?"

"I got my pistol out and cleaned it up. Now I'm already to go to the range whenever you are."

Well, this was encouraging. She not only remembered this idea but followed up on it. "How about this evening? The range is open until seven. We could go right after you get off then get something to eat. Unless you're starving when you get off work. In that case, we could eat something first, then go to the range."

"I always eat lunch, so I won't be starving when I'm done here. Let's go to the range first. But I'll have to meet you there, so my car doesn't get locked up in here."

"Or else I could just pick you up at your place. That way we can drive together." And that way, Ned thought, it would feel more like a date.

"That'll work," she said. "I usually get home by five-thirty."

"Five-thirty, it is. Wait a minute, I don't know where you live."

She pulled something out of her pocket, her business card.

She turned it over and wrote on the back. "Here you go, I'm sure your GPS will help you find it."

"Actually, I hardly ever use GPS, at least in this town. With this job, I'm driving all over town all the time. I think I know where every road is, even every back alley."

The side door opened again. Doc's assistant stood in the doorway. "I just put Parker back in his kennel," she said. "You can see him whenever you're ready."

"How did his checkup go?" Kim asked.

"Doc says he's doing fine. Healing up nicely. No surprises from the blood tests."

"That's a relief," Ned said.

"Well, I better get back," the assistant said and closed the door.

Ned stood. Kim did, too. "Do you have a minute to see him with me, or do you have to get back to your office?"

"Do you need me? How was he on Saturday without me there?"

"Fine. Same as Friday."

"Then I better get back. Have a bunch of phone calls I need to return. See you at five-thirty." She headed toward the side door.

"Looking forward to it," Ned said.

"Me, too."

Ned watched her walk back through the door and into the kennel. So, she really did come over here just to see him. Not Parker, just him. Even though she was busy enough that she had to rush back to her office to finish what she had been doing before. She'd actually stopped what she was doing when she heard he was over here, just to connect with him.

This was nice. A positive development.

He walked back to the kennel door and headed inside to see Parker.

THE UNCONTROLLABLE SHAKING had almost stopped.

Since that nice young woman had put him back in his cage, Parker remained curled up in a tight ball trying to get over whatever that was. They had brought him back into that strange room with all the funny smells. Dogs and cats all sat huddled in small cages, each one emitting various degrees of fear and anxiety.

Parker was certain he had added a fair share of his own.

The woman in the white coat had gently pulled him out of his cage and set him on a metal table. That's when the trembling began. She poked and prodded him and rubbed most of the painful red areas on his skin with her fingers. Something gooey was on her fingers. It had a funny smell but, somehow, when she'd rubbed it on his skin, it had actually made him feel better.

She knew his name, had said it several times. She and the young woman working with her were always nice to him. That helped ease his fears. Finally, after checking his teeth, shining a bright light in his eyes and sticking something cold into his ears, they were done.

Now he was back on this nice blanket in his own space. Fresh water in his bowl. He wasn't hot. None of the bigger dogs in the kennels nearby seemed able or even interested in doing him harm. Maybe, just maybe, he could catch a nap until the effects of this strange visit wore off.

"Hey Parker, how you doing, Boy?"

Parker looked up. That nice man. He came back. The one

who rescued him and brought him to this nice place. The one who always smiled, said nice things, and brought amazing treats.

Instantly, Parker stopped shaking. His tail began to wag as the man bent down and pulled out one of those yummy treats from his pocket. As before, he poked it through an opening in the gate and held it there.

"Come on, Parker. It's for you. You can have it."

Parker quickly got up and walked without fear toward the man's fingers. He looked up into his face for just a moment. Still smiling and looking right back at him. He took the treat gently between his teeth. The man let go and he hurried back to his blanket.

Mission accomplished.

"Wow, Ned," Kim said. "He didn't even hesitate. It was almost as if he was excited to see you."

"Yeah. That went even better than Saturday."

Ned, Parker thought. That must be the man's name, Ned. He'd heard it several times now. Ned.

Parker decided right then, Ned was officially a good person.

27

B efore Ned left to pick up Kim, he had decided to call Marilyn, Russell's mom, about Russell starting those classes tomorrow. She didn't pick up, so he'd left a voicemail. Now, halfway to Kim's apartment, she was returning his call.

"I'm sorry I missed your call, Ned. I was here, but I forgot to put your name in my contacts, so I didn't recognize the number. I never pick up the phone if I don't know who it is, so I'm glad you left a message."

"No problem. Just wanted to get back with you about Russell taking those classes. If it's not too soon, as it turns out, they're starting up a new one for beginners tomorrow. Same time as I mentioned before, 5PM. Here's the thing, I was able to change shifts with another officer. I was scheduled to work late into the evening, but now I'll get off a little before five. So, I can be there for Russell's first class. But I don't see how I can get him there on time if I have to pick him up beforehand."

"So, you need me to get him there by five. Is that it?"

"Pretty much. I know your work schedule's like mine. Any chance you can do that tomorrow?"

"I'm on the schedule to work till closing. But I can make it work on my lunch break. One way or another, I'll have him there by five."

"Great. Then I'll meet you there."

"Does he need anything? Anything he's supposed to bring?"

"Oh, I didn't even think about that. I texted you the information. Why don't you go on their website, see if they have any kind of checklist for beginners. If you could pick that stuff up and get me the receipt, I'll reimburse you."

"You don't have to do that."

"I don't, but that's what I want you to do. I'm sure it won't be expensive, whatever it is."

"Okay," she said. "I'll take care of that. And really, Ned, thanks so much for doing this. I can't wait for Russell to start taking this class."

"Today was his first day back to school, wasn't it? How did things go? With those bullies, I mean."

"Well, there weren't any more physical exchanges, but he said they were saying mean things off and on throughout the day."

"Like, *we're going to get you after school* kind of things?"

"Yeah," she said. "And, *this isn't over*. Things like that. But nothing happened after school. He walked home a totally different way."

"That's good. Speaking of him walking home, I have a surprise for you and Russell. Believe it or not, there's this guy I know who has a nonprofit ministry refurbishing bikes for kids. I picked up one for Russell. Didn't cost a thing."

"You're kidding, right? You got Russell a bike? And we don't have to pay a thing?"

"Not a thing. He approved Russell on my say-so. He's been doing this for years. Gets a lot of help from churches and volunteers. I'll bring the bike over soon."

"I can't even believe this, Ned. When we moved into this apartment complex, and I found out our next-door neighbor was a cop, I was kind of glad thinking no one will break in to our place with a cop next door. I had no idea we'd get all these other things besides. It's like living next to a superhero, or something."

Ned laughed. "No, I'm just a cop. No superpowers. I just remember what it's like to be afraid all the time and feel like I didn't have anyone I could turn to for help. So, when I see someone who was like me, I can do something about it. I even get to do it as part of my job."

"Maybe so, but I've never heard of any cop like you."

"I have. I know quite a few. Anyway, I better get going. There's somebody I'm supposed to meet in just a few minutes."

"Okay, see you soon," she said. "I'll tell Russell what you said. He'll be so excited."

Ned pulled into Kim's apartment complex. It wasn't very big, just a string of one-story triplexes built in a semicircle around a large retention pond. They were all landscaped nicely and the buildings appeared well maintained. But certainly, not high-end. Looking at the cars in the parking lot made him feel right at home.

He was just about to look at his cell phone to make sure he knew which one was hers, when he saw her coming out the front door on the left unit in one of the middle buildings. As he got closer, he noticed something a little different about her. Then he realized, she had changed out of what she'd been wearing at the shelter for work into something a little nicer. She had a natural beauty about her, but he was almost certain she had put on fresh makeup and did something a little different with her hair.

When she saw him, she waved. He noticed besides her purse, she carried what looked like a dark plastic gun case. He pulled in the parking space in front of her building, and she got in.

"Right on time," she said.

"Wow, you smell nice. What is that?"

"It's one of my favorites. It's called *Aromatics Elixi*r by *Clinique*. Did I put on too much?"

"Not at all. I don't mind being able to smell pleasant things. You can wear that anytime we're together as far as I'm concerned."

She smiled. "Glad you like it."

He waited a moment. "I knew it."

"Knew what? What's the matter?"

"You didn't say anything. You can't smell what I put on, can you?"

She lifted her nose slightly, sniffed the air. "Sorry. What is it?"

"Doesn't matter. Apparently, some cheap junk. Smells great when you first put it on. But then I don't smell it even ten minutes later. And it's obvious, neither can anyone else. Maybe you can help me with this. Seems like if you're going to go to the trouble to smell nice, you want to be able to smell the nice smell for more than ten minutes. Don't you agree?"

"I guess I do."

"Well, either I need to spend more on the cologne I'm buying, which is probably the case. Or, I need to squirt that thing about ten more times to get enough on so other people can smell it, too. At least for a little while anyway."

Kim laughed. "Well Ned, I don't think you need to put ten squirts of any kind of cologne on, regardless of how much you paid for it. But I'd be happy to help you with it. Maybe the next time we go somewhere together, we can swing by one of the stores at the mall and try on some men's cologne. I'm sure we can find something that'll work." Then she looked at him, lifted her nose in the air again and took a big sniff.

"Why'd you do that?"

"Well, at least you don't smell bad. So, we don't have a problem here."

Ned laughed. "So, I'm guessing that's your gun." He pointed to the case sitting on her lap. It had a familiar name and logo imprinted on the top. "Browning. They make excellent firearms."

"My Dad helped me pick it out." She unsnapped and opened the lid.

"Wow, a 1911-380," Ned said. "I've heard about those but have never seen one." The pistol sat in a fitted, molded space. Next to it was a clip. Obviously loaded with bullets.

"There's an empty clip in the gun," she said. "I don't usually keep them in this case. I store them in a gun safe under my bed. But it's kind of heavy to lug around. Is it legal to drive to the range with it in this?" She pointed to the case. "I don't have a concealed carry permit."

"In Florida, you're fine in the car, keeping it in this case. Obviously, can't have it loose or even on you, like in a holster, without the conceal-carry permit. But this is fine. I really like the look of this one, especially those Rosewood grips. It's similar to the gun I'm bringing. It's a 1911 model, too. Only full-size." The 380 version was fifteen percent smaller.

"I tried a full-sized one at the gun store, but it was too big for me. I couldn't even pull the slide back, on any of the models."

"That's what's so great about your gun," Ned said. "It's not just a good gun for women. A lot of folks are getting these as their concealed weapon, because of its size. And it's still got solid stopping power."

"Stopping power?" Kim sighed. "I hope I never have to find out about that firsthand."

"You probably won't," he said. "Chances are, you'll own this your whole life and only use it like we're about to do—at the range—then you'll put it in your will for one of your kids. But it's nice to know, if something ever did happen, you'd be all set with this."

"Well, I'll be all set if you show me how to use it properly. When I cleaned it I realized, I remember very little of what the instructor taught me. I even had to watch a YouTube video to put it back together." She closed the lid to the case and set it on the floor between her feet.

"I guarantee you, by the time I take you home tonight, the fog will be all gone. And if you enjoy yourself, we can do this more often." He put his car in reverse. "When you did go to the range the last time, were you any good? Ever get close to what you were aiming at?"

She smiled. "You just wait and see."

28

The parking lot at Buck's Gun Shop was only half-filled, which is what Ned had hoped by going there at this time. The right side of the building was a decent sized gun store, the left side a shooting range, which only had fifteen slots. There was no membership here, strictly first-come, first-served.

"We should have no problem getting two slots next to each other this time of day." He turned off the car and opened the door.

"It's an indoor range," Kim said, stepping onto the parking lot "I didn't know that. I'm glad. It's still kind of hot outside. But won't it be terribly noisy?"

"Not with the headgear I've got in my duffel bag. The guys on either side of us could be shooting mini-cannons, and we'd be okay."

She laughed. "I guess you would have the best stuff, considering your job."

"I've got some safety glasses in the bag, too," he said, as he walked toward the front door.

"I've got a nice pair of those. Got them on the internet. Mainly because they have pink trim. But they're supposed to be as strong as the other types."

"The ugly types, like mine?"

"Yes. Although, I haven't seen yours yet. But the pair my dad got me looked like goggles."

"Mine are actually pretty nice. No color, but they're kind of sleek." He opened the door for her.

"Thank you, kind sir."

"Just remember, we've got to put the glasses on before we go through that door into the shooting range. And keep them on the whole time we're in there."

"I remember that one," she said. "But maybe before we get started, you could run through the other safety rules with me again. Especially the ones about the gun itself."

"Be happy to."

A man behind the counter said, "Ned, good to see you my friend."

"You too, Buck." He walked toward a long glass counter filled with a variety of pistols stacked on three shelves. Then held out his hand to shake Buck's hand, which was already extended. Buck looked like a character from an old western, including a mustache and beard combo straight out of the 1800s. "Brought a friend with me this time. Kim meet Buck, the owner of this establishment."

Buck widened his grin and shook her hand. "I see you're carrying a case for a *Browning 1911-380*, young lady. A very nice little gun. Sell quite a few of them these days. How are you for ammunition?"

Kim looked at Ned. "I have a box of fifty. Will we need more?"

"Not sure. That might be all right. The nice thing about having the range next-door, we can always pop in here if we run out."

"That's right," Buck said. "And I'll give you a good deal on account of Ned being such a good customer, as well as an upstanding officer of the law." He looked at Ned. "So, you just want two charges for the range then?"

"That and a box of 45s for me."

"Put it on your tab?"

"If you don't mind."

"Happy to." Buck stepped away from the counter, reached for something on a shelf behind him. Came back and set a box of ammo in front of Ned. "You pretty much got the run of the place in there. Only four other slots in use. Targets are all set up on the empty ones. You can share one, or each get your own."

"Thanks, Buck."

"You kids have fun in there. Take your time."

"Thanks," Kim said.

"You're welcome. And do yourself a favor, young lady. Listen to everything he tells you. He's one of the best shooters that come in here, and he lives and breathes safety. He'll get you situated just fine."

"Thanks, Buck. That's my plan," she said.

They both put on their safety glasses, then Ned opened the first of two doors leading into the shooting range.

As soon as Ned opened the second door into the range, Kim wondered if they shouldn't have put the headgear on also. There were only four other people shooting, but the noise was incredible. At least to her.

"See that door on the left there, in the corner?" Ned said. "We'll go in there first. It's a soundproof room they use for training. If we put the headsets on now, you'd barely hear a word I'm saying."

"I was wondering about that. Lead the way. I'm right behind you."

The top half of the door had a window. You could tell no one was using it. Once inside, the sounds of gunfire almost disappeared after the door closed. Ned set his duffel bag on the table. Kim set her gun case beside it.

"Okay, why don't you open it up, take the gun out and, using the empty clip, show me what you remember. I'll stop you, if you do anything that's way off the mark."

Kim opened the lid and lifted the gun out of its compartment. It was amazing how solid and heavy it felt for something so small. She immediately pointed it away and slightly down.

"Good," Ned said. "Always keep the gun pointed in a safe direction, even if you're all alone. It's just a good habit to keep. What else do you remember?"

She held her index finger straight along the side of the trigger, not on it. "I remember you're never supposed to put your finger on the trigger until you're ready to actually shoot."

"Great. That's right. There's a few other important things, but if you think about just those two...if you follow them, there's no way an accident can happen. Do you remember the safety features on your gun, the ones specific to that model?"

"Not exactly."

He spent the next few minutes going over them with her. As it turned out, her gun had a few safety features most guns didn't have, which made her feel good. Then he spent about ten minutes showing her the ins and outs of working with the clip, including how to load it with bullets, how to insert it properly into the grip, and how to release it. Then they worked on how to use the slide, both to load and discharge a loaded round. They went over that procedure several times, until she no longer felt nervous.

"Good," he said. "You're getting the hang of it. Now let's make sure you know how to handle things once we get out into the range. If you ever hear the Range Safety Officer shout *cease-fire*, would you know what to do?"

"Stop...shooting?"

Ned laughed. "Yes, that's part of it. But let me show you the specific things every shooter is supposed to do with their gun." He went over these things for several minutes, then had her do everything he showed her until she could do it without thinking.

She loved how patient he was with her, and how gently he spoke. In fact, she realized, she really enjoyed just hearing the sound of Ned's voice.

They spent the next several minutes reviewing everything he'd taught her, only this time he let her do most of the talking and demonstrating how she did things with the gun.

"Good. I think we're actually ready to head out into the range."

"Really? You sure I'm ready?"

"I do. But that's not what's important. How do you feel? If you want to go over anything we talked about again, I don't mind. To me, the safety aspects of using a gun are even more important than driving a car. We're in no hurry."

She thought a moment. No, she really was ready. It was just such a big thing, shooting a gun. But she wasn't afraid anymore. "Okay, let's do this."

First, they put on the headsets then brought their gear out to the two slots directly in the middle. Kim liked that there was no one directly on either side of them. He set his gear down in the slot beside her but decided to continue working with her until she was comfortable doing everything on her own.

He used a button to set the target about halfway down the length of the range. Then he went through some more instructions about aiming the gun, breathing, and the right way to pull the trigger. She realized how distracted she became when he got close to her. A few times she had to ask him to repeat what he'd said.

"You got it?" he said.

"I think so," she yelled.

"Then fire when ready. Starting off, just fire one at a time to get used to the kick. It's not strong, but it is real. Once you get the feel of it, try firing two or three shots close together."

"Okay, here goes." She aimed, breathed in and fired as she exhaled. "Whoa!" It was so quick. She kept the gun extended. "Did I hit it? Felt like I did."

"Think so. Try it again."

She did. It was so exciting. He was right. There was a kick when she fired, but it wasn't hard to keep it still pointing where she wanted. She fired a third round.

"Okay, now fire two or three close together. Your gun holds eight rounds in the clip."

She fired two together, then three. Then the gun was

empty. She made sure the chamber was clear, left the slide locked back and set the gun down on the table, facing the target. "There, I did it. How did I do? Are you allowed to bring the target back close enough to see?"

"Sure, but I have a feeling, even from here, that you did all right." Ned pushed the button and the target came sailing back toward them. It stopped a few yards away. "Oh my gosh," he said. "Look at that."

She could see for herself. It was hard not to smile. The target was shaped like the top half of a man. A number of concentric ovals spread out from the center. None of her rounds had hit the actual center, an oval with an X. All but two of them were in the next oval out from that, marked with a "9." The last two holes were in the "8."

"Okay, Kim. Have you been taking me for a ride here? Is this like the way someone hustles somebody in a pool hall, only we're at the gun range?"

"No, I'm not kidding you. This is maybe the third time I've ever done this."

He smiled. "What can I say? You're a natural then. I'm not sure you need any more help from me. I'd say with a few more hours' practice, you'll be getting most of your shots dead center. Tell you what, why don't you load up another clip and try half for the center and the other half for the head area. See how close you come?"

"All right."

"Remember how to load the clip?"

"Think so."

"Okay, I'll get my gun set up then."

Just then the door opened from the gun store, Buck stuck his head out, a worried look on his face. "Say Ned, can I see you a minute? Could really use your help in here with an escalatin' situation."

"Be right there, Buck." He looked at Kim. "Are you okay here?"

"Go on. I'll be all right." She looked over. Buck had already disappeared behind the closed door.

29

Ned opened the main door that led into the store.

"I've got the money, in cash. I got a legal ID. I don't understand why I can't walk out of here with it as soon as I buy it."

Ned looked at a wiry but muscular looking fellow standing in front of the gun counter where he and Kim had purchased ammo a short while ago. The guy wore blue jeans and a T-shirt. A blue baseball cap sat backwards on his head. He'd just yelled those words at a guy named Bob, an employee who worked for Buck.

Buck stood next to him and looked over at Ned, then back at the customer. "Sir, I've heard my employee here explain the situation to you three different ways now. Every one of them made sense to me. What don't you understand? It's the law. It's not company policy."

"How can it be the law, as you say, when the Constitution guarantees me the right to bear arms? I've read the Second

Amendment. Have you? I don't see any clause about some three-day waiting period."

Ned walked up and stood close to the man. "There a problem here, Buck?"

"You and me are going to have a problem, Bud, if you don't bug out of here. This is none of your business."

Ned pulled his badge out of his pocket and let the man see his holstered firearm as he did. "Let me introduce myself. I'm Officer Ned Barringer." He held up his badge. "And I'm not just butting my nose in here where it doesn't belong. Buck here, the store owner, asked me to be a part of this conversation."

"Well, you can stand there if you want," the man said. "Still a free country last time I checked. But I don't see what difference you can make. No laws being broken here."

"Maybe," Ned said. "Not yet, anyway. But it sounds like you're getting a little heated here about your gun purchase."

"I ain't heated yet, Mister. I ain't even close to heated. But I might get there if this man keeps telling me he's willing to take my money, over five hundred dollars in cash, but he's not gonna let me walk out the store with the gun. Whoever heard of such a thing? Paying all that money and then you don't even get to take home what you bought. I know my Second Amendment rights."

"Apparently, you don't. It says you have the right to bear arms, but it doesn't get specific about the details. Buck here is not denying your rights. He's willing to sell you the gun. But there are other laws in play here besides the Constitution, sir. The state of Florida says you need to wait three days to take possession of it, so they can check things out. Make sure you are who you say you are. Make sure you're not a convicted felon, or someone else who shouldn't be buying a gun, legally or otherwise. The Constitution doesn't forbid that, and that's the law that's governing this situation. Buck would be breaking the law if he did what you're asking."

"That's just ridiculous."

"Maybe so. But that's not an issue for this moment. The issue here has already been settled before you even walked into the store. The only question is, do you still want the gun knowing you have to wait three days before you can pick it up?"

The man didn't say anything. His face got redder and his eyes more angry. He looked down at the gun sitting in the case then over at the front door, then back down at the gun.

"Sir," Ned said. "Did you hear what I said? I hope you're not thinking about grabbing that gun and making a run for it. That would be a very foolish mistake. You wouldn't get three steps down the aisle before I tackled you hard to the floor. Judging by your weight and mine, I'm predicting three or four cracked ribs, then the handcuffs, then the felony charges, then come the orange pajamas. Hardly seems worth it, don't you think?"

The expression on the man's face softened a little. He released a sigh.

"On top of that," Ned said, "you'd be doing this in front of three eyewitnesses. Not to mention the three cameras Buck has installed in the ceiling, catching everything going on here."

"Four," Buck said. "And they ain't the blurry kind, neither. I paid extra for color and Hi-def."

The four men stood there a moment in silence. Finally, Buck said, "So, do you want the gun or not?"

"I guess not," the man said. "There's a gun show in Orlando this weekend. I'll wait and get one then."

"You can try," Ned said. "But all the dealers there have to follow the same laws as Buck here."

The man started walking away. "I'll take my chances and my money somewhere else." He kept walking right out the door and toward his car in the parking lot.

"So glad you were here, Ned. I had a bad feeling about that guy. Like things were pretty close to turning sour, right quick."

"I was getting the same vibe too," Ned said. "Glad he decided to back off."

"You made a pretty convincing argument," Bob said. "Not just your badge, or the way you said what you said. But look at you... I wouldn't mess with you."

Buck agreed. "And look man, I'm real sorry to interrupt your time with your lady friend."

"That's okay," Kim said. "It was only for a few minutes."

"How long were you standing there?" Ned said.

"Long enough. Got a little curious. Glad things ended peacefully."

"That's why I asked Ned to come in here," Buck said. "He's got a way of handling people. If it had just been Bob or me, pretty sure things would've gotten ugly. But we're all snug as a bug in a rug now, Ned. You two can go on back to the range."

"Thanks Buck. Will do."

"Oh," Buck added, "And your range time is on the house today. For both of you. No arguments about it."

"Thank you, Buck." Ned walked toward the range doors. Kim had already gone through them.

Once Ned was back at their gun station, Kim said, "That was pretty impressive, the way you handled that situation."

"Thanks. Kind of used to it by now."

"Does that happen a lot with you? People dragging you into difficult situations when you're off duty?"

"Not too much." Actually, if Ned was being totally truthful he might have said, "A good bit." But he really never minded it, when it happened. But seeing her face then, the look in her eyes, he wondered if this bothered her more than she was letting on.

30

They had both gone through all their ammo at the gun range with no further interruptions. By the time Kim had gone through all fifty rounds, she wasn't nervous about shooting her gun anymore. And her aim had continued to improve.

When they brought the target back to where they stood, Ned pointed out that once again none of Kim's rounds were further from the center than the 8 or 9 rings, except for the head shots. And all of those were on point. She had even hit five bullets in the Big X.

He seemed properly impressed. Of course, he didn't want to show her his target sheet. But she had insisted. All his rounds were either in the 9 ring or the Big X. In fact, the X was actually missing. He'd hit the center so often the paper had disintegrated. A similar sized-hole was centered directly in the head.

"Yeah, but I do this all the time," is all he'd said.

Now they were sitting in a booth at Chili's, drinking ice

water with lemon while reading their menus. "I love their salsa here."

"Me, too," he said. "Let's get some. So, this is a place you go to pretty often?"

"I wouldn't say often, but I've come here enough."

"Then do we really need to be reading these menus? Don't you just come here for one thing?"

She shut her menu. "You're right. I get the Buffalo chicken salad. Whenever I get anything else, I always wish I got that."

"That's why I come here," Ned said.

"The Buffalo chicken salad?"

Ned nodded. "That and the salsa and chips."

The waitress walked up. "You guys look like you're ready."

Ned ordered for both of them. Kim added an un-sweet iced tea with lemon.

"I'll be right back with your drink and the chips and salsa."

As she walked away, Kim's cell phone vibrated on the table. She looked down. "It's Amy, my assistant at the shelter. You've met her, right?"

"Yeah."

"Mind if I get this? She never calls me outside of work."

"Sure. Do it."

"Hey Amy, what's up?"

"Sorry to call you on your time off, but I thought you'd want to hear this."

"No problem. What is it?"

"This happened just after you left. I was waiting at my desk for Chris and Finley to pick me up when the Doc came over and poked her head through our doorway. She was looking for you."

"Really? Why?"

"Well, it's good news. Don't want to keep you in suspense. But it's about Parker."

"Parker?"

"Yeah. Didn't you say you were going to see Ned tonight?"

"Yeah. He's right here as a matter of fact. We went from work to the shooting range. Now we're eating at Chili's."

"Shooting range? That sounds like fun. I've done that with Chris before. Well good, then you can talk this over with Ned as soon as we hang up."

"What's going on?"

"Well, I guess the Doc examined Parker at the end of the day. She said he's doing better than expected. He's eating normally, drinking plenty of water, and even all his skin problems are responding well to the meds. She thought that since Ned had already agreed to be his foster parent, there really wasn't any reason to keep Parker in the infirmary kennels anymore. As long as Ned didn't mind putting some ointment on his red areas for another week or so. And she's still got him on pain meds for a few more days. But apparently he takes them pretty easily. She said it's your call, whether you think Ned is ready, but if you do, she has no problem releasing him now. And as you know, they can always use an empty kennel back there."

"That is good news." She looked across the table at Ned and smiled.

He could tell this conversation was partially about him.

"I'll have to run it by Ned, see what he thinks. I'll let you know tomorrow when I come in."

"That'll work," Amy said. "Just thought you'd like to know."

"I'm glad you called. Thanks." She hung up.

"Good news?" he said.

"Well, I think you'll think it is. It's about Parker."

"I gathered that. You mentioned his name."

"Well, the bottom line is...the Doc has cleared him to go home."

"Already? I thought it might be a couple of weeks."

"So did I. But you never know with these things. Especially since his appetite is back, and he's fully rehydrated now. And she said he's responding very well to the meds. She thought since he's already got a foster home to go to, he'd be better off recovering there than in the infirmary. She left it up to me to decide if I think you're ready."

A nervous expression came over his face. "I don't know, am I?"

"I think you are. I mean, we've still got a lot more work to do in terms of training, but you did say you got all the things on the checklist already from the pet store, right?"

"Yeah. And I read that brochure you wrote about things to know when bringing home a shelter dog. Twice."

"Well, see? You're right on track. You're doing everything you should be doing to be ready. I mean, let's face it, compared to the existence poor Parker has known for most of his life, even if you make a dozen mistakes, living with you will be like living in a palace compared to what he's known. Not that I think you're going to make a bunch of mistakes. It's just, the pressure's off. You've got a great heart. We both know he already likes you. I'm only a phone call away if you have any questions. You can call me at work or when I'm off."

The confident look returned. "Well then, maybe I am ready. As ready as I'm going to be. But what about him? We haven't even taken him out of the kennel yet."

"Well, he's been out of the kennel several times, just not with you or me."

"Well, that's what I mean. I've never even touched him before. What if I do, and he freaks out?"

"Then we'll know he's not ready. There's no hurry, Ned. Right now, we're just trying to decide how ready you are to take him home. If he's not ready to go, we'll keep looking after him until he is. Then we'll just set up some times for the two of you to interact more directly. What I mean is, in the same space. Like out on the lawn or in a fenced area."

"Can we do that tomorrow?" Ned asked. "Oh wait, I changed shifts with a guy, so I can take Russell to his first self-defense class. I was going to have the morning off. But you know what? This is kind of a big deal. I'm going to call and see if I can take a personal day tomorrow. Then I can come down first thing in the morning, and we can see how things go with Parker. You know what your schedule is like in the morning?"

"No, but let me check." She looked at the calendar on her phone. She had a private dog training lesson first thing, but this was the third time she had worked with this dog and owner. Amy had been with her both times. "I do have something, but I'm pretty sure Amy can take care of it for me. Let me give her a quick call just to make sure. If she can, I can be freed up to help you with Parker."

"That would be great. Can I ask you a favor?"

"Sure, what is it?"

The waitress walked up and set down Kim's iced tea down and a big bowl of fresh salsa and tortilla chips. "Can we have some ranch dressing with that, too?" Ned asked.

"I'll be right back with it."

"So, what's the favor?" Kim asked.

"Before we eat, how about I call work to make sure I can get the day off, and you call Amy to make sure she can do the dog lesson for you. That way, I can totally relax and enjoy this meal. Otherwise, I know how I'm wired. I'll be totally distracted."

"Sure, we can do that."

"Okay, you can stay here and call Amy. I'm going to call work out by the sidewalk." He slid out of the booth and stood. "Be right back." He grabbed a chip and dipped it in some salsa and walked out.

Less than five minutes later, after Kim's call with Amy went as planned, Ned was back, all smiles. "No problem. Got the day off. The benefits of working in a small town with almost zero crime." He slid back into his seat. "And look, she brought the ranch. I love dipping them in both. Ever tried it?"

"I'm not just saying this," she said. "But that's how I always eat it. Go right ahead. I don't mind if you get the two mixed together."

"Great." He grabbed a big chip and dipped it in the salsa then the ranch. "Now I can relax and enjoy this." He chomped down on the messy tortilla chip and when he had finished chewing, said, "I sure hope Parker doesn't freak out at our big get-together tomorrow."

31

Parker could tell something was up. The established morning routine had changed. Not dramatically, but enough to make him wonder why. When he heard the door open at the end of the room, he hurried over to his blanket, laid down and curled up. Who would it be this time?

As soon as the voices talked, he relaxed. It sounded like Ned, the man who'd rescued him and that nice woman he had seen many times before. He needed to hear her name a few more times to remember it.

"So, we're going to take him outside for a walk?" Ned said.

"Not really a walk," the woman said. "Well, we'll be walking him a little. Just enough to get him to a fenced-in area we have in the back. I think it will be better if the two of you get more acquainted there. That way, if he's nervous about the visit, he won't be stuck so close on the end of the leash."

"By stuck, you mean stuck being so close to me? In a fenced area, he'll be able to get further away."

"Basically, that's the idea. We never want to force a dog to do something, especially one that's afraid and has been abused. For trust to grow, he needs to feel like he's making the choices himself."

Parker didn't understand a single word or phrase in their conversation. They were now standing right in front of him, looking down at him with kind eyes and smiling faces. Then he noticed something. The woman was carrying a leash in her hand.

Ned bent down. Out came the delicious treat, as before, stuck between his two fingers and poking through the gate. "How are you doing this morning, Parker? Want this? Go ahead, take it." He wiggled it back and forth.

By now, Parker knew this was a perfectly safe thing to do. He got up, walked straight to the treat and gently grabbed it with his teeth. Ned let go, but this time Parker only took a few steps back before eating it. Kim quickly slipped another treat into Ned's hands and whispered, "Break it in half and see if he'll stay by the gate."

Ned called Parker back, letting him see both halves. Parker approached sniffing in the air. As soon as he ate one, Ned showed him the second. This time Parker stayed while eating it. "That went pretty well. Don't you think, Kim?"

As Parker finished chewing, he looked at the woman. *Kim*, Ned called her. That must be her name.

"He didn't seem even a little nervous, Ned. I'd say he's pretty much accepted you into his little world. That's a good sign for what we're hoping to do here."

"How do you want to do this?" Ned asked. "I mean, putting the leash on him. We don't even know if he's ever had a leash on before, do we?"

"No, we don't. When he came in, he had that filthy collar

on. We put a nice clean one on, but there's no way to know what he thinks about a leash. I've only seen the infirmary staff carrying him from place to place. We'll just have to see."

"Do you have some kind of method you follow for something like this?"

"I do, but I think it would be better if you do it instead of me. He's definitely warming up to me, but you're in a better place in his little mind. I think we should work with that."

"Okay, so what do I do?"

Kim handed him the leash. "For starters, we're not just going to go in there and force the issue. That could set things back pretty far. Here, take this baggie of treats." She handed him an opened Ziploc bag.

Parker instantly smelled what just happened. Then he saw a bag of those delicious treats being given to Ned. She had already given him the leash. What did this mean? What was going to happen now?"

"The idea is, to get him used to the idea that touching his collar is a good thing. In a minute, we'll open the kennel door and you step inside. Just about a foot and still stay low. All the while, holding out a treat in the palm of your hand. Keep talking to him the way you've been right along. He'll probably freak out a little, seeing you in front of him without the safety of the gate between you. But I'm banking on his acceptance of you and that treat in your hand to get him over the hump."

"Think he'll take it?"

"I do. We might have to wait a minute or two. But I think he will. And when he does, this time I want you to gently scratch under his chin, moving down to touch his collar."

"Then do I grab it?"

"No. No grabbing. Simply touch it and let go."

"Then what?"

"He'll probably back up, maybe all the way to his blanket. Try putting a bunch of broken treat pieces in your hand to keep him there longer. And again, keep speaking to him kindly. When he comes back, let him take the treats. This time, pet him on the neck and gently grab his collar. But just for a second. And say 'Collar.' If things go well, we'll repeat this several more times, each time touch and hold his collar just a little bit longer."

"I get it," Ned said. "We're trying to get him to make a positive connection to me holding his collar."

"Right. Dogs are all about making associations, with things or with people. We want him to associate you holding his collar as a very good thing."

"I take it you've done this before, and it works."

"I've done it a lot. It works very well, and it should work here. We'll just have to take it slow and be patient. But I've seen dogs get to the place in one session where they'll cheerfully lift their heads when their owner says *Collar*, so they can click on the leash. So, what do you think? Ready to try it?"

"Sure. Like you said, if he freaks out, we'll just step back and take it slower."

"Right. But I don't think Parker will freak out. I've been watching his eyes the last several times he interacts with you. His mind is always in a relaxed state."

What were they going on about? Parker kept listening, trying to catch familiar words. It was clear they were talking about him. And whatever it was, it seemed likely they were planning on giving him more of those treats.

"Okay," Ned said. "Here goes." He unlatched the gate,

opened it slowly and took one step inside. Then quickly got low again.

What? What was he doing, Parker thought. He's coming in here?

Ned took out a treat, broke it up and placed it in the palm of his hand and held the pieces out toward Parker. "You want this, Boy? Here you go. Take it."

Parker relaxed a little. He wasn't coming all the way in. And look, he was offering another treat, or pieces of one. He looked back up in his eyes then at his face. Everything was still the same. Everything in his mood still seemed the same. Except Parker did detect a little nervousness in Ned. Or maybe he was just feeling that way himself.

"Come on, Parker. You can have it. It's just a treat."

Parker's fear disappeared. Ned had never given him one reason to be afraid. He decided to give this a try.

"Look Ned, he's doing it," Kim said softly.

Parker walked over, now inches from the treats. But this time it was in his open hand, not between his fingers. He hesitated for just a moment then stepped forward and ate them. As he did, he was suddenly aware of Ned's hand reaching for him. He froze a moment, not sure what to do. His instincts said to expect a blow, something painful. But that's not what happened. Ned scratched under his chin softly, then his neck. He then touched his collar and let go.

"That's a good boy, Parker. Such a good boy."

Parker backed up toward his blanket. Ned got out another treat, broke it up and, once again, held the pieces in the palm of his hand. "Here you go, Parker. Want another? You can have it."

Two in a row. Parker liked this. He came forward and took

the other treat without hesitation. This time he took hold of Parker's collar and actually said the word: "Collar." Parker expected to be dragged forward. That's always what happened whenever The Man grabbed his collar.

But that didn't happen. Ned let go. Then he scratched under his chin gently again. He took out another treat. "Good boy," he said. "Here you go." He handed the whole treat to Parker and grabbed his collar again. Again he let go. Parker happily took the treat. This time, he didn't even back up to eat it. Why should he? It was obvious, Ned had no intention of hurting him.

"I can't believe this, Ned," Kim said. "He's totally relaxed right now. He's not even backing up to eat the treat."

"I know," Ned said. "Isn't it wonderful?"

KIM SAW tears welling up in Ned's eyes. What a tenderhearted man he was. It almost made her get teary. He continued to follow the instructions she had given him about conditioning Parker to see Ned touching his collar as a good thing.

After repeating the behavior a few more times, Kim said, "Now this time hold the treat out, but just say the word, *Collar*."

Ned did. And Parker did just what she expected. He thought about it a moment, then stepped toward Ned until his collar was in his extended hand.

"He's doing it, Kim. Look, he's doing it."

"I know, so take it and give him the treat. Then do it once more but, this time, click on the leash and ask him if he wants to go for a walk."

"You think he's ready for that? I don't want to spoil this moment."

"I don't think we'll spoil it. Because he's going to like what comes next after he hears that click. Most dogs do. In time, he'll go bonkers when you ask him if he wants to go for a walk."

"Okay, I'll do it if you say so." He was just about to but paused and looked back at her. "Thanks so much for being here, for teaching me these things. You really are a wizard with dogs, you know?"

"You're welcome. But none of this would've worked as well as it did if you weren't so completely devoted to this dog. That's what he's sensing. That's why he's so relaxed. He's already bonding to you as his new owner."

32

A s Kim predicted, Parker froze momentarily when Ned clicked on the leash, but he didn't lose it. Ned and Kim kept reassuring him verbally then Ned gave him another treat. Soon, he was walking alongside Ned as he followed Kim down the aisle toward a door that led outside.

"He's doing so good," Ned said. "Guess he has worked on a leash before."

"Maybe he's just excited to get some fresh air," she said. "Or it could be, he's excited to be walking with you."

"I'm assuming we're heading toward that fenced area on the left?"

"Yep. Oh good, there's no one else using it." She looked down at Parker, still walking beside Ned as if they'd been doing this for years. "Look at the leash. Totally slack."

"That's good, right?"

"That's very good. This is what I'd hope to see after he'd

been trained. Looks like he's going to make my job an easy one."

They reached the fence gate. Kim opened it and walked through. Ned did, too. But Parker froze at the entrance. "What do you think is the matter?"

"Just give him a second. He's checking out the situation. You and I don't see anyone, but he probably smells the residue from the last several dogs who've been here. See how his nose is lifted up and twitching?" A few seconds later, he stepped inside. "Go ahead latch the gate."

Ned did and stood there. "What now? Should I unhook the leash?"

"Yes. Just do it very naturally and then the both of us will go take a seat on that bench."

Ned did what she said. Parker just stood in place staring at them. Then he sat.

"Should I call him over?"

"Let's give him a few seconds. See what he does."

PARKER WASN'T sure what to do next. Ned and Kim were both looking down at him. Their mood was the same, very pleasant. He thought about walking toward them but now that he was no longer on a leash, he realized he didn't have to.

He decided to check out this new space and all these conflicting smells. Clearly, several other dogs had been here recently. But it looked perfectly safe. He walked slowly around the perimeter smelling everything carefully. He marked several places and eventually came back around to where Ned and Kim were sitting.

Ned said something to Kim.

"Should I call him over now? Maybe use a treat?"

"I think so. He seems all done exploring. But let's don't use a treat first. See what he does if you just call him. Just call him using your regular voice. Too loud or too excited might frighten him."

"Hey Parker. Come here, Boy," Ned said with a smile. He bent over and held his hands near the ground.

Parker looked at them, then up at Ned's face. He didn't have any treats, but Parker felt inclined to respond anyway. He didn't feel any fear, because Ned wasn't yelling. The Man always yelled whenever he wanted Parker to come near and often would swat him hard if he hesitated even a few moments.

He didn't think Ned would do that. But still, how could he be sure? Parker had already hesitated long enough for The Man to have become very angry with him. He took a few steps forward then looked at Ned's face again. Such kind eyes.

"That's it, Boy. You can come here. I won't hurt you."

Parker didn't understand what he said, but the way he said it took all his fears away. He kept walking until he was close enough for Ned to touch him.

The moment of truth. What would Ned do?

"Should I give him a treat?"

"I don't think so. Just pet him gently and keep talking to him the way you are. He came without a treat. I think this is a very big deal." Parker waited and fought off the instinct to run to the other side of the fenced area. Then he felt Ned's gentle hand pat his chest then scratch the back of his neck.

"What a good boy you are. Such a good boy."

Ned did it again, just as gently. It felt so good. He wasn't mad. He wasn't going to hurt him. All the tension Parker had felt slipped away.

"Look," Ned said. "He's resting against my leg." He moved his hand down and scratched his chest. "He doesn't have any sores there, does he? I forget."

"I don't think so," Kim said.

"That would be terrible. I'm sure those areas are still pretty sore."

"Well, I guess it's okay. He didn't react. And he's still totally relaxed. Just keep talking to him."

Parker was enjoying this. He could hardly remember the last time he'd felt someone petting him so softly.

"LET'S see what happens if I insert myself into the picture a little," Kim said. "Just to be on the safe side, I'll come bearing gifts." She slid a little closer to Ned on the bench, took out a treat and lowered it toward Parker's head. "Hey Parker, you're such a good boy. You want a treat?"

His head instantly turned toward the smell, and his tail began to wag. She put it in her palm and lowered it to his mouth. As he took it, she scratched under his chin and neck.

"I don't feel him tensing at all," Ned said. "He seems totally fine with you."

"He's a total sweetie," Kim said. "I knew he would be. He's got lots of love left to give. He's just not had anyone to give it to."

"I'm really glad to see this. That gives me hope for how he might react to Russell."

"Russell?"

"Remember the little boy I'm helping out?"

"That's right. His name's Russell. What about him?"

"I don't think I mentioned. I was thinking I would get him to help me out with Parker. Not right off the bat, but after he'd been at my place a couple of days."

"In what way?"

"Well, I knew his mom wouldn't really like the idea of me paying for his self-defense classes. So, I thought of a way he could earn it. Maybe I should have asked you first, to make sure you'd be okay with it. But I told her I'd like to hire her son to look in on Parker on the days that I work. You know, just spend some time with him. Freshen his water. Maybe take him out to go the bathroom. Some days I'm gone for ten hours or more. I think I mentioned, some of the time I'll be able to check in on him myself at the halfway point. But if not, I don't really like the idea of him being shut up in my apartment all that time by himself."

"No, I can see your point."

"You think I should have waited to ask him?"

"I don't know. Some dogs respond really well to kids. But others get nervous. My mom has a little dog that's completely in love with people. She greets everyone who comes to the door with all kinds of happiness and excitement. Except kids. She totally loses it with kids. We don't know why. But she instantly tenses up when kids come around."

"That's strange. Isn't there some way to train something like that out of them? Some way to, as you say it, create a new association so that the dog sees kids as a good thing?"

"You'd think so, wouldn't you? Sadly, it doesn't always work. It kind of depends on the dog's upbringing and life situations. Dogs that start off with kids as a puppy--if the kids are taught to treat them right--can be great around kids for the rest of their life. But my mom's dog is never around kids. And at this point, I don't think she's ever going to warm up to them either."

Ned looked discouraged. "Man, hope I haven't jumped the gun by asking for Russell to help me."

"I wouldn't worry about it now. Either it'll work out, or it won't. You'll know almost right away when you introduce them. I'll explain the best way to do that. You just need to coach Russell about how to act and the way to talk, kind of like I did with you. Hopefully, Parker will be one of those dogs who likes kids."

"I just remembered something," Ned said. "The lady who lived across the street from Parker told me a little boy lived there for several months, and he was the only one who treated Parker well. He left five months ago."

"Well still, that gives us some hope," Kim said.

33

So far this morning, Russell's mood had been very upbeat and positive. How could it not be? He still couldn't believe it. Last night, Ned had stopped over to deliver a surprise. He'd given Russell a bike! Just like that. He said it wasn't brand new, but it sure looked like it. Bright blue, not a speck of rust. And then tonight was his first MMA class.

But standing there at his locker now, just after second period, all Russell felt was fear.

Edmund and Harley were walking down the main hallway, headed right toward him. So far, he had been able to avoid any confrontations with them. That didn't seem possible anymore. He quickly looked around the immediate area. No teachers in sight.

He had come to his locker because he'd accidentally brought the wrong book for his third class. He'd already made the exchange. He could just take off running in the opposite direction. It's not likely they would chase him and, even if they did, there's no chance they'd catch him. But then everyone would see it, the terrified boy running away from bullies.

But that was the truth, wasn't it? Still, that's not the reputation or brand he wanted to get saddled with at this school. Glancing up, he noticed they were still coming, now just ten feet away. He closed his locker, turned in the opposite direction and began to walk. Maybe nothing would happen. There was a hallway intersection just up ahead. Maybe there'd be a teacher standing just around the corner.

"Hey Monkey Boy," Edmund said, "don't run off."

Russell kept walking.

"Did you hear me? I said don't run off."

He was ten feet away from that hallway intersection when he heard a sudden rush of footsteps and felt a hand grab his shirt collar. He was yanked back and slammed against the lockers.

"We told you this wasn't finished. Didn't we?"

"I think he's been avoiding us," Harley said.

"I think you're right."

Edmund pinched Russell's chin as he lifted his face. "That eye's healing up pretty nice."

"Let go of me." Russell swatted his hand away.

Edmund stepped closer. "Feeling pretty tough now?"

"I'm not feeling anything. I just want to go to class."

"Yeah?" Harley said. "And people in hell just want ice water."

Edmund looked at Harley. "What does that even mean?"

"I don't know. Something my grandmother always said when we asked for something we couldn't get."

Edmund looked back at Russell. "You think you can just

kick me in the shin and Harley in his privates then just run off?"

"Uh...yeah," Russel said. "What did you think I was gonna do, just stand there and let you guys hit me? I told you I didn't have any money. So, I did the only thing I could." He pointed to his eye, "It's not like it didn't cost me anything."

"He's got a point there, Edmund," Harley said.

"Shut up, Harley. He does not. That eye doesn't come close to evening the score. And there's still the matter of paying the new kid tax."

"I told you, I don't have any money. And I don't have any way of making any. Now let me go, or I'll be late to class." He slid past Edmund and started walking toward the hallway intersection.

"Hey, where do you think you're going?"

Russell picked up his pace. Suddenly, someone punched him in the back. "O-o-w-w!" he yelled and fell forward, dropping his books to the floor.

"What's going on here?" A deep male voice said.

Russell picked up his books and straightened up. It was Mr. Augustine, his math teacher. Russell's back hurt like mad.

"Nothing's going on," Edmund said. "We're just working out something with Russell here."

"Is that true, Russell? Cause that's not what it looks like to me."

Russell decided, what difference did it make if he told the truth or covered for Edmund and Harley? It's not like they'd start treating him better if he did. "It's like this Mr. Augustine, this is your basic bullying situation. That's what's going on here, so your perception is correct. That loud noise you reacted to was me crying out in pain as one of these two jerks punched me in the back. Notice I said two. That's an important point. Two against one, and both of them older and bigger than me." He looked at the two bullies, their eyes filled with anger.

"I can see that," Mr. Augustine said. "Two against one, boys? That seem fair to you? If what Russell said is true, that makes you cowards in my book."

"What he said is not true," Edmund said. "Nobody hit him. He just tripped over his own two feet."

"I did not," Russell said. "I'd be happy to lift my shirt and let you take a look at my back, but I suspect the bruise won't show up until this evening or tomorrow. But you do see my eye, right? It's still swollen from being hit by them a few days ago. Although that time wasn't on school grounds. I do recall it had something to do with me not paying my taxes. If you check at the office, you'll see my mom came in to report it. There's even some pictures."

"That doesn't prove we did it," Harley said. "And you can't prove either one of us just hit him now. Look around. No cameras in this hallway."

"Funny that you would notice that," Russell said.

"Yes, isn't it?" Mr. Augustine said. He looked at Edmund and Harley. "Guys, I'm not stupid. I think we both know what's going on here. There may not be proof to back up what Russell said. But I'm letting you know, I believe him. And I don't believe you. And I am going down to the office after the next class to look into what he said. And if that report is there, I'm going to add to it what I believe just happened here. We have a zero-tolerance policy for bullying. Do you boys know that?"

Harley nodded. Edmund didn't respond.

"Now, I suggest the two of you turn around and start

heading to your next class. Russell, would you like to move your locker to a hallway that does have a camera? Because I can make that happen."

"Yes, I would."

"Then come by the office during lunch or after school. I'll get things set up so that you can do that right away."

No one said or did anything for a moment.

"Well, I've got a class to teach. What are you boys doing still standing here?"

"I'm going," Russell said. "And thanks for stepping in, Mr. Augustine."

"You're welcome." The teacher turned and walked back the other way.

Just before he turned and headed down the hallway toward his next class, Russell glanced up at Edmund. He pointed at him with an angry glare, then gestured with his thumb as though slitting his throat and mouthed the words, *You're a dead man.*

34

The visit with Parker in the fenced area had gone so well, Kim couldn't see any reason why they shouldn't take the next step and introduce him to Ned's apartment. His new home. At the moment, he was sitting next to Ned in the front seat, inside a dog crate, which they'd fastened snugly with a seatbelt. He whimpered a little as they carried the crate out from the shelter and set him it in place, but he didn't lose it completely. No howling or whining. And thankfully, no growling. But by this time, Ned wasn't expecting any of that.

As he turned off the main street leading into his apartment, he glanced at the rear-view mirror. Good, Kim was still right behind him. He wasn't worried about losing her, since she often used GPS for directions. But he was old-fashioned that way and felt responsible for her being able to stay behind him. He was so glad she could be there for Parker's first time home.

He turned right at the first corner as slowly as possible to minimize how much Parker slid around inside his crate. "You doing okay there, boy? Won't be long now, we're almost there." Parker was lying in the back of his crate curled up into a tight ball. One more left turn and there was his building. He pulled into one of his assigned parking spaces. Since he only had one car, Kim could park right beside him.

As he got out, he leaned over the front seat to look in on Parker. "We're here, boy. We're home." He heard Kim's car door open and close.

"How did he do?"

"Fine," Ned said. "He wasn't sedated before we left, was he?"

"No. Guess he took it pretty calmly then?"

"Yeah. I did like you told me and talked to him a good bit on the way over. He's a good listener and calm the whole way."

She laughed. "Calm is great. Way better than howling, peeing or throwing up."

"Stuff like that happens when dogs drive in cars?"

"All the time."

"Usually, when you see them on TV they're all happy with their heads out the window enjoying the breeze."

"That's because they pick dogs who love to ride in cars. Wouldn't make much of a commercial to have a dog leaning over the front seat *roop-rupping* on the carpet."

"Did you say *roop-rupping*?"

"Yeah, throwing up. That's the sound my mom's dog makes when it gets sick. *Roop-rup, roop-rup, roop-rup,* then...*blech!*"

Ned laughed. "That's a very vivid picture, Kim. Thanks for sharing. But thankfully, no *roop-rupping* this time." He closed his door and went to open the passenger side. "Should I put his leash on right away and walk him in, or carry him in his crate the first time?"

"I say carry him, just to be safe. Don't want to take a chance of him breaking loose out here. I don't think he'd do that but better safe than sorry."

"Good idea."

PARKER WAS TRYING to stay calm, but inside he was terrified. He had no idea where he was, but it was definitely not the nice place he'd been in the last week or so. He was still with Ned and he was still being nice, but Parker was all shut up in a small box with only a small cage door in front.

For the last twenty minutes, the box had been vibrating constantly. Every so often, he'd feel himself sliding one way or another, then it would stop. Now, the vibrating had stopped completely. Ned had disappeared for a moment but appeared again behind him. Now the box was high off the ground. Parker braced himself. It felt like he was falling, but he was still inside the box.

Ned kept saying kind things to reassure him. Then Kim's face appeared in front of him, smiling and saying his name along with other nice things. He couldn't even focus on her face; the box was moving so much.

"It's right up the stairs," Ned said. "I'm the first apartment on the corner. Russell's apartment is right next door to that."

"That'll be convenient."

Now, they were moving up. That's how it felt anyway, but the ride became very bumpy.

"Say Ned, I had an idea on the way over. Remember how I had you bring a toy to Parker in the kennel? We could do the same thing with Russell. To make Parker feel more comfortable with him when they first meet. Just pick something out and ask Russell to sleep with it in his bed for a few days. Then put it in Parker's crate a few days before they meet. As soon as Parker smells Russell, he'll already seem familiar."

"Great idea. I'll talk to him about that today."

The bumpy ride stopped. Things felt a little more stable.

"Here we are."

Parker heard Ned make a jingling sound. A door opened and they stepped inside to a brand new place. The door closed. Things became much quieter. Instantly, Parker began to relax a little. As he sniffed the air beyond the crate, he realized everything here smelled like Ned.

"Should I just let him out to explore?"

"Not yet," Kim said. "We want him to get off to a good start. That won't happen if he has an accident right off the bat."

"Right. I should take him for a walk first. We have a nice little field right across the street. I'll walk him on the leash there."

"That'll be fine. That's a good habit to get into anyway, whenever you take him for a car ride. And don't forget, as soon as he's done his business, give him a treat. Then let him walk around a bit before bringing him back here. That's another good habit to get into. We want to always make him feel rewarded for doing his business outside. I know that may sound a little odd but, in time, it'll become a valuable conditioned behavior."

"Sounds like a great idea. Think I should try the collar idea we taught him a little while ago where he gives it to me voluntarily?"

"We could try it. Hopefully, he's not too nervous to remember. If he is, don't make a big deal about it. Just click on the leash and start walking."

Ned got the leash out and a treat and bent down in front of Parker's travel crate. "Remember this, Parker?" He unlatched the crate door. "Collar, remember?" The door swung open, and he held the treat out in one hand. The other he held open and waited to see what Parker would do."

"Well, look at that," Kim said.

Parker stepped right out of the crate and put his collar in Ned's empty hand. "Good boy, good boy," Ned said and gave him the treat. Then he clicked on the leash. When Parker finished chewing, Ned stood. "Want to go for a walk?" He started walking toward the front door. Parker walked right beside him.

35

As Ned walked Parker outside, Kim walked around the living area of his apartment, trying to strike a balance between curiosity and outright nosiness. The furniture wasn't anything special. The pieces matched each other in a general way and the upholstered couch and loveseat looked more designed for comfort than style. On one side of the coffee table sat a large photographic history book of World War I aviation. On the other, a cute little bonsai tree in a ceramic pot. She thought it must be fake until she touched it.

Across the room, was an overstuffed suede recliner facing a midsize flatscreen TV. Then she saw something rather comforting on a little table beside it. A well-worn Bible sat atop a Christian devotional book she recognized. Another thing that struck her in an encouraging way was how clean it was. The place looked lived in but it was clear: Ned definitely cleaned up after himself. She was just about to check out the kitchen when the front door opened. Ned and Parker had returned.

"So, how'd it go, your first walk?"

"Guess he really had to go bad," Ned said. "He squatted down just about as quick as we cleared the sidewalk. But he walked great on the leash. Didn't pull a bit, there or on the way back. After he went, I gave him a treat and let him smell all around the grassy area. Figured he needed to feel comfortable there, since it was going to be his new bathroom."

"Well, that's one area of training I can check off the list, walking on a leash. Are there any other immediate questions you have before I go? I mean, we have lots more to talk about. I'm talking about specific things you'd want to know for his first time at your place?"

Ned thought a minute. "That brochure you wrote was pretty thorough, so I feel like I'll be okay. I've got his meds and the Doc explained how to give them to him. Did you see where I put his dog crate and food and water bowls? Think I put them in a good enough spot?"

"They look fine where they are."

"How about the one in the bedroom. Let me show you that one." He walked down the hall and opened a closed door.

She followed him and stepped inside his bedroom. The bed was made. The only clothes she saw were piled up in a hamper.

"I put it against the wall there, because that's the side I sleep on. Figured he could see me during the night. Or at least hear me."

"Hear you? Do you snore?"

"I don't think so. Then again, if a man snores when all alone in his bedroom, does he really make a sound?"

Kim laughed. "I get it. Like the tree falling in the forest. But starting tonight, you won't be the only one here."

"True. But if I did snore, how would Parker tell me? Anyway, I don't think I snore."

"You probably don't." She looked at her watch. "I better get back to work. So, you're okay if I leave you alone with him?"

"Think we'll be fine. Figured I would just let him off the leash as soon as you're gone then take a seat in the living room while he explores. Still got a couple of hours before I have to leave to take Russell to his first self-defense class. That'll give Parker and me a little more time to get used to each other before I have to leave him by himself."

"Sounds like a plan," she said. "You've got my number. Call if you have any questions, at any time."

"I will."

She walked toward the front door.

"Can I call you sometime...even if I don't have any questions?"

She stopped and turned. "I hope you will." She smiled and walked out the door.

Ned hurried over to the window behind his recliner and watched Kim as she walked to her car, right until she went out of sight. Parker, still on his leash, was forced to follow right behind it. "Well how about that, boy? I think the young lady is starting to like me back." Parker looked up at him, his tail wagging. "And I'm already talking to the dog."

He came around the recliner and sat on the edge. "Bet you'd like to be off that leash, wouldn't you?" His instinct was to pull him closer using the leash, but he remembered what Kim had said about choices. He still had the baggie of treats in his pocket and decided to see what would happen if he just offered Parker his open hands near the floor. "Come here, Boy," he said softly. "Let me take that off."

Parker sat about three feet in front of him, looked down at Ned's hands then up at his face, then down at his hands.

"That's it, Boy. You can do it. Come."

Parker still didn't move. Ned was just about to get the treat out of the baggie when the little guy stood. Ned gestured with his hands again, inviting him closer. Parker responded and came right to Ned's hands. Ned scratched under his chin with one hand and behind his ears with the other. "Good boy, Parker. Good to come. Let's get that leash off you. Let you check out the place for a little while." He unhooked the leash and, to his surprise, Parker stayed put for little while longer.

Ned began to pet his back and sides, being careful to avoid any of the wounded areas. They were looking better, much better than the day after they cleaned him up. But he was still quite a sight to see. Parker had already captured such a place in his heart, Ned almost forgot how bad he looked to other people. He got a quick reminder while taking Parker out to the grassy area a few minutes ago.

Parker had already done his business and then began to explore the perimeter. Ned had followed close behind, leaving just enough room to keep the leash slacked. Two teenaged girls walked by on the sidewalk, noticed Ned then looked down at Parker. Both girls reacted with instant, freaked-out expressions, as if Ned had taken a little green goblin for a walk. Their heads immediately shot forward and their pace quickened. One of them looked back for just a second, as if to convince herself she had really seen the hideous creature.

Ned looked down at Parker now, sitting contentedly between his legs. "You look just fine to me, Buddy," he said.

"Wait till all those sores heal up and that hair grows back. Those girls will be stopping dead in their tracks to come over and love on you." Parker's tail wagged.

Ned leaned back in his recliner. "Go on, Boy. Check the place out. This is your new home." He looked down at the dog, who looked up at him as if trying to decipher what he just said. He didn't move for several moments. Just sat there staring at Ned.

"Okay, I'll make the first move." Ned got up and walked over to the dinette table, picked up the manila folder filled with things from the shelter, and dumped them out. Picking up that photograph of Parker the lady across the street had taken, he held it up. Then looked down at Parker, who was now standing just two feet away, looking back at him.

"Hard to believe this is you, boy. Still see you in the face, but that's about all." He walked over to the fridge and stuck the photo on the freezer with a magnet. "We'll just put that there to help me remember where this little restoration project of ours is going."

Parker, of course, followed him there and just looked up, tail wagging. Now his mouth opened in that half-pant, half-smile look dogs get. "Welcome home, Parker."

36

A few hours later, it was time to head next door to pick up Russell for the drive to his first self-defense class. Ned slipped out the front door and locked the deadbolt behind him.

He knocked on Russell's door rather than use the doorbell. His mother answered. "Right on time. Russell's been so excited about this, and I am too. You want to come in a minute? He's just brushing his teeth."

"Sure." Ned stepped inside, and she closed the door.

"I was thinking I'd have to bring him this first time. I thought you had to work and needed to meet him there."

"That was the plan, but that little dog I told you about, the one that I'm adopting, got the green light from the vet to go home already. He was supposed to be in there another week, but I went down there to pick him up this morning. So I took a personal day. Didn't want him spending his first full day in a strange apartment all by himself."

"So, he's in there now?"

"Yep. Left him in his crate, sound asleep. That's why I knocked instead of ringing the bell. Hoping Russell and I could sneak by him on our way down to the car. He's still recuperating. The more he sleeps, the better. I'm hoping he stays asleep the whole time we're gone. But if you hear some whimpering or whining next door, you'll know why. Hope you don't hear anything. I have no idea how thick these walls are."

"You never hear me yelling and screaming at Russell?" she said, straight-faced.

"No. Does that...happen a lot?"

She laughed. "No, I'm just joking. I try to never raise my voice with him. And we don't listen to loud music, either. But don't worry about the dog making noise. Unless he's howling at the moon, I'll be fine."

Russell walked out into the living area. "I'm all ready."

"Great. I see you got your duffel bag."

"It's got everything in it from the online checklist," his mother said.

"Then let's go." Ned put his hand on the doorknob. "There's just one thing. Remember that little dog you're going to start watching for me?"

"Yeah."

"I brought him home today. He's next door sleeping. I'd like to keep it that way, so no talking when we go by my apartment and let's talk quietly on the stairs. Can you do that?"

"He's already here? When can I see him?"

"Not for a few days, I'm afraid." Ned took his hand off the door. "I was talking with the dog trainer, and she's a little concerned about whether Parker will accept you right off the bat. We have no idea what he's like around kids. I'm sure you know, he's had kind of a rough time of it with his old owner. He's got some--"

"Issues?" Russell said.

"Right, issues. So, it's nothing about you. But the trainer had an idea we could try to help make your introduction to him a little smoother. I'll explain what it is in the car. I promise, as soon as we can, I'll let you see him."

"Okay."

Ned opened the door. Russell closed the distance between them.

"Wait a minute, young man," his mother said. "I didn't get my kiss."

"Mom..."

"Want me to step outside?" Ned said.

"No, he doesn't." She gently grabbed Russell's shoulders.

Russell leaned forward and kissed her goodbye.

"Never be ashamed to kiss your mom," Ned said.

"Can we go now?"

As they stepped out into the corridor, Ned held up his index finger to his lips and made the *Sh-h-h* sound. When they got to the bottom of the stairs, he stopped to listen. "I don't hear anything."

"Me, neither," Russell said. "Think we did it."

They walked toward Ned's car. He hit a button and the doors unlocked. "That eye's looking almost normal."

Russell's expression instantly turned sour.

"Something wrong?"

"Nothing we can do anything about right now. Going to this place will help, if I live that long."

Ned opened the car door and got in. Russell did the same. "What are you talking about?"

"Nothing. I just wish I had taken this class about eight weeks ago."

Ned started the car, backed out and headed in the direction of the gym. "Those boys bother you again today?"

"Yeah. Getting a little bolder, I guess. First time they've messed with me at school. If a teacher hadn't happened by at just the right moment, my whole face would've looked like my eye did last week."

Ned had to suppress a surge of rage. "Did the teacher see them?"

"He didn't see anything incriminating, if that's what you mean. One of them had just punched me in the back. He might've heard the thump, but he came around the corner just then, so they stopped before he saw anything else. I think he believed me, though. It was pretty obvious what was going on."

"Did you check to see if there were any cameras in the hallway? A lot of schools have installed them in recent years. It might've picked up what happened."

"No such luck. As it turns out, my locker happens to be in one of the few hallways that have no camera. And as dumb as they seem, Edmund and Harley had apparently picked up on that, which is why they felt okay coming at me at my locker."

"Then you need to move. That needs to change right—"

"It's already happening. The teacher figured out the same thing and set things up, so I could move to a different locker."

Ned sighed. "Well, that's something anyway."

"And he also said he'd stop by the office and make a note about what happened, to hopefully deter these guys from trying anything like this again."

"Think that'll do any good?"

"No, I know it won't. As soon as the teacher turned around

and started heading back to his class, the guys basically looked at me like they wanted to kill me, and one of them whispered, you're a dead man." Tears welled up in Russell's eyes. "I hate this so much. I don't understand why it's happening. Why they can't just leave me alone." He wiped his eyes, tried blinking away the tears. After releasing a deep sigh, he said, "I'm really glad we're doing this, Ned. Really, I am. But the class is eight weeks long, right? That's what it said on the internet. I'm guessing they teach you the basics upfront, right? And the good stuff, the stuff that might actually help me, toward the end. I don't think I can wait five or six weeks to learn what I need to do to stop these guys. I'll be in the hospital long before that. They're not going to leave me alone. I know it. I just know it."

Ned wanted to say something comforting, something that would ease his pain, take away his fear. But Russell had a point. This thing with these bullies wasn't sitting on idle; it was escalating. His own instincts confirmed what Russell was saying. He needed help now.

But what could Ned do? He had to figure out something.

37

"Here we are," Ned said, as they pulled into the gym parking lot. It occupied three storefronts of a fairly modern strip mall. You could see the gym layout pretty clearly from the street. A class of clearly older kids was already underway in the left suite. Two kids, all suited up, were sparring with a sensei nearby giving directions. About a dozen other kids were squatting down around the perimeter of the mat.

"That's not our class, is it?" Russell said.

"No, they look at least two or three grades older than you." He saw a huddle of kids about Russell's age gathering around another instructor in the suite on the right. Two other children of similar age just walked through the front door and headed in that direction. "Think that's where we go."

Russell grabbed his duffel bag and sighed heavily.

"You ready for this?" Ned asked.

"Ready as I'll ever be, I guess." He unlatched the car door and opened it.

They both headed inside and walked toward the group of kids. Ned noticed they were all filling out little half sheets of paper attached to small clipboards. He walked up to the instructor and extended his hand. "Are you Roberts?" Ned asked. "I mean, Sensei Roberts?"

The man shook his hand. "That's me."

"Ned Barringer. I'm the police officer. We spoke on the phone."

"Right, Ned. I remember."

"Are we late?" According to the clock, they weren't.

"No, just giving the kids a short questionnaire to fill out. Something to help us get to know them a little more on a personal level. This is Russell, right? And you're not his dad but a family friend?"

"Good memory. Yeah, I'm his next-door neighbor."

He handled Russell a clipboard with a page and pen attached. "You can have a seat over there on the mat. Just fill that out as best you can. This isn't a test, so no sweat about getting wrong answers."

"Okay," Russell said. He found an empty space on the second row of kids.

"Is there anything you want me to do right now?" Ned said. "I'd be happy to help out if I can."

"Not really. Tonight's pretty much going to be laying some foundations. Have you ever pursued any mixed martial arts training before."

"Some. Not a ton. Our police fitness training includes some of it."

"Any Muay Thai?"

"Some."

"That's probably the discipline we'll be teaching the most," Roberts said. "How are you with kids?"

"Great. I do pretty well with kids. I've done quite a few community service projects and safety seminars in public schools for the department. It's not my job, but they often tag me for stuff like that because of how well I connect with kids. Just let me know if there's something I can do to help."

"That's good to hear. What I could mainly use is help with coordinating drills with the kids in my place, so I can give individual attention to certain kids that don't seem to be getting it. Really simple stuff. You'll see me do it, whatever the thing is I'm teaching, and if you see me need to leave for a minute, you just come up and keep the kids going doing the same thing until we're done. I'm sure I'll need your help for other things, too. How about we just play it by ear?"

"Fine. Whatever I can do to help."

Ned stood a few feet off from Roberts and watched Russell as he sat there filling out the questionnaire. There was a wall clock behind them. Roberts looked up at it then stood at the center of the little semi-circle of kids in front of him. Ned counted nine others besides Russell.

"Is everyone finished?" Roberts said.

"Almost," a few said. The rest were already done.

"You don't need to write long answers," Roberts said. "It's really time for us to begin, so finish up quickly."

The remaining kids, including Russell, began writing frantically on their pads. Then one by one they were done.

"Good. I want to welcome you all to your first lesson in our self-defense class for kids. Has anyone ever been to a class like this before?" No one raised their hand. "That's fine. This is a beginners' class, so you're at the right place. We'll be teaching you a lot of different things over the next eight weeks. And I'm sure most of you are pretty anxious to start learning all the fun stuff, right? The punches and kicks."

"Will this be like the UFC?" a kid in the first row asked.

"Not exactly," Roberts said. "How many of you have seen MMA fights like the UFC, where two fighters face each other in a fenced-in cage?"

Several kids raised their hands. One of them said, "My dad watches that stuff all the time." Russell kept his hand down. Ned thought most of these kids looked way too young to be watching UFC fights.

"Well, that's definitely MMA, mixed martial arts," Roberts said, "but that is seriously advanced stuff, and those guys are intentionally trying to hurt each other. That's how that sport works. But that's not what we're doing here. You might be learning some of those same skills, but the goal here is self-defense, not trying to knock someone out. Are we clear on that?"

Everyone nodded. Roberts continued. "This class is about you knowing how to protect yourself if someone is trying to hurt you. We want you to have the confidence that comes from knowing what to do if someone is trying to hurt you and words alone won't make them stop."

That's exactly the situation Russell was facing now, Ned thought. He glanced over at him. He was leaning forward, his eyes locked onto Roberts' face. He obviously liked what he'd just heard.

"But we're not just going to teach you about punching and kicking."

"How about ground and pound?" said the same kid who asked about UFC.

Ned knew the term. It was when one fighter had the other pinned to the ground and just pounded away with his fists until he was knocked out or the ref stopped the fight.

"No," Roberts said sternly. "Remember I said, our goal isn't knocking anyone out. And please don't interrupt while I'm talking. If you have a question, you raise your hand. What I was going to say is, part of what you will learn are different things you can say to, hopefully, de-escalate a tense situation. So that you don't have to use the punches and kicks you will learn here. Who knows what de-escalation means?"

Three or four kids raised their hands, including Russell. Roberts picked Russell to answer.

"It's when you say things that lower the tension in a conflict. And hopefully avoid a fight altogether."

"Very good. It's Russell, right?"

Russell nodded. "My mom has taught me a lot about de-escalation. The problem is, even if you're pretty good at it, it doesn't always work. That's been my experience anyway."

Ned couldn't believe how intelligent this kid was. In some ways, he already had the mind of an adult.

"No, you're right," Roberts said. "Sometimes words are not enough, which is why this class is so important. But learning how to lower the tension in a conflict is also important, because sometimes it *does* work. And if you can avoid physical contact in a confrontation, work things out some other way, that's always a better way to go."

He took a few steps back. "Okay, so here's what we're going to do. Everyone stand. One of the most important things about mixed martial arts is being physically fit. From my experience, way too many kids in your generation are not physically fit. They spend way too much time watching TV or playing video games. Some of that is fine, but if you're in this class and you are serious about learning the skills I plan to teach you, you need to be in good physical shape. So, for the remainder of this first lesson, I'm going to show you a number of fitness and strength exercises I want you to do at least three or four days a week from now on. Starting with jogging. Line up in single file and set your clipboards down on the table as you pass by. For the next several minutes, I want you to jog around the outside of this open area. I'll let you know when to stop. Ready? Okay go."

And that's how the rest of the class was spent. Teaching the kids different exercise routines, including things like jumping jacks, doing pushups the right way, even jumping rope. A few of the heavier kids couldn't keep up. Roberts was very patient with them, even encouraging, but still he told them they had to work at this faithfully, even if they couldn't do it as long as the others.

When the time was up, Roberts had everyone come back and sit on the mats in a semi-circle again.

"I know this wasn't any fun, right? Did any of you enjoy all this exercise?" No one said a word. "Well, I promise you, we will start learning all of the different punching and kicking techniques soon. In fact, starting the next lesson, we'll spend the second half doing some of that stuff. But I really want you to get how important it is to get in shape and stay in shape. So, I'm giving you this assignment...do the exercises you've just done for at least twenty minutes, three or four times a week. And I'm going to ask you about it at class. Are we clear on that?"

Everyone nodded, but no one was smiling.

Roberts picked up on that. "And I promise you, we will

start getting into the fun stuff beginning with our next class. Well, that's it for tonight. See you all next time."

As the class began to disperse, Ned looked over at Russell. He was obviously already in great shape. His face wasn't even red. But Ned saw the sadness in his eyes. He walked over to Roberts and said, "Can I talk to you for a few minutes? It's about a pretty serious situation Russell is facing right now. I'll make sure he does everything you say about fitness. But as you can see, he's already got that part down. We really need your help with a bully situation he's dealing with right now. I don't think this thing can wait."

Roberts looked over at Russell. "Hey Russ, why don't you take a seat there behind the table for a couple minutes. Ned and I are going back to my office to chat."

"Uh...okay. Over here?" He walked to the table.

"That's right. Sit right there. We'll be back in a few."

38

S ensei Roberts' office was pretty small and sparsely
furnished. It was obvious he only spent time here
when absolutely necessary. Ned noticed a straight
back chair sitting in front of a gray metal desk.

Roberts closed the door. "Go ahead, Ned. Have a seat." He
walked around and sat in a black ergonomic-looking swivel
chair. "So, what's up? What's going on with Russ?"

"Before I tell you, it's probably a small thing, but I've never
heard him or his mom refer to him as Russ. It's always Russell."

"Good to know. So tell me, what's he dealing with? School
bullies?"

"Yeah, but after school as well. Seems like two punks have
decided to target him for the treatment. As you can see, he's on
the smallish side. And he's also the new kid."

"I don't know why that one thing is so attractive to bullies,"
Roberts said. "But you combine that with a kid being small,
and it's almost like an irresistible lure for these cowards."

"Cowards is the word," Ned said. "Anyway, my introduction to Russell happened in the hallway just outside of my apartment. He lives next door. We bumped into each other, and I noticed he had a black eye. Turns out, these two kids had just jumped him in the park down the street from our complex. He'd gotten away by kicking one of them in the groin and the other in the shin. Which, of course, only made them madder. If they had been strangers, that might have been the end of it. But they go to the same school, and this thing had been building for weeks."

"And let me guess," Roberts said, "these guys have been making his life a nightmare ever since."

"Basically, yeah."

"Did he report this at the school?"

"Yeah, and they started a file on the matter."

Roberts laughed. "Yeah, the school system is pretty much a wash on this issue at the moment."

"And technically," Ned said, "this ambush didn't even occur on school grounds or during school hours. And while it was bad, it wasn't bad enough to involve any legal consequences."

"Have there been any more incidents? I mean ones that got physical?"

"Yes, one other. Today, in fact. But it's mostly been verbal abuse. They did try to hurt him today by his locker. One of them figured out the hallway near his locker didn't have any cameras. Russell said he tried to walk away. One of them punched him in the back. Just then, a teacher walked by, figured out what was going on and stopped it."

"But he didn't actually see anything physical?" Roberts asked.

"Nope."

"Well, I'm sure he made a fresh entry into the file, for all the good that'll do."

"Well, this guy offered to do a little more. He got Russell's locker moved to a hallway with a camera. Of course, that's not going to stop these guys. Just change the location for the next assault."

"And I'm sure they let Russell know this thing isn't over after the teacher left."

Ned nodded. "One of them whispered, *You're a dead man.*"

Roberts shook his head in silent disgust. "It never changes."

"And I'm telling you, this kid is not some kind of oddball. He's not doing anything to bring this on himself. He's a really good kid, smart, easy to talk to, great sense of humor. But he's basically being terrorized by these punks and wakes up dreading every day. And I think this thing's escalating. I wouldn't be at all surprised if they don't come after him again before the week is out."

Roberts leaned back in his chair. "I'm inclined to agree with you. We need to bring this boy some relief. And soon."

"Glad to hear you say that. What have you got in mind?"

"You guys coming back on Thursday?"

"Planning on it."

"Then I'll plan on staying after an extra hour or so for some private tutoring. I could teach him some moves that will guarantee he gets the better outcome the next time they clash."

"Really?"

Roberts nodded. "Will you be there?"

"Yep. One way or another."

"Good. Then you can work with him after the session, make sure he gets all the moves down right. He needs to do it enough to where it's almost second nature, so he doesn't forget what to do in a panic."

"I'll definitely work with him. Look, I really appreciate you doing this." Ned stood.

So did Roberts. "Happy to help. It's why I'm here. One of the main reasons I started this place, was for situations exactly like this. You tell Russell for me, keep your chin up. Don't give in to fear. We'll give him the tools to turn this thing around." He extended his hand.

Ned shook it and left the office, greatly encouraged. He found Russell and said, "All set. Let's get in the car."

Russell waited till they got in to ask Ned how it went with Sensei Roberts. He hoped they were talking about his situation. The look on Ned's face when he came out of the office gave Russell a spark of hope. Russell always looked at people's faces, especially their eyes. If you caught them right after something happened, before they had a chance to figure out how they should react, you could usually see how they really felt about something.

Ned's face had started off positive and stayed that way all the way to the car.

"So, what did he say? Were you guys talking about me? Is he going to help?"

Ned started the car and backed out. "The short answer is yes."

"When? How many weeks do I have to wait?"

"Not weeks, days. Like, two. How's Thursday sound, right after class?"

"Really? Thursday? He's going to do it on Thursday?" Russell was so happy, he almost felt like crying. He couldn't believe it. Thursday. That wasn't so long. He could make it till then. "What did he say? What's he going to teach me? You think it'll work?"

Ned laughed. "Slow down, little buddy. Give me a second. First off, to answer your question, he didn't get into the details of what he's going to teach you. But he made it perfectly clear, on Thursday night you will learn some moves that will guarantee—those were his words, not mine— that you come out on top, not the bullies, the next time they come after you."

"Really? He said that?"

Ned nodded. "He did. He also said, after I explained everything you're going through, that situations like yours were the very reason he opened up this gym in the first place."

"Dojo. I think they call it a dojo."

"You're right. That's what martial arts gyms are called. Anyway, did you hear what I said? He's all about helping kids like you learn the skills they need, so they don't have to live in fear anymore. Does that sound great?"

"Sounds almost too good to be true."

"But it's not. It's going to happen. Starting Thursday. Now, do you think you can stay out of trouble until then?"

"I know I can. I've got a friend named Pete. I told him about what we're doing, about you taking me to this place. He knows all about Edmund and Harley. I can ride my new bike to his place after school the next two days until my mom gets home."

"Sounds like a plan," Ned said.

They drove in silence for a few moments. But for Russell, it felt like the weight of the world had lifted off his shoulders.

Finally, Ned said, "Hey, before I forget, there's something I want to give you tonight when we get home."

"What is it?"

"Well, actually, it's a stuffed animal."

"Really? Why?"

"Remember what I said about something we could do that would make it easier for Parker to accept you?"

"Yeah."

"Well, that's what this is about. Kim, the trainer at the shelter who's been helping me, said that dogs are all about smell and scents. You're supposed to take the stuffed animal home and sleep with it a couple of days. I guess, even keep it near you when you're home. Your scent will get on the stuffed animal. Then I'll give it to Parker and let him have it for a couple of days. Then when the two of you meet, you won't seem like such a stranger to him."

"Because he'll be smelling me on the stuffed animal."

"Right. It's no guarantee that he'll accept you, but she thinks it will improve the chances."

"You mean, there's a chance even if we do this, Parker won't like me? And I won't get to watch him for you when you're at work?"

"There's a chance. But like I said, this idea will greatly—"

"If that happens, then will we have to stop taking these classes?"

"What? No, why?"

"Well, you're paying for them, and I'm supposed be paying you back by watching Parker for you."

"No Russell. No. That's not gonna happen. Listen to me, if something happens and Parker winds up being too afraid of you, you and I are still going to do these classes together. Nothing's going to change that. Besides, what kind of friend would I be if I let you pay the price for something you have no control over? So, you don't worry about that, okay? Even for a minute."

"Okay," Russell said. He took a deep breath and let some hope back into his heart again.

Parker huddled in the back of his crate. For the last few hours, he had been trying to nap off and on, but he kept hearing strange sounds outside that woke him up. He was nervous about being left here all alone, but not enough to start shaking. He kept clinging to the hope that Ned would return. If not Ned, then that nice woman, Kim, from the last place he had been.

They seemed to be the two people who interacted with him the most for the last several days. He hoped that Ned was going to be with him from now on. He had only and always been kind to Parker, almost the exact opposite of The Man. It was beginning to look like Parker would never have to be around that man again. Which would be wonderful.

Ned was the one who had put him in this crate and brought him to this new place. There's always a measure of fear whenever he faced a new or uncertain situation. But Ned's kindness, not to mention those wonderful treats, helped keep Parker's fears at bay. And before putting him in here the most recent time, Ned had let Parker roam freely all around the place. Even encouraged him to do it. Parker didn't sense anything dangerous or alarming. And Ned's scent permeated everything, even here inside his crate.

Parker heard a new sound. His ears shot up. Sounded like footsteps outside, not far away. Then voices, coming from the front. That's where most of the other noises had come from, too. He listened some more. The voices got louder. Sounded like two people. A man and a child. Then a jingling sound followed by a loud click.

The front door opened.

"Well, I'm glad you had a good time. And I'm really looking forward to Thursday night, too."

It was Ned. Parker was sure of it. He stood and walked to the front of his crate, tried to look out through the grate, but he couldn't see him.

"You said to remind you about giving me that stuffed toy, for Parker."

The child's voice. Clearer now. Sounded like a little boy. His mind instantly flashed back to pictures of the little boy who had lived at his old place for a little while. He loved that little boy so much and was so sad when he went away. He kept looking for him and longing to see him for weeks and weeks, then finally accepted that he was gone for good.

This little boy's voice sounded almost the same.

"You're right," Ned said, "I did say that, and I completely forgot. You wait right here. I'll go in and get it and be right back out."

Parker found himself experiencing a sensation he hadn't felt for so long. Excitement. He heard Ned's footsteps hurrying into the apartment. At one point, he'd brushed right past Parker's crate. Parker was so glad he was home and actually wanted to see him face-to-face. His tail was wagging. He felt the urge to bark out loud but restrained himself.

Ned hurried past him again and now stood by the front door. "Here it is," he said.

"What is this?" the little boy said.

"It's supposed to be a fox," Ned said. "If you stretch it out, it looks a little more like one. Don't press them now, but the head and tail squeak."

"Okay. I don't have to play with it. As long as he's happy. I'll start sleeping with it tonight."

"Good, you do that. Well, I better get in here so I can let Parker out to go the bathroom."

"Okay, well, thanks again for doing this. It really means a lot to me. I actually already do feel kinda better."

"Great. So glad to hear it. See you soon." Ned closed the front door.

NED WALKED down the hall from the front door and turned on a few more lights. He had left just a couple on before he'd left. He grabbed Parker's leash off the hook and brought it with him. "How's my boy?" he said, as he walked toward the crate.

Looking down, he saw Parker's face pressed up against the crate door. "Look at you, wagging your tail. Did you miss me? Did you think I wasn't coming back?" Ned squatted down. "There's my good boy." He stuck two fingers through the crate door and scratched under Parker's chin. Parker actually licked them.

"I bet you're ready to get out of there, aren't you?" He opened the crate door, reached in with the leash. Parker really got excited now. Well, for him. He sat politely but his tail continued to thump the crate floor. "Let's see if you remember. Collar." Sure enough, Parker stood and brought his collar to Ned's hand. Ned clicked on the leash.

"What a good boy. And so smart." He pulled a treat out of his pocket. "Good boy." He handed him the treat and led him out of the crate. "And I can see we didn't have any accidents, either."

Kim had said Parker would probably be able to hold it, since he was a full adult now and dogs don't like to mess in their crates, unless they've been left way too long.

Parker walked right beside Ned as they went through the front door toward the steps leading downstairs. He hesitated at the steps, as if he had never seen anything like them before. "It's okay, Boy. You can do it." Ned went down a few more steps then turned to face him. "Come on, Parker. You can do it." He held out a treat, just far enough that he would have to come down at least one step to reach it. Ned stood quietly, giving Parker time to make a choice.

Parker stared at the treat, then down at the steps, then back at the treat. He did this two or three more times but still didn't move from the top step. Ned knew not to drag him down with the leash, so he decided they would face this challenge some other time.

"That's okay, Boy. I'll pick you up." And that's what he did. He carried Parker down the steps and set him gently down on the pavement. Parker resumed his steady pace walking right beside him as they crossed the street and headed to the grassy area where Parker could relieve himself. Thankfully, no one else happened to be walking their dog now.

Parker didn't need any prodding. He quickly did what he

had to do, scuffed the grass behind him after going number two, then proudly returned to Ned's side. "Good boy," he said, and gave Parker a treat. "You ready to go back in, or do you want to take a walk?" Ned realized he was saying this to himself. Parker probably only understood the word *walk* out of everything else Ned had just said.

"A walk it is, then." It would do them both good to get some fresh air. And Ned figured, Parker probably needed to burn some energy after being cooped up in the crate for several hours.

As they walked along, Ned wrestled with the idea of calling Kim. He could do it under the guise of giving her an update about Parker's first day at his place. But the truth was, he found himself thinking about her more and more throughout the day, in every idle moment. And he really just wanted to hear her voice.

40

W hen Russell awoke the next morning, the usual cloud of doom that greeted him seemed a little less intense than normal. He knew the class last night was the reason why. Well, not the class exactly but what came after. For the first time since this whole bullying ordeal began, he felt a tinge of hope that a real solution could be just around the corner.

Of course, he tried not to dwell on the fact that the solution still involved him having to fight Edmund and Harley. But he'd seen enough movies and played enough video games to know, the hero doesn't become the hero without facing the bad guys head on and beating them. Then again, he didn't know any heroes who were less than five feet tall and weighed less than a hundred pounds.

He brought his backpack with him as he headed out to the breakfast table.

"There you are," Mom said. "Thought I was going to have to come after you. You didn't tell me how things went last night. I wasn't going to let you head off to school without filling me in. Did you learn anything?"

"Nothing I didn't already know. We didn't get into any actual karate or Kung Fu moves. The sensei, that's what they call the instructors, spent the first half just giving us a lecture. You would've liked it. Pretty much said the same things you always tell me. About how the goal is not beating people up or getting into fights. About how important it is to learn how to de-escalate a conflict before it gets physical. Of course, he didn't spend too much time talking about what to do if the guys who want to fight you are brainless and have zero interest in a friendly chat."

His mom laughed. "But they are going to teach you that stuff, right?" She set a plate of pancakes in front of him. "I already buttered them. Doesn't look like it, cause it already melted."

He grabbed the syrup and started pouring.

"That's enough."

"Mom, you're the one counting carbs, not me."

"Still, you don't need that much sugar."

He grabbed his fork and knife. "Anyway, yeah, we are going to learn that stuff eventually. But I can tell, they are going to constantly be emphasizing the kind of stuff you care about. The moral high ground stuff, the positive values and such."

"So you said they only spent the first half on that. What did you do the rest of the time?"

"Nothing fun, as the president says, *That I can tell you.*" He took a big forkful of pancakes, plopped it in his mouth.

"So what did you do?"

"You want me to talk while I'm still chewing?"

"This morning you can. I want to hear what you're saying, but I don't want you to be late for school."

"Okay, basically, the rest the time we were just exercising. Lots and lots of exercising. And of course, that came with a lecture about the importance of fitness. About two thirds of the kids there probably found this lecture very relevant. A few looked like they hadn't done anything physical since they left the crib. But as you know, that's not really a problem for me. I can run for miles, if I have to. Or should I say, *when* I have to."

"You sound a little discouraged. Are you worried you're not going to learn how to defend yourself before you get in another scrap with these bullies?"

"I was, pretty much for the whole class. But then thankfully, Ned must have been tracking the same wavelength, because right after he asked to speak to the sensei privately."

"Really, about that? About you not having to wait so long to learn what to do?"

"Yep. The very thing. I wasn't there when they were talking, but Ned filled me in on the drive home. He pretty much explained my situation to the guy and told him I couldn't wait until he got around to teaching us how to fight a few weeks from now."

"So, what did the guy say, this sensei? Is he going to help?"

"Yup. He said if we would stay after tomorrow night's class, he would teach me exactly what I needed to do to keep these guys from hurting me if they come after me again. Which they will. All I have to do is steer clear of them until then. Then hopefully, I'll be able to do what he teaches me and be ready when the showdown finally comes."

His mom got tears in her eyes. She reached over and patted his wrist with one hand, wiped her eyes with the other.

"What's the matter, Mom? This is actually good news."

"I'm just so sorry my little boy is having to deal with this. It's just so awful that there are kids like these two guys making your life so difficult now. It isn't right. I keep praying and praying this will all be over soon."

"Well Mom, maybe your prayers are being answered. Just in a different way. Instead of the problem just disappearing like that, God's going to help me make it go away, by teaching me how to beat them. I wish I didn't have to. And if I think about it too much, I start feeling sick inside. But I gotta say, if I can really learn how to stop these guys, so they stop treating me or anyone else this way, I'm gonna feel a whole lot better when I wake up each day. I'm so tired of being afraid."

"I know, Honey. Come here." She held her arms open.

Russell got out of his chair, walked over and disappeared into a big hug.

41

Ned had awakened about twenty minutes ago to the sound of Parker whimpering in his crate. It wasn't loud, but Ned wasn't used to any sounds in the morning, except his cell phone alarm. He hadn't set it last night because his shift didn't start until midmorning.

Parker had responded to Ned very well, just like last night when he'd let him out of the crate in the living room. Even though he clearly had to go to the bathroom, he sat when asked and gave Ned his collar. Ned walked carefully down the stairs with Parker and across the street. Parker had squatted the moment he reached the grass.

But hey, Ned thought, it could have been a much tougher night. Parker had at least slept through and again, he didn't mess up his crate.

Ned had continued walking Parker in the grass until he was sure the little guy was done. As he waited, he'd met a middle-aged woman walking her dog for the same reason. Fortunately, after sniffing each other thoroughly, the dogs lost interest in each other. Ned could see the woman kept staring at Parker's appearance with a concerned look.

Not wanting her to think he was responsible, he'd said, "I picked him up from the shelter yesterday. Came from an abused home. He's actually looking a lot better than he did a week ago."

His explanation had done the trick. The woman's face instantly changed to sympathy and compassion toward Parker. Before she left, she'd said, "That's a wonderful thing you're doing."

Now they were back in Ned's apartment. Ned was sitting in his recliner eating a previously frozen breakfast sandwich, reading a couple of Psalms in the Bible. Parker was sitting at his feet, clearly interested. But he had this cute little thing he did, trying not to appear obvious. In his peripheral vision, Ned could see him staring at his sandwich but when he looked at Parker he turned his head sideways, feigning disinterest.

When he got to the last bite, he set his Bible aside and leaned forward. Holding up the piece of food in front of Parker secured his undivided attention. "You want this?" Parker's tail started to wag. "Do you?" He was already sitting. Ned couldn't think of any trick he wanted to work on with the dog. Then he had an idea.

"I wonder if you'll let me pick you up." He pulled the piece of sandwich back to his lap. "You want this, Parker? Do you, Boy?"

Parker stood, his eyes laser-focused on the food.

"Here you go. Up, Parker. Up." Ned patted his lap with the other hand. Parker just looked at him, confused. Ned repeated the same words and made the same motions, only this time he lowered the food to within a few inches of Parker's nose then said "up" two or three times as he raised the food to his lap.

Parker got the idea. He jumped onto Ned's lap and was instantly rewarded with the piece of sandwich. Parker munched it down quickly and licked his lips. Then he looked Ned over, as if hoping to find more.

"That's all I have, Boy. But you are such a good boy." Ned quickly but gently patted him on the head, then scratched behind his ears and rubbed his back." Such a good boy. You want to stay up here with me?" Ned really hoped Parker would be that kind of dog, one who liked to sit close. He patted the side of his right leg and said, "Sit Parker. Sit, Boy."

Parker looked at his hands, then at his face. Ned repeated it again. This time Parker obeyed. He sat down on Ned's lap. Ned scratched his back a little and Parker lay down. Ned rested his arm on Parker's back and continued to scratch behind his ears. He took a sip of his coffee, reached for the remote and turned on the news.

He was rather enjoying this, having a dog sitting there on his lap. Soon, Parker got even more comfortable and laid his head down. They sat there watching TV together for the next hour or so. At some point, Parker fell asleep.

WHEN IT WAS time for Ned to get up and start getting ready for work, he was pleased to discover not only did Parker enjoy sitting with him, apparently he preferred following Ned around the apartment to whatever other little doggy things he could be doing. Wherever Ned went, Parker was right there. After a shower, he opened the bathroom door to let some of the steam out, and there was Parker lying right near the doorway in the hall.

Of course, Ned talked to him the whole time. After a while, you kind of forget that, in reality, dogs only understand a fraction of what you're saying. The look on their face as you speak and the level of interest in their eyes creates the impression that they're incredibly good listeners. The kind of friend who genuinely cares about whatever you're going through.

Ned realized... that's why he was telling Parker all these things.

After Ned finished his getting-ready routine, he took a look at the clock on the stove. "Better give you your medicine, little buddy, before I forget." Kim had said to try offering the pills wrapped in either butter or peanut butter, whichever one Parker seemed to enjoy more. For Parker, it was butter. Then Ned sat on the couch and lifted Parker onto the coffee table. It was time to apply ointment to his sores. Thankfully, they were all looking much better now, so it wasn't nearly as disgusting a task as it could have been. Parker didn't seem to mind, so the medicine must not have bothered his skin. Kim said it tasted bad enough that dogs usually didn't try to lick it off, either.

"Well, that's it, Boy. You're all set. Let's take you out before I put you up for the day." Parker seemed to be learning the word "out," because he instantly ran to the spot in the hall where his leash hung on a hook.

Once they reached the grassy area, it took a little longer for Parker to go than earlier, but he finally did. Ned was about to turn and head back toward the apartment when a thought, or maybe more like a feeling, came over him. He hated the idea of sticking Parker back in his crate for the next nine to ten hours. They were getting along so well, and Parker was responding to him ten times better than Ned had expected by this point.

How would Parker interpret being stuck in that crate for so long without any interaction from anyone? They hadn't had enough time together for Parker to establish any routines. Considering what his life had been like for so long, wouldn't he simply feel abandoned by Ned? And confused? Here he was experiencing all this friendship and companionship, for the first time in forever, and then he's shut up in this little box all day.

Ned reached for his cell phone and called Kim. He never did call her last night. Just chickened out. Hopefully, he wouldn't get her voicemail.

"Hey Ned, glad you called. I was wondering how things were going with you and Parker?"

How about that? She was glad he called. "They've been going great. I mean, really. Way better than I would've expected by now."

"Really? Tell me about it."

So Ned did for the next five minutes.

"Wow, that's really cool. And you're right, that's way more interaction than I would've expected at this point. I'm really glad to hear it."

"Here's the thing, Kim. And the real reason I called." He explained all his misgivings and concerns about heading off to work and leaving Parker stuck in his crate all day.

"Isn't there a chance that you could check in on him during your lunch break? Didn't you say something about that?"

"There's definitely a chance. But there's also a chance I might get a call on the other side of town and not have enough time to check in on him before my break's over."

"I can see that. And I guess things aren't far enough along for the little boy to check in on him. What's his name, Russell?"

"Yeah, Russell. And yes, it's too soon. I just gave him the fox last night. Hopefully, things will work out with him in a few days, but we're not there yet. Maybe I should just take another personal business day. Or maybe just a half-day. What do you think?"

"I think you can probably just take the chance that either you'll get a chance to see him on your break, or he'll just have to wait till you get home. I mean, if you think about it, Ned, he's probably already received more love and attention in the last twenty-four hours than he's known in years. He's not used to companionship. He's used to being totally ignored and neglected by everyone for days at a time. I don't think we'll see any big setbacks from you just going off to work on a regular shift. The crate you bought him is plenty big. Lots of room for him to move around. Besides, it'll only be for a few days, right? Then Russell can get involved."

"You really think so?"

"I do. He'll probably just sleep all afternoon if you're not able to get back. It's amazing the amount of sleep a dog can pack in when they're bored. Even if they've slept all night. You know that saying, *I worked like a dog*? When do dogs ever work? Most of them anyway. The saying should be, *I slept like a dog*. That's what they do most of the day."

Ned laughed. This call to Kim really helped. "All right, I'll take your advice. Any chance we can go out again soon?"

"I'd say there's a very good chance."

Ned smiled. "Great. When I get into work, I'll check my schedule and figure out a good time. So...call you later?"

"Yep, sounds good."

42

Russell came through the lunch line at the cafeteria and paused for a moment, looking for Pete. They usually sat together when they ate now and usually at the same table, which they usually had to themselves. Pete wasn't there, though, so Russell walked in that direction.

Pete came in from the front door carrying a flat Tupperware container. He found Russell with his eyes, waved then pointed to the far corner of the cafeteria and held up his container. Russell understood. The microwave.

He set his tray down and took a seat, eyeing the cafeteria for any signs of trouble. So far, he'd been able to avoid it. Well...*them*. He started eating today's offering: a chicken filet sandwich, sweet potato nuggets, a small cup of baked beans and diced pears. Not too bad. After a few bites, Pete joined him.

"Mom made homemade pizza last night," Pete said. "It was so good. I like it even better the next day."

"It does look good," Russell said. "I don't think I've ever had homemade pizza. Kind of like Sicilian style, right? Extra thick?"

"I guess so," Pete said. "Never had that before."

Both boys ate in silence for a few moments. It was totally understood and agreed that you could talk with your mouth full, as long as it wasn't too full, which they both agreed was disgusting.

"So how did it go last night? Learn any good moves?"

"Not really. Well, not at all. Last night was kind of like orientation night."

"Vision and values stuff?" Pete said.

"Pretty much. That and a bunch of exercising."

"That doesn't sound like any fun."

"It wasn't. But they did say we're going to start learning fight moves soon." Russell thought about Pete doing the exercise part. He wouldn't have fared too well. "I was half expecting you to be there. Didn't you say you were interested in this?"

"I was. Still am. I've got transportation problems. But hey, maybe you can teach me some moves once you get them down. I can be your practice partner."

"We can do that." Russell took a spoonful of baked beans. "Might get a chance to do that sooner than later."

"How's that?"

Russell explained about his disappointment in not learning the moves he'd need to protect himself for several weeks, and about how Ned had gone to bat for him with the sensei. "Looks like he's going to teach me what I need to know, one-on-one, tomorrow night after class. Me and Ned together. Which brings up a favor I need to ask you."

"The answer is yes, whatever it is. Unless it's money. I'm all out until my next allowance."

"You get an allowance?"

"Yeah, but it's not much. Ten bucks a week."

"Ten bucks a week? I'd rob a bank for ten bucks a week."

"Anyway, what's the favor?"

"Me and Ned figured I need some place to hide out the next few days after school. At least today and tomorrow. You know, from Edmund and Harley. I told him I thought I could hang out at your place."

Pete wrestled with a bite of chewy pizza crust. "Sure, man. No problem. I'd like to do that anyway."

"Great," Russell said. "I was hoping you'd say that."

"So, what else is new? You started earning your keep yet? You know, watching the cop's dog?"

"Not yet, but that should start soon. That is, if the dog doesn't wind up hating me. Supposedly, abused dogs can be kind of iffy about who they'll accept. He's already accepted Ned, but they're not totally sure how he'll do with me."

"Who is *they*? Ned and who else?"

"A lady from the dog shelter named Kim. She's kind of an expert on dog matters. You'll never guess what they asked me to do to improve my chances with the dog?"

"What?"

"Before I tell you, you gotta promise you won't tell anyone."

"Wow, really? Okay, I promise."

"They want me to sleep with this furry toy for a couple of nights. A fox."

"Okay...how's that supposed to help?"

"The idea is, my scent gets on the dog toy and they give it to him for a few days. He gets used to my scent, so that when I meet him he's already used to me."

"Well, I can see that working."

"But seriously, you can't tell anyone about it."

"Can't tell anyone about *what*?" a familiar voice said from behind.

Russell instantly tensed up. It was Edmund. He turned and saw Harley right behind him. Where did they come from?

"He wasn't talking to you," Pete said.

"Shut up, fat boy. I wasn't talking to you. So Russell, what secrets are you telling Chubby here that you don't want anyone to know?" They came around to the head of the table and could now look straight down at them.

Oh, how Russell wished he'd already learned those moves. But he needed to keep cool; these guys wouldn't try anything with so many teachers in plain view. "Well, if I told you it wouldn't be a secret anymore, would it? That's kinda how secrets work."

"So, we got a funny man here, Harley. You know Twerp, this thing between us ain't over yet. You've got some payback coming."

"I think you two boys should leave my friend Russell here alone?"

"You do, huh? Well, I think you should just butt out and mind your own business, unless you want to get some of what we plan to dish out on your little friend."

"You think the two of you can take the two of us?" Harley said.

"I don't know," Pete said. "But that's not really the right question to ask at this point, Harley. Do you agree, Russell?"

Russell couldn't believe Pete's confidence in this situation.

Must be sweet to have enjoyed that big-brother-bully card your whole life. Problem was, he had no idea what Pete was referring to, so he just played along, feigning the same confidence. "I agree, Pete. Not the right question."

Edmund's face became instantly angry and red, like he wanted to hit either one or both of them right now. "I think you just bought into this trouble, fat boy. Whether you intended to or not."

"See, I don't think I have Edmund. I'm guessing you don't really know who I am. Or maybe, who I'm related to."

"I haven't, eh? Well, unless it's Batman or Spider-Man, I don't think it's gonna do you any good."

"No, I'm not talking about a fake superhero. I'm talking about a real big brother. Maybe you've heard of him. His name's Rob. Rob Sanford? First string running back on our football team? And I'm Pete, his kid brother."

A look of fear instantly came over Edmund and Harley's face.

"And you know something Rob told me the first day I came here to this middle school? He said, Pete, don't worry about a thing. Anybody messes with you, they'll have to answer to me." Pete stood up just then and looked around. "There he is. Over there. Eating with some of his football friends. Turn around and look. Hey Rob," Pete yelled.

Everyone turned in the direction Pete was referring to. Russell saw Rob; he'd just stopped talking and turned toward his brother's voice. Pete waved.

"You need something, Pete?" Rob yelled.

Pete looked at Edmund and Harley, who had already started to leave.

"I don't think so. Just talking about you with my friend here." He sat back in his seat.

Two tables away, Edmund turned back and glared at Russell. "He might be in the clear," he said. "But for you? This thing isn't over."

43

Ned pulled into his regular parking space at the apartment complex. Things had worked out in his shift so far today. He found himself on the right side of town when it came time for his lunch break, so he was able to stop in and check on Parker.

Before shutting off the car, he glanced at the dashboard clock. Just a few minutes after 2PM. He got out and headed up the stairs toward his place. Pressing his ear against the front door, he listened but didn't hear any sounds coming from the dog and hoped he had been this quiet the whole time Ned had been gone.

Of course, if Parker had barked his head off Ned would certainly hear about it from the apartment manager. But so far, he didn't seem like a yippy kind of a dog. As soon as he unlocked and opened the front door, though, Parker instantly reacted. He could see his crate straight down the hallway in the living room and hear his tail thumping on the crate floor. Sounded like he was prancing, too.

Ned grabbed his leash from the hook, walked straight to him and squatted down. "Hey Boy, how are you doing? You been a good boy?" Parker was visibly excited, even more so now that he could see Ned. Ned wondered if it was happiness or if the poor thing just really had to go the bathroom badly. He couldn't imagine living under such restraints. Imagine being locked up in a room and having to go to the bathroom for hours but being forced to hold it.

Without being instructed, Parker presented his collar to Ned almost as soon as the crate door opened. "Look at you, so smart." Ned latched the leash and led him out of the crate. "Let's get you out of here and across the street."

But before he started walking down the hall, Parker did something that made Ned smile. He stopped and looked up at him and wagged his tail. "What is it, Boy? What do you want?" He raised his paw and scratched the inside of Ned's pant leg. Ned reached down, patted his head and scratched behind his ears. "What a good boy you are. Are you glad I came home?"

Ned wasn't sure, but it seemed like that's all he wanted, to connect with Ned. Because right after that, he got up and started walking toward the front door.

HE CAME BACK. Parker was so relieved. Ned had left him in the crate again. But again, he came back. This time the wait seemed even shorter than the last. And now he was about to go outside. He didn't even have to go that badly yet. He had expected to have to wait several more hours.

But he was thirsty. Ned stood by the front door, about to open it. Parker looked to the left at his water bowl just inside the kitchen. He really wanted a drink. He moved toward it hoping Ned would get the message and not yank him back into the hall.

"What's the matter, Parker? You want something in here?"

Good, Ned was following. He reached his water bowl and started lapping it up.

"Okay, guess you're thirsty. I get it. Take your time. We can wait."

That tasted so good. When he was done, Parker headed back to the front door. Now he did have to go. Something about drinking water always sped up the urge. Thankfully, Ned was right behind him and opened the door before Parker even reached it.

He carefully navigated down the steps, took a quick whiff of the air. Didn't smell any competition nearby, which meant he could relax. They walked to the street, paused briefly then crossed. He was beginning to recognize this grassy area. Of course, it was filled with a thousand smells. Sniffing around, he found an area to call his own and squatted. After walking around a few minutes more, he could tell that's all he needed to do down here.

He started to walk back in the direction they came, but it seemed Ned had other plans. He led them toward a nearby bench and sat down. Parker was fine with that. He liked being outside with Ned, so he just took a seat beside him. Ned took out a little black object and started talking into it. Parker figured that meant they might be here for a while. At least long enough for him to lie down.

NED LOOKED TO HIS RIGHT. This was so cool. Parker was lying

down beside him. As he listened to Kim's phone ring, he reached down and scratched his back.

"Hey Ned. This is good timing," Kim said. "I'm actually sitting here at my desk returning phone calls. But I'd much rather be talking to you."

"I'm actually sitting on a bench in that grassy area across the street from my apartment. Parker has just done his business, and now he's lying down right beside me while I'm talking to you, as if he's been my dog for years. This is really working out well."

"I'm so glad to hear it."

"And once again, he didn't mess up in his crate. Of course, it's only been about four hours, but still."

"No, that's a good thing. Hope things keep going smoothly from here on out. How's he doing with his meds?"

"No problem there, either. I'll be glad when that part of things is over, especially applying the gooey skin stuff."

Kim laughed. "Yeah, that's no fun. But it'll be over before you know it. And soon his hair will start growing back. In a couple of months, he'll look as good as that picture you showed me."

Ned looked down at him. Parker noticed and looked up at him, gave him something of a dog smile. "Yeah, he's still a little hard to look at, if you stop and think about it. So I try not to do that."

"Try not to do what?"

"Try not to think about how he looks. I'm focused on the dog inside this not-too-handsome exterior. And *that* dog looks just fine."

"So, I'm glad you were able to make it home halfway through your shift."

"Yep. Not sure where I'll be for the second half, but that doesn't matter, because after I can come back here and let him out again. That's really why I called, to talk about after work. Still interested in going out?"

"Sure, what do you have in mind?"

"Well, you do remember I don't get off till about seven, so I was thinking we wouldn't include dinner, so you don't have to wait so long."

"I don't mind waiting. I mean, if that's the only reason you're not wanting to do it. I don't have a fixed dinner hour. Sometimes I eat right when I get off work, other times it can be an hour or two later."

"Okay then, if you're sure, why don't we go to one of your favorite places this time?"

"Hmmm, I've got about three or four places I like."

"Okay, you've got some time to think it over. You can tell me when I come by to pick you up."

"Okay, that'll work."

"Great," he said. "See you shortly after seven then."

"Okay, bye. Stay safe."

"I will."

Ned stood. Parker instantly did, too. "Okay boy, guess we'll head back upstairs. Get you situated for round two." As he headed upstairs, he couldn't stop smiling. It definitely had something to do with how well things were going with Parker, but even more this budding romance with Kim. He hadn't felt this way about a girl in a very long time.

Upstairs, he spent as much time with Parker as he could before putting him back in his crate and taking off. He decided he'd grab a burger at a drive-through nearby to save a few minutes.

He just made it through the drive-through line and fixed up his burger, when a call came over the radio. He recognized the voice. It was Angela, one of the dispatchers. He could hear the tension in her voice as soon as she began to speak and, after hearing what she said, he understood why.

There was a bank robbery in progress. The silent alarm had gone off. It was happening right now at a Wells Fargo Bank less than five blocks from where Ned sat. He set the burger down on the seat, wiped his mouth with a napkin, then responded to the call.

"Angela, this is 315, responding. Be there in five."

"Copy that, 315. Be advised, 315, just received 911 call. Someone leaving parking lot said suspect is armed, Hispanic male dressed in camo fatigues, observed heading into the bank."

"Copy that."

"All available units," Angela continued, "please respond to 410 Hampton Road, Wells Fargo bank. Robbery in progress. Suspect is armed. Repeat, suspect is armed."

44

Ned raced his patrol car toward the scene, lights and sirens on. Other officers chimed in, informing dispatch that they had heard the alert and were on their way. He guessed that he'd be the first to reach the bank and could be there by himself for at least a few minutes.

His cell phone rang. It was fellow officer, Jeb Hodgins. He hit the speakerphone button. "Hey Jeb, heard you on the radio."

"On my way, partner. Maybe a mile behind you. Wait for backup, if you can. Don't be a hero."

"I'll wait. See you in a few."

He turned another corner and moved on to Hampton Road, the street where the bank was located. According to his GPS, it was two blocks ahead on the right. He said a quick prayer, asking God for wisdom and protection.

Just one more intersection to get through. He must've been going eighty but slowed to half of that when the light turned red. Didn't want to be T-boned or T-bone anyone else. Fortunately, the cars approaching the intersection all stopped, leaving him just enough space to wiggle through. He gunned it again and moments later reached the bank parking lot.

It was a freestanding building surrounded by stores on both sides. He glanced at the front door. No people in sight but a black mid-sized SUV had parked sideways, taking up at least three spaces. Must be the suspect's getaway car.

Ned sized up the likely route the robber would take leaving the parking lot and parked sideways just in front, blocking his path. He radioed in and described the scene then heard the dispatcher relay that information to everyone else.

"Be advised, ETA three minutes." It was Jeb.

Ned opened the door and got out but remained behind it. He was just about to reach for his shotgun when he heard a commotion at the front door.

He quickly looked around at the stores on either side. No one on the left side but a young couple stood huddled behind a stone pillar, staring at the bank. The man was holding his cell phone up, catching everything on video. "I think he's coming out," the man yelled.

"You people need to get back," Ned shouted. "That way." He pointed in the opposite direction.

The young man moved the camera toward Ned, got him in his little production, but stayed put. Ned was just about to yell again when he heard a banging sound in front. The bank door flew open and a young Hispanic-looking man came out wearing a hoodie over a baseball cap. A revolver in one hand, a duffel bag in the other.

He started running toward his car.

"Freeze," Ned shouted. "Drop the gun and get on the ground!"

The man stopped, glanced in Ned's general direction, saw Ned crouched behind the patrol car door. His eyes focused on Ned's gun pointing right at him.

"I said, drop the gun and get on the ground. It's over. You've got no way out of this parking lot. Three or four more patrol cars will be here any second." As if on cue, suddenly police sirens could be heard behind them.

"I ain't dropping this gun, and I ain't dropping the money. But I'll tell you what I will do, if you don't get in that car and back out of my way. I'm going to run back into the bank and start shooting people. How'd you like that?"

"I can't let you do that," Ned said.

"How you gonna stop me?"

"You're kidding, right? I've got this gun aimed right at you. You take one step toward that front door, I'll drop you where you stand. Now, do what I said. Drop the gun and the bag and get on the ground."

The young man looked at Ned then glanced over his shoulder at the bank's front door, as if sizing up his chances. "You a gambling man, Mr. Pig? As you can see, I broke the door. It's standing there wide open. I can be back in there before you can blink. You want to gamble with those people's lives. I ain't shot no one yet, but I promise you, I go back in there, people die. You want that on your head?"

"That's not how this is going down, son. I'm telling you, for the last time...you do anything but drop that gun, I will shoot you. And I won't miss."

"You just call me *son*? You ain't five years older'n me."

"Drop the gun." That was pretty stupid, calling him son.

Suddenly, screeching tires came from behind and a wailing siren turned off. A patrol car skidded to a stop fifty yards to

Ned's left. He glanced over and saw Jeb getting out, holding a shotgun. Then back at the suspect, who was looking at the same thing.

"It's over, man. Drop the gun. Don't be stupid."

A strange look came over the robber's face. Then he noticed the young couple standing behind the stone pillar. The guy must've moved to get a better camera angle. He lifted his gun in their direction. "Put your gun down, or the camera man dies. And I won't miss, neither. I been practicing."

Ned realized he had only seconds to act. He stepped out from behind his car door, held his gun out to the side, away from the robber. "Don't shoot them, shoot me," he yelled at the same time.

"Ned, no," Jeb yelled.

The robber turned his gun on Ned and fired.

Ned returned fire a half-second later. Felt a thud on his chest, like someone hit him with a hammer and fell back to the ground.

The robber dropped straight down where he stood.

Jeb fired a shotgun blast at the suspect but hit the wall behind where he'd just been standing.

The young couple screamed.

"He shot the cop, he shot the cop," the young man said.

"Ned, are you okay?"

Ned heard Jeb's voice, sounded far away.

"Shot's fired, shot's fired. Suspect down, officer down."

"The cop's down. He's been shot."

Ned lay there, trying to breathe. He could, but it hurt. Was he shot? He looked at his hands. No blood. He rubbed his chest, felt a hard piece of metal stuck near the center of his ribs."

Now Jeb was standing over him. "You okay? You get hit?"

"I'm alright. Vest took the hit."

"Well, stay down man. I'm gonna check the perp. He ain't moving, but I wanna make sure. Help's on the way."

"Go ahead. I'm okay." Ned sat up, leaned against the front tire. Felt like someone had punched him, hard. He instantly realized how much worse this could have been. "Thank you, God," he whispered.

"Man, you saved my life."

Ned looked up into the face of the young man who'd been filming the whole thing with his phone. He still was.

His lady friend stood next to him. "I thought we were dead," she said. "Are you okay?"

"Would you mind turning that thing off?"

"Turn it off? Man, this thing's guaranteed to go viral. You're a hero, Sir. Don't you know what you just did?"

He'd probably just killed someone. "But it's over now. If you've got any gratitude for what I did, show me by turning off the video?" He winced. "Hurts to talk."

"Sure, I got what I need anyway." He put the phone down.

Ned tried to stand.

"Here, let me help you."

As soon as he stood, the girl wrapped her arms around Ned and started to cry.

"It's okay," Ned said. "You're fine."

"Dang," the young man said. "That would have been a great ending for this."

More patrol cars pulled up, lights flashing. Ned heard the sound of fire department vehicles coming.

Jeb came over. "He's gone. I told everyone inside the bank

to stay put a few minutes. You doing okay? Like getting hit with a bat people say? That how it felt?"

"Close."

"You took him out with one shot," Jeb said, "while he was firing at you."

"I saw it," the young man said. "It was amazing. Got it all on here." He held up his phone.

"I'm going to need you to step back out of the way," Jeb said. "This is now a crime scene."

"Where you want us to go?"

"Stay close. We need to get a statement."

"How about we go back over there, where we were? You come get us when you're ready."

"Fine," Jeb said. "Just don't leave the area." He looked at Ned. "Glad to know these vests really work."

"Yeah, me too," Ned said. He looked behind them, saw the cavalry coming, all headed this way.

45

Thirty minutes later, Ned was sitting on the edge of a hospital bed in the emergency room. It was really a precautionary decision. Ned didn't think he had any serious injuries, but the captain insisted he come and get checked out. Jeb had driven him. Someone else was supposed to drive his car home.

Of course, another consequence of this was that Ned had to be relieved from active duty, with pay, pending an investigation. It happened whenever there was an officer-involved shooting. Jeb had witnessed the actual shooting and told everyone at the scene what happened. The captain made it clear, Ned would be absolved of any responsibility in the matter. "It was a good kill," he'd said.

A good kill.

Ned couldn't believe it. It still hadn't sunk in. He had killed a guy. He had no choice, obviously. But still. He didn't feel any guilt at the moment. He wondered if that would come later.

"How are you doing?"

Ned looked over at Jeb, sitting in a straight-backed chair a few feet away. "Pretty much the same. I've been punched in the gut before. Feels kind of like that. I'm sure the x-ray will come back clean. Doesn't hurt to breathe at all."

Jeb pointed to his head. "No, I mean how are you doing in here? With what happened? You okay?"

"I feel like I am, I hate that I had to do it. Can't believe that kid was so stupid. Why didn't he just cooperate?"

"Who knows? Obviously, this kid wasn't too bright. I guess he imagined he could just trot out of the bank, get in his car and drive off, a big bag of cash sitting in the passenger seat. But I heard how you handled it, Ned. You gave him every chance. There was nothing you could do, especially when he pointed the gun at that couple. Man, that was a pretty gutsy thing to do. Making yourself a target like that."

"It just popped into my head. I had to distract him. Thought I could take him out if he turned on me."

"And he did. And you did."

"Yeah, but I didn't think I'd get shot."

"Well," Jeb said, "the kid did say he'd been practicing. Pretty much got you center mass."

"Good thing he wasn't practicing head shots," Ned said.

Just then the nurse walked in carrying a chart. "Well it's good news. Just like you said. Nothing broken. The doctor said you're going to be pretty sore in that area for a few days. Here's a prescription for some pain meds. Take them if you need to." She held out a slip of paper.

"Thanks. How much longer do I have to stay here?"

"Not too much longer. Someone else will be in a few minutes from now. They'll get you checked out." She started to walk away but stopped. "Oh, thought you might want a little heads up. There are some reporters out in the waiting room hoping to talk with you. Apparently, someone uploaded a video of what happened at the bank. They got word that you were sent here, and they'd like to interview you."

"Rats, I don't want to talk to any reporters. Not now."

Jeb stood. "Is there any way we can sneak out of here without seeing those guys?"

The nurse thought a moment. "Yeah, I can help you out with that. Come see me once you get checked out, and I'll show you where to go."

"Thanks," Ned said. Then the other thing she said struck him. *Someone uploaded a video.* It was that guy at the bank standing behind the pillar. Ned should have figured this would happen.

"Wow," Jeb said. "I'd like to see that video."

Ned felt a knot growing in his stomach. He didn't want this. Then he thought about trying again to call Kim somehow. He wanted to on the way here but discovered when he'd fallen after being shot, he'd crushed his cell phone.

KIM HAD JUST COME into her office and sat at her desk. For the last two hours, she had been working through a challenging private dog lesson. As was so often the case, the challenging part wasn't the dog but working with a stubborn owner. Some people think way too highly of their uninformed opinions. With almost every suggestion she made, the owner said she either already knew that, or else she had reasons why that just wouldn't work with her dog.

Of course, Kim was able to then show her the dog could do everything she was saying, but that still didn't get the woman to back off and start paying attention. She usually left such training sessions mostly feeling sorry for the poor dog she had to leave behind.

Her office door opened and Amy walked in with one of the kennel workers. Both wore serious expressions on their faces and were looking straight at her. "Hey ladies, what's up?"

Amy walked in and sat in Kim's office chair. The kennel worker, Linda, followed and stood beside her. Kim noticed her holding her cell phone. Phones were off-limits during working hours, except on lunch hours or breaks.

"I guess you haven't heard," Amy said.

"Heard what?"

She looked up at Linda. "I was in the lobby and Linda came rushing in from outside."

"I was on break, having a smoke."

"She was holding that up," Amy said, pointing to her phone, "and her eyes were bugging out."

"Why?" Kim asked.

"She showed me what she was looking at." Amy rested her hand on Kim's wrist, as if to comfort her.

"Why Amy? What's going on?"

Amy took a deep breath. Something very serious has happened, Kim."

"Something that involves me?"

Amy nodded.

"What? How?"

"It's about Ned. There was a robbery at the Wells Fargo Bank. I guess it was just over an hour ago."

Kim's heart sank. A wave of dread washed over her.

"You know, the one over by where the old Kmart used to be," Linda said.

Kim looked at Amy. "And what happened? Something happened to Ned?"

Amy made a face Kim could not interpret. "We don't really have any facts yet. This video doesn't include any information other than what you can see."

"What video?" Kim said.

Linda held up her phone. "Like I said, I was out having a smoke, thought I would go on Facebook. Got this notice about this bank robbery that just happened, so I clicked on it. It was the local news website. They had just sent a reporter there, and the report was pretty basic at this point. But she did say, the Wells Fargo was robbed at gunpoint. None of the people inside were hurt. But apparently, a silent alarm was triggered and the cops were called. There was a confrontation outside and shots were fired."

"Oh, no," Kim said.

"The suspect was killed," Linda said. "Apparently by the cop, but the cop was also shot. They didn't know yet about his condition but said he was sent to the local hospital. The article mentioned a video that was taken that captured the whole thing, by a guy nearby."

"But you guys said this involved Ned. Did they mention his name in the story?"

Linda shook her head no.

"But I looked at the video," Amy said. Tears welled up in her eyes. "It was Ned. You could see him plain as day. He was the one that confronted the robber as he came out of the bank. You could hear them yelling back and forth to each other. Ned's mostly telling him to put the gun down. The guys yelling something about why he won't. Then he actually points the gun, the robber I mean, at the guy holding the camera. Ned yells something to the robber. And then..."

Amy got choked up. "Ned does this crazy brave thing. The robber points the gun at Ned, and the camera swings back to him. Ned is standing there. He came out from behind the car door, making himself a target, trying to draw the robber's attention back on him. Then the camera gets a little shaky when two shots ring out. You see Ned fall backwards, out of sight behind the patrol car. The camera swings back to the robber. He's lying on the sidewalk by the front door of the bank, not moving."

Kim starts crying. "And then what? What happens next?"

"We don't know," Linda said. "That's where the video cuts off."

Amy reaches for a box of tissues. Takes one and hands one to Kim. "He might be fine, Kim. They said they don't have any word on his condition. They didn't say he was killed."

"No, they didn't," Kim said. "But we know he was shot. You saw him go down."

"Do you want to watch the video?" Linda said.

Kim reached for another tissue. "I don't think I can."

46

"Thanks Linda," Amy said. "You can go back to what you were doing in the kennel."

"So sorry, Kim," Linda said. "Didn't mean to upset you. I had no idea you knew the guy."

Kim dabbed her eyes with another tissue. "It's okay, Linda. I'm glad you showed it to Amy." Did she really believe that? "But seriously, I'll be okay. You should get back to work. We don't want to get you in trouble with your boss."

"Okay then, see you later." Linda headed down the hallway.

Amy got up and closed the office door. Kim burst into a fresh flow of tears. "Oh Amy, what if he's dead? Or mortally wounded?"

"The report said they took Ned to the hospital."

"That just means he wasn't dead then, at that moment. You know how many cops have been shot the last couple of years? Stories like these are happening all the time. And how many times do you hear about the officer being taken to the hospital, only to be told a day later they passed away?"

Amy came over and put her arm around Kim. "Why don't you try calling his phone? You know if he can, he'll pick right up when he sees your name."

"That's what I'll do." Still holding the tissue, she pulled her cell phone out of her purse, swiped it on, hit the phone icon and Ned's name. "Please pick up." It rang several times, then finally..." No, it's going to voicemail." She hung up and set the phone down and cried some more.

"It might not mean anything," Amy said.

"But you said it yourself, he would pick up if he could. Obviously, he can't."

"I know, I know. But maybe he's been taken down for a test, or maybe he's even in surgery."

"Maybe," Kim said. "I wish I knew for sure. Maybe I should go down there. See for myself." She thought about it a moment. "But why would they let me see him, or tell me anything? I'm not family, we've just started seeing each other. I don't even know if any of his police friends know who I am."

"That gives me an idea," Amy said. "Chris has some police friends. I could call him, see if he could check with them. They'd tell him what's going on."

"Would you do that? I've got to know what happened to him."

"I will," Amy said. "Why don't you go down to the restroom and get freshened up. If the news is good, we can drive to the hospital together."

If the news is good, Kim thought. *Please God, let the news be good.*

As soon as Kim was far enough down the hall, Amy called her

husband, Chris. He would still be at work at the golf course, but she was sure he would pick up if he could.

It only rang three times, "Hey Babe, what's up? How are you doing?"

"Not great at the moment."

"Why, what's wrong?"

She heard the big ride-on lawnmower in the background. "You might have to turn that thing off for a few minutes. I need to ask you a favor."

The mower sound stopped. "Okay, what's wrong? What's going on?"

"It's Kim. Well, not really her. You know the police officer she started dating the last few weeks? I told you about him, right?"

"Fred, or Ed?"

"His name's Ned."

"Right. Well, what about him?"

"We just found out he was involved in stopping an armed robbery at that Wells Fargo Bank near the old Kmart. It happened like, less than an hour ago. Anyway, there was a shooting. Some guy outside caught the whole thing on video and already uploaded it. One of the girls here saw it on her break and showed it to me. Chris, Ned was the cop who shot the robber. Killed him apparently. But he got shot, too."

"Oh, no."

"I saw the video myself. It was definitely Ned. He was trying to get the robber to put the gun down, but the guy pointed at the guy taking the video. Ned stepped out in the open to draw the robber's attention back on him. Then you hear two shots. Ned was definitely hit. You can see him flying backward behind a patrol car. But there's no information about his condition. They took him to the hospital, so we know he was alive, at least a little while ago."

"Did you try calling him? Maybe he's fine."

"We did. Well, Kim did. But he didn't pick up. And you know he would if he could, as soon as he saw it was her. It's obvious, the guy is crazy about her. Could you call some of your policemen friends, see if any of them know what happened? How Ned's doing?"

"I'll do it right now. Then I'll get back with you as soon as I know something."

"Thanks. Love you."

Ten minutes later, Kim was sitting on the edge of her seat. Amy's husband Chris had just called back. While she waited, Kim had called Ned's cell phone three more times. All three times, it went straight to voicemail.

Kim focused on Amy's face as she listened. It changed from seriously-concerned to something more hopeful. Now, she was smiling. Oh thank God, she was smiling.

"Thanks for calling back. You just made my day. I'll tell Kim. See you and Finley when I get home. Love you, bye."

"So, he's alive?" Kim said. "Ned's okay?"

"Looks that way. One of Chris's friends is a sergeant, who's actually been to the hospital. Apparently, the bullet struck Ned almost dead center in the abdomen, right below his rib cage."

"But he was wearing a vest, right?"

"Yep. And the vest stopped the bullet. He wasn't hurt at all. Well, they said it was no more than being punched in the gut. The force of it was enough to knock him down, but the sergeant said they sent him to the hospital more as a precaution. He's supposed to be getting released any minute."

"Maybe he'll call," Kim said. "I hope he does. Did he say anything about why Ned isn't answering his calls?"

"I asked him, but he said he didn't know anything about that. He did say, though, everyone's thinking Ned deserves some kind of medal for what he did. Why don't you try calling him again?"

"Okay, I will." She was so relieved. *Thank you, Lord*, she prayed quietly. As she reached for her cell, it began to ring.

"Who is it? Is it Ned?"

"I don't know. I don't recognize the number."

"Well, pick it up."

Kim did. "Hello?"

"Kim? Is that you?"

It was Ned. "Ned," she said, then burst into tears.

"Aww, Kim," Ned said. "Don't cry. I'm okay, really."

"I know you are, but still..." Kim reached for the tissue box. "We saw the video from the bank. Well, Amy did. She saw you go down after being shot, but we had no idea what happened to you."

"I'm sorry you had to find out that way. I can't believe that video is already online."

"The story's already on the local news website, with a link to the video."

"I'm sure that kid is thrilled," Ned said.

"What kid?"

"Never mind. Doesn't matter. I'm just really sorry you had to find out that way. I would've called you while I was on the way to the hospital, but unfortunately I destroyed my phone. Happened when I fell back after being shot. Crushed it."

"Well, that makes sense then. I tried calling you a bunch of times, always got voicemail. Of course, each time that happened we thought the worst."

"I'm sorry. Who's we?"

"Amy. She's the one who found out about the video. We just found out, like two minutes ago, from her husband Chris that you were okay."

"How did Chris know?"

Kim explained. "The important thing is, you're not dead, or seriously injured."

"I'm not really injured at all. They're telling me I'll probably feel bruised up right where the bullet hit for a few days. After that, I'll be good as new."

Good as new. Kim thought but didn't want to say, *you won't be good as new. You almost died today. If you weren't wearing that vest, or if the gunman had aimed for your head, you wouldn't be here on the phone with me.*

"Kim? Are you okay?"

"What? Yeah, I'm fine. Now that I know you are."

47

Kim talked with Ned a few more minutes, but he had to give the borrowed phone back to his friend. He mentioned that he'd been relieved of duty, not so much because of his injury; it's something they always did after an officer-involved shooting. She suggested he might want to take some time to get a replacement phone, since his other one was destroyed. He said he'd head over to the store and take care of that now. The last thing he said was to confirm that they were still on for tonight.

Of course, she said.

Now she sat at her desk, staring out the window, feeling mostly numb.

"Talk about emotional roller coasters," Amy said. "Are you okay?"

Kim turned and looked at her. "I guess I am. Thankfully, I'm not having to deal with the tragedy I thought we would be facing. But I gotta tell you, that felt pretty horrible back there when it looked like that's where this thing had gone."

"You mean if Ned had been killed?"

"Yeah, or seriously wounded. Instead, he's heading off to the phone store, like nothing ever happened."

"But that's a good thing, right?"

"Yeah, it's a real good thing. On one level anyway. The one that matters most."

Amy walked over and sat in Kim's office chair. "What are some other levels? I can tell something's bothering you."

Kim released a pent up sigh. "I don't know if I can talk about it yet."

"Well, I certainly don't want to push you here. But I know from all the help Chris has received in dealing with his PTSD, seems like it's always better to talk about things like this, rather than bottle them up inside. You don't have to talk with me. But somebody. You've said Ned's a good listener."

"I can't talk *to* Ned. What's bothering me is *about* Ned."

"Oh." Amy leaned back, thought a moment. "Let me guess. It's about him being a cop and how dangerous it is. If that's it, I totally get it."

"That's pretty close. But I think it's more about whether or not I'm cut out to deal with it. It's obvious to me, Ned is doing what he loves to do. And it's clear, he's very good at it. I haven't seen the video, but—"

"No, you're right," Amy said. "He's very good at it. What he did was amazing. And he did it without hesitation, which means he reacted instinctively. If that's not protect and serve, I don't know what is."

"See? Ned is doing what he was meant to do. And I really like him. The more we've been together, the more I'm thinking he could be the guy. You know, *the one*. And if he was an engineer or an accountant, or even a mechanic. Really, in almost any other line of work, I wouldn't be struggling with what I'm struggling with. Because he wouldn't have been there today confronting an armed robber." She looked up at Amy. "He almost died this afternoon. And he really could have died. And not just this afternoon. Any afternoon, morning or evening he heads out the door for work."

"That's...definitely true," Amy said.

"I don't even have the luxury anymore of believing that he's relatively safe, because we live in such a small town. That's kind of what I've been telling myself since we started seeing each other, when this fear first cropped up. But now that hope is gone. I know for a fact, at any given moment of the day, I could go through the horror of what we just went through, only I don't get the happy ending. I get a phone call that says he's gone."

"I'm sorry, Kim. I wish I had the words to make this all better. But I don't. I know when I first started falling for Chris, in a way, I was so glad that his military days were over. That I didn't have to deal with the day-to-day fear most military wives have to face. We've definitely had our struggles, some because of the PTSD, some because of the extra challenges he faces with his prosthetic leg. But to me, those are small things compared to dealing with whether or not I might lose him in combat in some faraway country."

She reached over and grabbed Kim's hand. Kim squeezed tightly. Amy may not have the magic words to make Kim's anxiety disappear, but it certainly felt good to be with someone who listened and tried to understand, versus someone who felt compelled to hammer her with a lecture. "Thanks for not making me feel guilty. Well, any more guilty than I already feel."

"Guilty? What would you have to feel guilty about? What-ever it is, I guess I'm guilty of it, too."

"I don't know, it just seems like such a selfish outlook to have. Guys like Ned, and women officers, too, are willing to be out there putting their lives on the line every day. And I'm thinking of ending a relationship with someone I really care about, because I don't want to have to deal with worrying about their safety all the time."

"That may be true, but I don't think it's anything you should have to feel guilty about. Some occupations are really more of a vocation. Something certain people feel almost compelled to do. Like they're born to it, hardwired for it. When you ask them about it, like how they confront their own fears every day, they'll say, what fears? People like that have a gift. I'm glad God gives it to them. Where would we be without policemen, or soldiers, or ER nurses and EMTs? I could never do their job, but I'm glad they're out there doing it every day."

"I guess so," Kim said.

Neither one said anything for a few moments.

"What are you thinking?" Amy asked.

"I'm wondering about all these women, the ones married to the policemen or to the soldiers. How do they keep their sanity? How do you turn off the fearful thoughts? Especially nowadays, for spouses of police officers. You're not just dealing with the kind of situation Ned faced this afternoon, but the very real possibility one of these cop-hating lunatics will just come up and shoot you for no reason at all."

"I don't know, Kim. But I just remembered, both of Chris's police friends are married. I don't know the women well, but I have met them. If you want, I could see if one of them would meet you for coffee. I'd give them a heads up, so they know what you're wanting to talk about. See if either of them is willing."

"I don't know, Amy. Seems like something you would do if you were thinking about marrying someone. I like Ned. Actually, I like him a lot. But this relationship is pretty new."

"That's true. It is fairly new. But you're not like some high school or college-age girl. You're past the girls-just-want-to-have-fun stage. Right? You agree to go out with a guy now, neither one of you might be using the M-word right away, but you're sizing him up for the job."

Kim laughed. "That's definitely true. And so far, by every measurement I've taken, he measures up pretty well. To be a husband and a cop. I'm just not sure I measure up to be a cop's wife."

48

About an hour later, Kim pulled into the parking lot at the city center. It was situated on the banks of a large pond, bordered by tall cypress trees. They had created a beautiful park at the midpoint, with lots of benches, finely landscaped. She had texted Ned a little while ago, asking if they could meet at one of those benches to talk before their date.

The truth was, this talk would be *instead* of their date.

As she closed the distance between her car and the bench where they were supposed to meet, she couldn't help replaying the images of that uploaded video, the one where Ned confronted and then shot the armed bank robber. She had decided to watch it, now that she'd talked with Ned and knew he was fine.

If anything, seeing the video solidified her concerns even more. She simply wasn't ready for this. She wondered if she would ever be.

Glancing up ahead, she saw Ned coming toward the bench

from the parking lot at the other end. He noticed her, nodded and waved. She waved back, but she could tell by the look on his face he knew something was up. Still, it was good to see him in person, living and breathing and looking very normal.

She tried not to keep looking at him as she neared the bench. But when she did look up, he was always looking at her.

They reached the bench and hugged briefly before they sat. "Great to see you," he said. "And really, I'm sorry I crushed my phone when I fell. It must've been awful to find out about what happened from a YouTube video. And then not to know whether I was dead or alive. I should've called you much sooner than I did."

She took a deep breath. "It was pretty awful. I'm not gonna lie. But Ned, I don't blame you for not calling me sooner. You had your hands full. I'm just glad you're all right. That must've been a terrible thing to go through. When we talked on the phone earlier, everything was so normal. You were so upbeat. Who could've ever guessed an hour later you would be in a gunfight with a bank robber."

"Yeah, right? How crazy is that? And in a town like this. The chief told me they haven't had an armed bank robbery in almost a decade here. And that one didn't involve a shootout."

"You seem to be doing all right," she said. "Are you?"

"For the most part. Definitely sore where the bullet hit the vest. The doc said I'll probably have a pretty decent bruise forming there the next day or so. But other than that, I'm fine."

"You're talking physically. I want to know about that but, really, I was talking about in here, and in here." She pointed at his head and his heart.

"Oh, oddly enough, I am doing...okay. You kind of know

when you become a policeman, there's always the chance that someday you might have to use your gun in the line of duty. But you can't really prepare for it, I don't think. Not emotionally anyway. Because day after day, you strap on that gun, and nothing happens. It just becomes part of the get-ready routine. Then here today, a day like any other day, and I not only have to use it, I have to shoot a guy. And not just shoot him, but kill him. Wow, just saying it out loud...I still can't believe it."

Neither could she. "So, do you feel anything? Numb? Remorse or regret?"

"I don't think I feel numb. I do feel some remorse and regret. Not so much for what I've done, but for that kid forcing my hand. All he had to do was drop the gun. It would've been so easy. There was no way out. He had to know that. But when he pointed the gun at that couple, I had no choice. You see that, right?"

Kim didn't know what to say. But he had put his finger right on the point of it for her. "To be honest, I'm so conflicted about this, Ned."

"Conflicted? I'm not sure I know what you mean."

"I'm not sure I can explain it, either. But I'll try. That's really the reason why I wanted to meet with you here, so we can talk. See, on the one hand, there's part of me that's ridiculously proud of who you are and what you've done this afternoon. To answer your question, no, you really didn't have a choice. You saved that couple's lives. Obviously, he shot you, so he would've shot them. When I saw you, step out from the safety of that car door and put yourself in harm's way to protect them...well, that might've been one of the bravest things I've ever seen anyone do." Kim started tearing up. She knew she would. She reached for tissues sitting on the top of her purse.

"But see, Ned, the part of me that was proud was, I guess, for the lack of a better word, the *citizen* part of me. But the other part of me, the part that's interested in being your girl-friend and, who knows, someday maybe something more... absolutely hated it. It terrified me. I didn't want you to do it. I wanted you to stay behind that car door until help arrived. Or maybe yet, to not even respond to the call in the first place. To let someone else go for it. Let someone else save the day."

"But Kim, I couldn't have done that. It wouldn't be right. I was the closest one to the robbery. It's my duty to respond. And then when I got there, I did everything I could to talk the guy down, to get him to drop the gun, to end this thing peacefully."

"I know, Ned. You did the right thing. As an officer of the law, you not only did your duty, but I think people are going to say you went above and beyond the call of duty. You shouldn't feel the need to apologize. Certainly not to me."

"Then what are you saying, Kim? I don't understand."

"I'm saying...you're not the problem here, I am. I don't think I can do this."

"Do what?"

"This. Us. I don't think I can do...us. I don't think I have what it takes to be in a close, romantic relationship with someone who has to do what you have to do for a living." The tears started coming again. She reached for the tissues.

"So, you don't want us to see each other again? I mean, in a dating kind of way?"

She shook her head no. "I'm sorry, Ned. But I don't think so. I really care about you, and I've really enjoyed getting to know you better. But I think, at least for now, I'd prefer just being your dog trainer. I'll do everything I can to help you out

with Parker. But for now, I think maybe that's all our relationship should be. I'm sorry."

Ned sighed. "I'm sorry, too, Kim. But I think I understand. I
know some of the guys have even said being a cop has ruined
their marriage. I don't know if it's because of things like this,
the danger part I mean. But I know this job comes with some
baggage. I really don't want to lose what we've started here, but
I'll respect your wishes."

"Thanks, Ned. I really am sorry."

He stood. "But listen, twice you said *for now*. I won't bug
you or pressure you in any way, but I'm also not in a hurry. If
some time passes, and you have a change of heart, promise me
you will let me know. I'm not going anywhere, Kim. If all you
need is time, I'm willing to give you as much as it takes."

"Thanks Ned. I'm not saying I'll feel different in time."

"I know. But you did say, *for now*. Twice. That has to mean
something. Just promise me. If you change your mind, you'll
let me know."

"Okay, I will."

PARKER WAS SO EXCITED. Ned had gone out and left him in the
crate again. Parker had prepared himself for a long stay by
himself, but the front door had just opened. Ned was back
already.

Parker stood, then sat. His tail wagging, his front feet
prancing. Ned walked by, bent down holding the leash. "Better
let you out again."

The crate door opened, Parker offered his collar to let Ned
click on the leash, and out he went. As they walked down the
hall, down the steps and across the street, Parker could tell

something was wrong. Ned wasn't paying any attention to him. He was relieved to see no evidence of anger, but something was troubling him.

He quickly did his business and came back to Ned, sitting quietly at his feet. For several moments, Ned didn't even notice. Then he looked down. "You done already? Good boy." Ned stood, started walking back across the street.

Parker realized, that was the first time Ned had ever said *good boy* without any excitement in his voice. And for the rest of the walk to the front door, he didn't interact with Parker at all.

What was wrong? Had to be something.

They walked inside. Ned unhooked his leash and hung it up. He walked over to his big chair and sat. But he didn't lean back and prop his feet up as before. Instead, he leaned forward and lowered his head into his hands.

Ned began to cry.

"God, I need some help here. When I turned my day over to you this morning, this is not what I expected. I had to kill a guy. I know you know that. But now I've lost Kim because of it. I don't blame her. But God, it hurts. I was afraid she might not be okay with this part of what I do, but I was hoping we'd have a whole lot more time together before anything happened to test it, you know? That you'd let her fall for me, and our relationship would have time to get strong, so much so that it wouldn't matter to her that I'm a cop." He sat up, wiped his eyes on his sleeve.

"But now it's too late. I guess it's wrong to care more about this than having to shoot that guy. I hated having to do that. But I..." The tears came again. "I hate way more losing Kim."

Parker had no idea what Ned had just said. Didn't catch a

single word, but he couldn't wait to be invited into his lap any longer. He stood up between his legs and got as close to him as he could, licked under his chin.

"Now look at you, buddy," Ned said. "Trying to make me feel better. After all life's put you through." Ned sat back. "You come on up the rest of the way."

Parker jumped into Ned's lap. Though he didn't understand what had made Ned so sad, he had to try to take at least some of it away.

49

R ussell had made the bike ride home from Pete's house just in time to rendezvous with his mom in the parking lot. She had just arrived home from work. "Hey Mom," he said as she got out of the car.

"Hey Honey, you have a nice day at school? No...problems?" She held out one arm, signaling a hug was required.

"It was fine. No problems. I hid out over at Pete's after school, remember?"

"That's right."

They walked past Ned's patrol car. His mom instantly made a face. "I almost forgot," she said. "Did you hear about the bank robbery?"

"No? Here? In this town?" They started walking toward the apartment stairs.

"Yes, here. At the Wells Fargo Bank. Ned was involved. One of the cashiers at work told me he had to shoot the bank robber."

"Ned? He shot someone?"

"That's what she said. Apparently, there's a video online."

"Really? I wonder what happened, to the bank robber, I mean."

"He was killed."

"No, killed? By Ned?"

They reached the steps and started climbing. "That's what she said. And it sounds like he didn't have a choice. I guess the bank robber was going to shoot some people nearby, so Ned had to shoot to stop him."

"Wow, that's crazy. I wonder how he's doing?"

"Maybe we should find out," Mom said. "Be good neighbors. Let me just put my things away, and we'll go over and check on him."

Russell walked his bike into the apartment and back into his bedroom. When he came out, he glanced over the railing at Ned's patrol car. He couldn't believe it. Ned had killed a bank robber. That was a big deal. He never knew anybody that had ever killed anybody before. Obviously, the guy must've had it coming. Ned wasn't the kind of guy who'd ever do something like that unless it was absolutely necessary. Not that he knew Ned that well, but he seemed to be such a calm, in control kind of person.

Russell wondered how much they could ask Ned about it. He had so many questions. But it didn't seem like the kind of thing you could talk about freely with someone, unless they opened up the conversation and you could tell they were totally cool with it.

Just then, his mother came out and closed their apartment door. She walked right up to Russell and gently put her hand on his shoulder. "Now listen to me, we're not gonna ask Ned all kinds of questions. Like how did it feel to kill somebody? How do you feel now about doing it? Or anything like that. Do you understand?"

"I do. And I wasn't going to anyway."

"Good. I'm glad."

"You just follow my lead." She walked over and knocked on Ned's door. Russell stood behind her.

Instantly, a dog started barking. That's right. Russell had forgotten about Parker. He heard footsteps and then the door opened. There stood Ned dressed in regular clothes.

"Hey folks," he said, "nice to see you. That eye's looking almost completely better, Russell."

"Uh, yeah. It is."

"Hi Ned," his Mom said. "We don't want to bother you. Just wanted to come over and see how you were doing. We heard about what happened this afternoon. You know, over at the bank."

"Yeah, well, that was pretty terrible." He looked behind him. "That's funny, Parker stopped barking as soon as I opened the door. I put him in his crate before opening the door. Just in case. You want to come in?"

"Maybe just for a minute. But really, we don't want to bother you. You probably need some time to yourself."

"Well, looks like I'll be getting plenty of that now." He made a face Russell didn't understand. "Well, come on in. Parker doesn't seem to mind."

PARKER WAS STUNNED at what he saw when Ned opened the front door. Was that...was that his little boy? The one who was so nice to him at the old house? Was that his mother? He couldn't see them clearly because of the light coming in behind them and the bars on his crate door.

Now they were coming inside. He sniffed the air. The scent wasn't right.

"Well, would you look at him?" Ned said. "He's looking right at you two. And his tail is wagging. You see it?"

"I don't," Marilyn said. "But I believe you. It's nice that he stopped barking so quickly."

"Yeah, that too."

"You seem to be doing okay," Marilyn said, "considering what you've been through."

Ned closed the front door. "I guess I am."

"Did they give you the rest of the day off?"

"More than just today," Ned said. "I'll be off for several days, maybe a week or more. That's standard procedure after an officer-involved shooting."

"That hardly seems fair," Marilyn said. "It's like being punished for doing your job. And the girl at work who told me about it said you were like a major hero for what you did."

Ned laughed. "I don't know about that. But it's not a punishment. They give you the time off with pay."

"Oh, that's different then. So, it's more like a vacation."

"Yeah, I guess so."

"Does that mean I won't get to babysit Parker?" Russell said. "I mean, if you're not at work."

"I don't know. Maybe not during this break. We'll see. But I'm still surprised by how well he's doing with you two being here. Look, now he's lying down. Like he's totally relaxed."

Parker lifted his head. He could tell they were talking about him. Now, they were looking at him. One thing was sure, this wasn't the little boy he knew, or his mother. The scent was all wrong and their voices were different. But they seemed very nice. Everyone was smiling. Even Ned, who hadn't been happy for a while.

"Do you mind if we try an experiment?" Ned said. "With Parker, I mean."

"Sure, what do you have in mind?" Marilyn asked.

"Well, I wasn't thinking of Parker and Russell meeting for at least a couple more days, you know, doing that thing with the toy fox. But maybe that's unnecessary, judging by how he looks now. I was thinking, maybe you guys could go in the living room and sit down. I'll take Parker out of his crate, but hold him, and see how he reacts to you. If he starts getting all tense, or starts barking, then I'll just put him back until you leave. But who knows, maybe he'll be fine."

"I'm okay with that," Marilyn said.

Ned hesitated. "I should warn you. He's not looking his best right now, from all the abuse. But he's healing up nicely, and he's clean. No diseases, nothing contagious."

They walked into the living room and sat.

Parker wasn't sure what was up, but the boy and his mother just walked by his crate. He could still see them through the little openings in the side. They were sitting down. His crate door opened. It was Ned, squatting down in front. He had one of those amazing treats in his hand.

"Here Parker, want this? Come on now, Boy. It's okay."

Parker stepped out of his crate and took the treat. He wasn't afraid of Ned anymore. Ned lifted him up off the ground. What was he doing? He held him close to his side and stroked his head and neck gently. This wasn't so bad. He turned to face the little boy and his mom in the living room. They were looking up at him and smiling.

"What should we do?" Marilyn said.

"You see that little baggie with treats on the coffee table? Each of you take one out. When I bring Parker over just hold it out in your palm. I think this is going to be fine. I can already tell, he's not tensing up. His tail is still wagging."

Parker heard the word *treats* and saw the baggie on the table. The boy and his mother both took one. Now they were holding them out for him. Ned carried him closer and bent down.

"Good boy, Parker," Ned said. "You want the treats? Go ahead. Take it."

Parker looked up at Ned then back at the treats. Marilyn was closer, so he stuck his neck out to reach it and took it from her hand. It was so good. Ned patted him as he ate. This was nice. The little boy held out his treat, so Parker ate it, too.

"Wow," Ned said. "I guess this answers the question of whether or not Parker will accept you. He's fine with both of you."

"Can I pet him?" Russell said.

"Yeah, I think that would be fine, too. But start under his chin. Kim said it's always better to come underneath their head rather than over it."

Parker finished the second treat. The little boy scratched under his chin gently. Parker licked his hand.

"He licked me," Russell said. "And now his tail is wagging even more."

"I'm going to let him down on the floor. Call him to you, see if he comes."

Parker felt himself lowering to the carpet. The boy held out his hands and called to him. Parker couldn't help the joy he felt at the sight of the little boy's outstretched hand. His tail, then his whole body began to wag. He trotted over and began to lick the boy's face.

"I think he likes me," Russell said.

"Well, look at that," Ned said. "I guess it's safe to say, you can stop sleeping with that toy fox. You and Parker are already pals."

50

The following day around midmorning Ned sat in his recliner watching cable news. Nothing world shaking was going on, so the news people were just trying to make a lot out of a little by talking about the same small-minded themes they usually talked about, over and over again, with each other and with special guests who were supposed to know more than they did.

Ned had stopped listening a while ago. He wished there was something major going on in the world, something big enough to grab his attention and keep it, to force his thoughts to stop returning to the conversation with Kim yesterday. The one where she'd basically ended their relationship.

The only bright spot in his day had been the visit with Russell and his mom, seeing Parker respond so well to them. He really was a great dog. After all the abuse and neglect he'd experienced, you'd think he'd want nothing to do with people. But there he was wagging his tail, licking them, eager to feel their touch. Even now, he could sit anywhere he wanted in the apartment but, here he was, half-sitting on Ned, half resting on the armchair.

Ned scratched Parker's neck and massaged his shoulders. "You're a good boy, Parker. I'm really glad you're here." His tail swished back and forth. Ned thought about calling Kim to tell her how well things went yesterday, and that they didn't even need to do the stuffed animal bit with Russell. Before she dumped him, he would have called her, first thing. And she would have been so excited and encouraging.

But now, it would just be awkward. She would be polite, but probably aloof, trying not to keep the conversation going too long. He would quickly run out of things to say that didn't sound like he was trying too hard. She did say she would still help him train Parker, but what did that really mean? Were they going to meet once a week, twice, for something like a class? Pretty much have no contact beyond that? Before, she'd said he should feel free to call her anytime, no question was too small.

But that hardly seemed appropriate anymore. That invitation included all kinds of interest in getting to know him more. Using the dog training as a bridge to branch into many other areas of life. All with a view to spending more time together, testing the ins-and-outs of the relationship to see how things fit. And all that discovery time seemed to be going so well, for both of them.

Right up until it didn't anymore. Until yesterday. When Ned shot and killed a bank robber. That didn't fit.

It didn't fit in anywhere. And how could it? Whose romantic relationship has to make room for one of the partners being shot at occasionally and killing bad guys?

Ned sighed. It wasn't her fault. He's the one who chose this profession. She had chosen to become a dog trainer, to help people understand how to get along better with their dogs. Why did he have to choose this? To help protect the good people, the innocent people from the bad ones, from those who wanted to do them harm. It really was a noble profession, and he knew he had nothing to be ashamed of. But it wasn't a question of right or wrong, or pride and shame.

The simple truth was, it was a dangerous way to live. She was right. He deliberately put himself in harm's way. At that moment, because of who he was and what he was called to do, it was his duty to step out into the line of fire and try to save that couple. And if it happened tomorrow, he'd do it all over again.

She hadn't really dumped him. He could at least take comfort in how difficult it seemed for her to end things between them. She really did care for him. What she couldn't live with was the fear created by what he did for a living. But what if he could do something else for living? There were lots of other occupations he could pursue. Normal things. Safe things. Things that didn't involve shooting people, or being shot at.

He didn't know anything else that interested him right now, but he could look into it. He wasn't even thirty years old yet. Most policemen only stayed on the job for twenty years, some thirty. But a relationship like this, like the one he and Kim had going...this had the makings of something that could last the rest of his life. She was the kind of woman he'd want to have kids with, and grandkids someday.

He wondered, would she reconsider getting back with him if he stopped being a cop? Was that even a possibility? And if so, how would he even get a conversation like that started? He could tell, she was the kind of woman who wouldn't feel right being the reason why he stopped doing something he loved.

Not for a relationship like theirs, one that was still so new.

KIM STEPPED into her office carrying a container that held all but a few bites from her lunch outing with Amy. Amy had offered to treat her, take her someplace nice, hopefully help her dig out of the hole she'd been stuck in all morning.

It didn't work.

Amy came in behind her, sat at her desk. "Well, at least you have your dinner already. That's something."

Kim smiled. "I really appreciate you doing this, Amy. Even though I wasn't much company."

"That's okay. I didn't take you out so you could entertain me. I just wanted to lighten the load a little, if I could."

"Well, you did that," Kim said. "I just wish I could be sure I did the right thing. Maybe I should've waited a few days, or maybe a week. See if a little time might have given me a different perspective."

"You did act pretty quickly on this, but I've never thought of you as a hasty or irrational person. In fact, if anything you seem just the opposite. Very levelheaded and low-key. I could tell, this thing really bothered you, on a pretty deep level. Which is why I've hesitated to share any of my opinions or advice."

"But I wish you would," Kim said. "I know, technically, you work for me. But I also feel like we're pretty good friends."

"We are. I agree. But this isn't the kind of thing, I think, a friend can sort out for you. It's too deep. Something you have to discover for yourself. I think maybe God can help you. You know, like that verse in Psalm thirty-nine: *Search me oh God and know my heart, know my anxious thoughts...* Sometimes when I'm stuck I pray like that, ask God to turn the lights on for me. I prayed like that when Chris and I were starting to get serious. It's not exactly the same situation. His life's not in danger anymore. But the missing leg and the PTSD. I didn't want to lead him on for a number of months, only to bail on him when things got tough. I needed to know if I was up for it. I discovered I was. But I don't think anybody else could've told me what to do back then. I needed to be sure of my own heart."

That really was Kim's problem. She wasn't sure. If she had been, she wouldn't be this depressed and unsettled about letting Ned go. But she also didn't know how she could possibly live every day worrying about whether each time they parted, if that was the last time she would ever see him. She looked over at Amy. "You really love Chris, don't you?"

"More now than I did then. And really, that's what makes the difference, isn't it? The love. It cuts the hard times down by at least half. The bottom line is, for me, Chris matters more. Being with him matters more than any of the downsides in the relationship." Amy leaned forward. "I think that's the thing you have to discover Kim. Where does Ned factor into your equation, the one that's clearly still forming in your heart?"

51

R ussell was all set. He'd finished dinner, got all cleaned up and ready for his second self-defense class. Ned had just called his mom to say he was heading out the front door, and to send Russell out. "Okay Mom, I'm going. See you in a few hours."

"Not without a hug," she said.

Russell ran over, gave her a quick hug, picked up his gym bag and headed out the front door.

Sure enough, Ned was already there locking his deadbolt. "Hey Partner, you ready to go?"

"Yep. I've been waiting for this for two days." They started walking down the stairs.

"Those guys give you any trouble?"

"Just dirty looks and evil stares. But both days I was able to head over to Pete's house until my mom got home. Took a different route each time. But hopefully, after tonight, things are going to change."

"According to the sensei, you should be all right." They

reached the car. Ned unlocked it, and they both got in. "But remember, don't go looking for anything."

Russell looked at him. "Ned, do I look like the kind of kid that would ever go looking for trouble?"

"No, I guess not. Felt like I had to say it anyway. You know, the adult thing to say."

It was a fairly short drive. They chatted about different things along the way. Russell really wanted to ask him about the bank robbery. There's so much he wanted to know. You see stuff like this on TV shows and movies and, here he was, sitting right next to a guy who's been through a real-life one, that included a shootout, and he'd lived to tell the tale. But Russell's mom had said, don't you dare ask him about it, and Ned didn't even bring it up once.

They got to the dojo and pulled into a parking space. Russell recognized several of the kids getting out of cars and heading in. Several of them looked their way, stopped and pointed, and were clearly talking about them. Then he realized, they weren't talking about them. It was Ned. Of course, they had seen the video of the robbery. It had played on local news several times that day.

"You see what's going on?" Russell said. "I think you're a celebrity now."

"I see it. Can't wait for this thing to blow over. Do me a favor, let's don't make a fuss of it."

"Sure. If that's what you want."

As soon as they walked in the front door, the sensei noticed, smiled and headed their way. "Hey Ned, can I have a quick word?"

"Sure. What's up?"

"First off, that was an amazing thing you did yesterday. I wasn't even sure if you'd make it here tonight."

"Really, I'm fine. It's just a little sore where the bullet hit the vest. But listen, could we not make a big deal out of this? I really want tonight to be about Russell, not me. You do remember about giving him some private tutoring after, right? Help prepare him to face those two bullies I told you about?"

"Yeah, I definitely remember. But if you don't mind, I'd like to make a thirty second fuss about what you did. It's the elephant in the room. I think if we ignore it, everybody will be thinking about it all night. We'll just address it quickly and move on. Are you okay with that?"

"Sure, I see your point."

Russell wasn't sure if that was a private conversation, but he was close enough to hear every word. He was mostly relieved to hear the sensei mention they were definitely going to have the private lesson after.

The sensei gathered everyone together in a half circle like he did last week. He asked for a show of hands to see how many had heard about the bank robbery and the shooting that Ned was involved in. Every hand went up, including the parents standing in the back. The sensei mentioned how glad they were that Ned and all the innocent civilians involved were safe which, he said, was because of Ned's heroic actions.

He had just begun to suggest they all thank Ned for what he did when the room erupted into spontaneous applause. Russell could tell Ned felt very uncomfortable. He waved and smiled. The applause died down, and the sensei asked everyone to now give him their undivided attention for the remainder of the class.

The rest of the class went pretty much as Russell expected. A lot of exercise, like last week, only not as long. Another fifteen to twenty-minute talk on confrontation and learning how to de-escalate conflict. The last part of the class was spent teaching everyone the proper stance, and how to quickly get in position if it became clear that words were not enough, and you had to defend yourself.

Russell looked up at the clock. Only ten more minutes of this. Fortunately, the sensei actually spent this time teaching them the basic one-two punch, and let them keep doing it as he walked around and gave specific pointers. Finally, the class was over and everyone started packing up and heading for their cars.

Ned and Russell stayed by the main table, sitting in chairs. When the last class members had left, the sensei came back to the center of the room and asked Ned and Russell to join him.

Russell was so excited.

"I really should just watch tonight," Ned said. "I don't think I can do any of the moves."

"That's fine. But I am glad you're here, so you can make sure Russell gets them right." He turned his full attention to Russell. "Now listen, the things that I'm going to show you tonight are really supposed to be a last resort. When it becomes painfully clear, the guys who are bothering you aren't going away without a fight. They were both bigger than you, right?"

Russell nodded. "And two years older, too."

"Here's the good news. You do the things I'm going to teach you, and none of that matters."

Russell smiled.

"Now Russell, the first thing you have to grasp is, in a situation like this, in order to win a conflict with two bigger guys, especially guys who have no business bothering you, you have to accept the reality that you're going to have to hurt them, quickly and decisively, to get them to stop. You probably have been raised right, to think of sportsmanship and fairness, things like that. But these guys aren't playing fair, and if you try to play fair, they are going to hurt you. Just by virtue of the fact that they are both willing to come after you in the first place, two against one, attacking someone they know is physically smaller than they are, shows they are cowards. So, they don't deserve your respect. Do you understand what I'm saying?"

Russell nodded.

"The moment it becomes clear, they are in-your-face and this isn't going to end without a fight, you have to make the first move. You have to strike like a snake, fast and quick. Only unlike a snake, which often just strike once, you will have to strike several blows, one after the other. With fists, elbows, knees and kicks. I will show you moves in just a few moments, ways to use each of these body parts as weapons, to put these two bullies down, hopefully once and for all."

"Do you understand what he is saying?" Ned asked. "Are you okay with this?"

Russell looked at Ned. "I understand. At least I think I do. I can't wait around until they start punching me. Which is what I think I usually do, hoping they won't do it. Hoping they'll just leave me alone. But I can tell, the way they're acting now... they're not gonna leave me alone anymore. So yeah, I get this. Being quick is something I'm good at. If I knew what to do to stop these guys, I think I could do it quick."

"That's good Russell," the sensei said. "I can see you're a real sensible kid. I'd love to keep teaching you after this ordeal is over. So, in just a minute we'll start working on these moves, but I want to say this first. Although I'm going to teach you how to hurt these guys, and what you're going to do will definitely hurt, no one will be hurt seriously. They might have a black eye, a bloody nose, several bruises and aches and pains all over, but we don't want to send anyone to the hospital. You got that? As soon as they're down, and you know they'll be staying down, you stop the attack. Are we clear?"

"Yes, Sensei. We're clear." Although at this point, Russell had the hardest time imagining he could ever actually cause Edmund and Harley enough pain to put them down in the first place, let alone make them stay down. But the way the sensei talked just now, Russell was starting to believe that maybe, just maybe, it might be true.

52

The following day, Kim was still struggling with her emotions. So, she called her mom, asked if she could come over for lunch. The things that Amy had said certainly helped, but she felt like she needed to hear her mom's thoughts on these things. Thankfully, Mom was a great listener and, when she did give advice, it was rarely with strings and never pushy.

Kim pulled into the familiar, shady driveway. Since it was Friday, many of the managers at the shelter met for lunch at a restaurant and always went a little long. So, she didn't need to be in a hurry.

Once inside, her mom heated up some homemade beef stew from two nights ago, served with some fresh bread. "This looks and smells wonderful," Kim said.

"I don't mean to brag, since I made them both, but they really are." She smiled. "So, my darling girl, what's going on? I could tell by the tone of your voice on the phone and now by the look on your face that something is troubling you. My guess is, in a pretty big way."

"As usual, I can't hide anything from you." Over the next twenty-five minutes, interrupted only by her mom's insightful questions and several tasty swallows of beef stew, Kim did her best to share her dilemma about Ned, her feelings about him, and her serious misgivings about his occupation, especially in light of the bank robbery and shooting. Of course, it wasn't long before the box of tissues was set on the table.

Kim concluded with, "What I really want is for you to just tell me what to do. I feel like I've lost my way."

Her mom didn't say anything for what felt like several minutes, but was just probably a few seconds. "Well, for starters, I had no idea my daughter was in love."

"In love? I didn't say I was in love with Ned."

"You didn't with your words. You did it with your pain. But in a way, you did it with your words, too. You spent the first ten minutes talking about the many wonders of Ned. You went on and on about all the things you deeply respected and thoroughly enjoyed about him. If I'm being honest, I've never heard you talk that way about a man before."

"Really?"

"Really."

"So, that's why this is so hard? Because I'm in love with him?"

Her mother nodded.

"But we haven't known each other long enough."

"Long enough for what? To be in love? I was in love with your father in less than a week. I've been in love with the man ever since."

"Okay, maybe I am. But that doesn't help me. And it doesn't

change the level of danger associated with Ned's job. Mom, someone shot at him yesterday and almost killed him."

"That's true. But you know what else is true? I read the article about the shooting this morning. We haven't had an incident like that in this town for over a decade. That doesn't mean it won't happen again, but it's not like Ned is serving in downtown Chicago, either. He could serve the rest of his career without ever being shot at or shooting his gun again in the line of duty."

Kim sipped her cup of coffee. "Or it could happen again tomorrow."

"It could. But really, Kim. Ultimately, it's not just a question of odds or chances. What's that verse say in the Bible, *Our times are in his hands*?" She got a look, like a thought had just popped into her head. "Do you remember what happened to Mr. Curran? That nice man who was an usher in church? It was almost two years ago."

Kim did. It was horrible. Shocking and horrible.

"He had a safe job," her mother continued, "worked in a cubicle every day, staff accountant I think they said. Drove home the same way every day from the same job, for nearly twenty years. Always got home at the same time, his wife said. Five thirty-five. But not that day. You remember what happened?"

"Yes." And Kim remembered how unsettled it made her feel for months afterward.

"Less than five minutes from home, a speeding driver ran through a red light and smacked right into his door. He died instantly." She paused a moment. "Do you get why I brought that up just now?"

"Perfectly," Kim said.

"Just to humor me, say it out loud."

"Our times are in his hands."

"No matter what we do for a living. All those people who've died in all these different terror attacks, had no idea when they went to that concert, or got on that plane, or went to that office party, or whatever, that today was their last day on earth."

Kim sighed. Everything she said was true.

Her mother smiled.

"What are you smiling about?"

"I just remembered how much your father and I were against you becoming a dog trainer. Do you remember that?"

"Barely, but yeah."

"We only told you a fraction of our fears. We knew you were too old for us to tell you what to do anymore, and we knew you absolutely wanted to do it. But we were terrified for you. Especially when we realized you were going to be training shelter dogs, including pits and Rottweilers and Dobermans. We were sure you were going to get your arm bitten off. Or some dog was going to ruin that beautiful face of yours."

"I had no idea it bothered you guys that much."

"Well, it did."

"So how did you get past it? Because, obviously you did. You never seem to worry about it anymore, unless you're hiding it really well."

"I'm not sure how we got past it. I guess it was just prayer. Trusting God. Every day I'd ask God to protect you. Every time you got off the phone, and I'd hear those dogs barking in the background, I'd pray: *Lord, please don't let one of those dogs bite my girl.*"

"Well, look. God's answered your prayers." She held up her

arms. "Still here after all these years. No scars. Never bitten in the face, either."

Her mom smiled. "Yep. Still here after all these years. Safe and sound."

Kim got the message.

53

Russell hurried home from school on his bike, nervously looking about, hoping he wouldn't see Edmund and Harley. Even though he felt more ready now to face them, he still hoped he'd make it home without a fight. It was Friday afternoon, their last chance to try something until Monday.

When he crossed the street into the apartment complex, he breathed a sigh of relief. Home free. Now he would get to spend some time with Parker while Ned was at the police station for his meeting. And he'd have at least the rest of the weekend to practice the moves the sensei had taught him last night before facing the boys on Monday.

He quickly put his stuff away in their apartment and headed next-door, Ned's spare key in his hands. As he unlocked it he remembered Ned's instructions. *Talk to Parker in a happy high-pitched voice. Give him plenty of treats. And always keep him on the leash unless he's inside the apartment with the door closed.*

And there was one other thing, something that went before the others. *If Parker doesn't seem happy to see you, if he seems even a little bit tense or growls, just close the door and we'll try again later.* Fortunately, that concern disappeared the moment the door opened and Russell called out his name. "Hey Parker, there's a good boy. It's me, remember me from yesterday?" Parker instantly stood in his crate, his tail wagging and his front feet prancing. "What a good boy you are," Russell said as he grabbed the leash from its hook and headed for the crate.

He opened the crate door and handed Parker a treat. To his surprise, Parker ran right past the treat, jumped up and began licking under his chin. Russell carefully rubbed his back. "Are you happy to see me, Boy? Happy to get out of that crate?" He quickly latched on the leash and offered Parker the treat again. Parker gobbled it right up.

Russell stood and started leading him toward the front door. "First things first. Let's get you across the street to go the bathroom." It felt funny to Russell, referring to a patch of dirt and grass as a bathroom. Parker walked right beside him until they got through the door. Sat while Russell locked it, then stayed by his side all the way across the street.

Parker did what he needed to do within two minutes. He sniffed around a little bit more, but it didn't seem like he had to do anything else. Russell didn't feel right bringing him back inside so quickly. Ned had mentioned, if he wanted, he could take Parker on short walks. That big park was just down the street a little ways.

But that was also where Edmund and Harley had first ambushed him. It's not like a dog Parker's size would scare them off. He decided to give it a try, but to tread carefully. He walked Parker to the entrance then stood behind a cluster of trees. From there he had a pretty good view of the park, at least all the open areas. Lots of kids playing. Some parents with their toddlers in the kiddie section. But no sign of Edmund and Harley.

"Looks like the coast is clear, Parker." There was a main concrete walkway that meandered around the perimeter of the park. Russell decided that would probably be the safest route to take.

For the first ten minutes, everything went fine. Then he reached the back section, which made an irregular loop around a section of live oaks. It was a beautiful shaded area but it also put the populated area of the park out of sight for a few minutes. Russell hesitated, wondering whether he should skip it. He decided to be brave. It's not like anyone knew he was coming here and was hiding out, ready to jump him.

Things went fine for the first two-thirds of the loop. But when he came around to the other side where he could see the main section of the park again, he froze at the sight just ahead. His heart started pounding.

Parker immediately tensed up and began to growl.

"Hey Monkey Boy," Edmund yelled. Standing next to him was Harley. Both boys were coming this way.

"We couldn't believe our luck," Edmund said. "We've been looking for you after school for three days. We decided to check the park one last time before calling it quits and what do we see, but you heading here into the back section, where things are nice and quiet."

"Like it was meant to be," Harley said, laughing.

They got a few steps closer. Parker's growl turned into a fierce bark.

"What you got there, Monkey Boy?" Edmund said. "That supposed to be a dog? If it is, that's gotta be about the ugliest dog I ever saw."

"Looks more like a hyena," Harley said.

Edmund laughed out loud. "A hyena. That's a good one, Harley. Monkey Boy and his hyena, out for a nice walk. But you don't really think a little dog like that is gonna stop the beating you've got coming, do you?"

The entire time the boys spoke, Russell replayed the moves he'd learned last night in his mind and repeated his sensei's instructions:

Try to walk away.

If that doesn't help, you turn and strike fast. No words.

Incapacitate the leader first.

When he goes down, quickly demolish the second.

Go back and finish off the leader before he recovers.

Now come the words.

Russell turned around and started walking in the other direction. "Come on Parker, it's time to go."

Parker resisted, stood his ground and continued growling and barking.

"Parker, come!" Russell yanked on the leash and continued walking. This time Parker obeyed, turned and followed.

"Where do you think you're going?" Edmund yelled. "This thing ain't over."

Russell heard stomping footsteps coming up fast behind him. Then someone pushed him hard in the back. He fell forward but caught himself and turned around. It was Edmund, Harley right behind him.

Parker let loose a loud, horrible growl and lunged at

Edmund. The end of the leash caused him to miss his mark by inches. Russell couldn't believe what Edmund did next.

"Stupid dog!" Then Edmund drop-kicked Parker in the side. He yelped and flew several feet back in the air, landing in the dirt with a thump.

"Parker!" Russell screamed and ran over to him. His eyes were open and blinking, but it was obvious he was badly hurt. Russell stood and faced the two boys.

He didn't feel an ounce of fear anymore.

"Now we can finish this," Harley said.

Russell walked straight up to Edmund, staring right into his eyes.

"What are you going to do?"

Russell faked a punch to Edmund's face. Edmund raised his hands to block. Russell executed a spinning back kick, with almost lightning speed, straight into Edmund's exposed gut. All his air came rushing out of his mouth in a roar as he doubled over in pain and fell to the ground.

Stunned, Harley stood there dumbly, his mouth dropped open and his eyes bugging out. Russell quickly set in position and threw an almost perfectly placed side kick to Harley's jaw. His head snapped back. Russell bent down, and in one quick motion, spun his right leg around behind Harley's legs and swept him off his feet. He fell crashing to the ground with a thud.

Russell jumped on top of his chest and delivered four hammer punches to his face. Harley screamed for him to please stop. So Russell did. Then he ran over and kicked Edmund in the side, as he tried to get up. Edmund groaned and fell on his back again. Russell now jumped on top of Edmund's chest, and raised his fist.

Now the words.

"This thing ain't over, Edmund? Is that what you said?" Russell let loose a barrage of hammer punches to Edmund's face. Edmund tried to block them, but most got through. "How about now, Edmund? This thing over now?"

"Yes, yes! Please stop, yes."

Russell got up. He stood over Edmund, still fuming inside, and looked at his battered face. "If I see you or Harley bothering anyone else at school, or even hear that you did, we'll be doing this again. Do you understand?"

Edmund looked away.

"Edmund, do you understand?"

"Yes, I do. Would you please leave?" He started to cry and covered his face with his hands.

Russell turned and walked toward Parker's poor crumpled body across the way. Filled with fresh anger, he turned back and looked at Edmund. He imagined running back and drop-kicking Edmund in the side, just like he did to Parker. But he remembered what the sensei said about when to call off the attack and resisted the urge. Instead, he ran over to Parker. "You poor boy. I'm here, Parker. You're gonna be okay. I'm going to get you some help." He gently scooped him up in his arms, flung the leash over his shoulder and ran for all he was worth toward the park entrance. Crying as he ran.

When he cleared the loop area, he saw a teenage girl had been filming the whole scene with her phone.

"I saw what you did," she said. "Got the whole thing on tape. It was amazing."

As he ran past her, he yelled. "Then please stop filming me and call the police. Tell them what happened. I've got to get this dog some help."

He didn't stop to hear her response. He just kept running, all the way till he reached Ned's apartment. Exhausted, he gently held Parker's body up to the door, so he could pull out the keys. Once inside, he set Parker down on the couch, grabbed his cell phone and called Ned.

The phone rang and rang. "Please answer, Ned," Russell said aloud.

He did. "Hello, Russell? That you? My meeting's almost done."

"Ned please, you have to come now! Parker's hurt. Bad!"

"Parker's hurt? What happened?"

"The bullies, I was taking Parker for a walk in the park. They found us and attacked me. Parker tried to stop them, but they kicked him, hard. You gotta come, quick. I don't know what to do."

"Are you okay?"

"I'm fine. But Parker. He's hurt bad. It looks like he's hardly breathing."

"I'll be right there."

Russell heard a click.

54

N ed stood. "Sorry guys, I gotta go. This should have been a 911 call. Jeb, can you race over to the park across the street from my apartment complex? I've got to get to my apartment."

"Sure, Ned," Jeb said, standing. "What's going on?"

Ned was already moving toward the door. "Don't know all the details, but two middle school bullies just attacked my next-door neighbor somewhere in that park. The kid's half their size. He says he's fine, but looks like they almost killed that little dog I took in."

"So why you heading to your apartment?"

"The kid they attacked--my neighbor--ran there carrying the dog."

"What if the bullies are gone? If I were them, I wouldn't stick around."

"Then ask the people standing nearby. Maybe somebody saw something, or got a video on their phone. I gotta go."

Ned stopped by the dispatcher on his way to the front door.

"Have you received any 911 calls in the last few minutes? From that park over on Wilmette Avenue?"

She stopped typing on a keyboard and looked up. "Matter of fact, I did. A teenage girl reported seeing a fight. Two bigger kids picking on a smaller kid. But the thing is, the two bigger kids are the ones on the ground, not the kid they attacked. Or at least they were when she called. The kid they attacked ran off. She said it looked like the bigger kids attacked his dog, or something. I've got someone headed there already."

"Great. That's actually my dog they attacked."

"What? Your dog?"

"Jeb is heading there now, too. Can you contact him, tell him everything you just told me?"

"Will do."

Ned hurried for the front door. He ran across the parking lot and jumped into his car. As soon as he backed out, he turned on his lights and siren and hit the pedal. Once on the main road, he glanced at the clock. A few minutes before five. He called Kim, hoping to reach her before she'd left the shelter for the weekend.

She picked up on the second ring. "Hey Ned. I'm actually glad you called."

"Kim, sorry to interrupt you. But we have an emergency. Any chance you could meet me at my apartment?"

"An emergency? Yeah, I can meet you there. When?"

"Like, right now. I'm driving there at full speed, lights and sirens going."

"Oh my. I'm getting up right now. Can you tell me anything about it?"

"It's Parker. He's hurt. Russell was watching him for me.

Those bullies attacked him in the park again. Sounds like Parker got the worst of it."

WHEN KIM ARRIVED at Ned's apartment ten minutes later, she saw his squad car parked parallel to the curb nearest the stairway. The car was off, and so were the lights and siren. She ran upstairs and found his front door opened. She walked in to find him hovering over Parker, who was lying on the couch. Russell was sitting next to him, his eyes were all red from crying.

"Is he going to be all right?" Russell said to Ned.

Ned must've heard Kim come in. He turned and offered a weak smile. "I hope so, Russell. But whatever happens, you did the right thing coming here."

Kim hurried over and looked down at the dog. She wasn't sure what to expect, but at least there didn't appear to be any blood. His eyes were open, but just barely. He seemed to be having trouble breathing. She looked down at Russell. "Did you see what they did to him?"

"Yes, I was right there." He started crying again but quickly wiped the tears away. "I did exactly like the sensei told me. I tried to walk away. I didn't want to fight them. But they wouldn't stop. Parker was trying to defend me, but I didn't want him to. I just wanted us to get out of there. But Edmund shoved me from behind. Parker growled and lunged like he was trying to stop him, but Edmund just laughed. Then he kicked him in the side, like he was kicking a football. Parker went flying through the air and landed in the dirt. He was barely moving after that."

She looked at his face. "You don't look so bad. Are you all right?"

Ned gently patted Parker's head. "Sounds like they didn't lay a hand on him after that. Before I left the station, the dispatcher said she'd already gotten a 911 call. The two bullies were still on the ground. At least they were then." He looked back at Parker. "What can we do for him? Is the vet still there at the shelter? I know it's Friday."

"She is," Kim said. "I called her on the way here, asked her if there's any way she could wait to leave till I got back with her. So, let's get Parker over there now. I've got some blankets in the backseat. How about you carry him down, Ned, and gently lay him on them. Russell, can you sit in the back seat next to him?"

He nodded. "My mom's not home from work yet, but I called her and told her what happened. She'll be fine with that."

"Okay then," she said. "Let's do this and try to keep him as still as possible. I'll update the Doc once we're on the way."

NED FOLLOWED Kim in his patrol car. He wished he could justify driving to the shelter the same way he had raced toward his apartment. Back then, he at least had some concern about Russell's welfare. But Russell was fine, and Ned couldn't turn on the sirens and lights to escort a dog.

His phone rang. It was Jeb. "Hey Jeb, what did you find out?"

"Well, I got two kids sitting on a bench in handcuffs. Mostly to scare them. I'm not sure I got enough to make anything stick. But I did watch this teenage girl's video, and we might be able to get them for misdemeanor animal cruelty. It was hard to watch, the way that one kid kicked your dog. Is he gonna be okay?"

"Don't know. I'm driving him out to see the vet at the shelter."

"Well, hope the little guy heals up all right. But I gotta tell you, watching what that little kid did to these two bullies. You know, your neighbor? If this thing gets on YouTube, it's definitely going viral. I've never seen anything like it. These boys had him by at least twenty, thirty pounds each. And several inches in height. But man, he made quick work of them."

"Really?" Ned couldn't help but smile. *Good for you, Russell.*

"You should see them now. Black eyes, fat lips, aching all over. I asked them if they need to go to the hospital, but they insisted they don't. They're both crying, promising me they'll do anything if I take these cuffs off and let them go."

Ned could tell, Jeb was asking for advice. They didn't typically arrest kids for fistfights like they did adults. Something Ned didn't always agree with. Especially when a bully situation was involved. But seeing that this time the bullies got the worst of it... "Is the video pretty clear?" Ned asked. "Is it totally obvious my neighbor's in the clear? These boys started the fight?"

"Oh yeah, it's all on them. Your boy was trying to walk away. He didn't do his Karate Kid bit until after they had drop-kicked your dog. Then he was on them like a buzz saw."

"Well how about this, Jeb? Still not sure I want to let these punks off the hook after what they did to my dog. Why don't you bring them down to the station? Keep them in handcuffs. See if you can get their parents to come down. Let the boys sweat it out a bit. I'll give you a call after we hear from the vet about what kind of shape Parker's in."

"Fine with me, Ned. Then that's what we'll do."

Ned looked up. Kim's car was turning into the shelter parking lot.

55

They had been waiting for almost ninety minutes. It turned out, Parker needed a surgical procedure to repair the rib damage. And since there really wasn't a patient waiting room in the infirmary, Doc Porter suggested they either wait in the shelter lobby or Kim's office. She'd let them know the minute he was in recovery.

They chose Kim's office. More privacy in there.

"It was really nice of her to stay after hours to take care of him," Ned said to Kim. "I don't know where we would've taken him if we couldn't have come here."

"I'm not surprised she's doing this. She really cares about these animals. Obviously, she could make a ton more money in a private practice."

Ned looked over at Russell, his face buried in a comic book. About thirty minutes ago, Ned had gone out and picked up a pizza. The place was next door to a convenience store, so he'd stopped in and grabbed some Marvel comics. Thought that would give Russell's mind someplace to go while they waited.

They still hadn't talked much about what took place at the park. Ned was very curious to hear Russell's version but decided to let him wait a while. If they wound up pressing charges on those boys, Russell would have to give an official statement. Ned figured that could wait until after they got news about Parker.

One thing was pretty clear: Russell didn't have a scratch on him. And from what Jeb had said, the other boys were in pretty sad shape. He would have loved to see it go down. But then again, if he really had been anywhere near, his instincts would have been to step in and stop it before anyone got hurt.

This way was actually better.

By the sound of it, Ned doubted these boys would ever give Russell any trouble ever again. And when word got out about this, no one else would bother Russell, either. And that thought was very satisfying. Ned even offered up a silent prayer of thanks.

Something else he was thankful for, unless it was just a figment of his imagination. Kim's whole demeanor during this time of waiting seemed to have changed toward him. He knew Kim to be a basically compassionate, caring person who would naturally be very supportive of him and Russell at a time like this. But he thought he detected something more than that going on.

She was supposed to be knocking out a few emails while they waited, but several times when he looked up at her, he caught her staring at him. Before she turned away, she smiled.

Now what did that mean? Hadn't she just put an abrupt end to the personal side of their relationship? It wasn't surprising to find her stealing glances at him. He was doing the same thing. That could have been nothing more than curiosity.

But why the lingering smile after? That's what didn't make sense.

Suddenly, the phone rang, startling them all. Kim picked it up. "Hello? Hi, Doc. Kinda hoping this was going to be you. What?" Kim released a sigh. "I'm so glad. Okay, we'll be right down."

She stood. Ned and Russell's eyes instantly focused on her face. "Well, Parker made it through the surgery fine. She thinks he'll make a full recovery, but she wants us to come to the infirmary, and she'll fill us in."

"Then let's go," Ned said.

"Will we be able to take Parker home tonight?" Russell asked as they walked into the hallway.

"I don't know," Kim said. "I think you should prepare yourself for him having to stay here a little while."

"Okay," Russell said. "I guess I don't really care where he stays as long as he's okay."

They walked in silence through the mostly empty halls until they reached the infirmary. Dr. Porter was waiting for them outside in the hall. She looked tired.

"So, is Parker going to be okay?" Russell said.

"I think so. He took quite a blow to his side. Cracked three ribs. But the good news is, nothing was punctured and there doesn't seem to be any internal bleeding. Both of those are very good things. I did have to repair things surgically, which involved attaching some pins and wires and screws, to keep his ribs in place. He's still out and will be for another thirty minutes or so."

"Then what?" Ned said. "I'm guessing he won't be coming home tonight?"

"No, I'm going to keep him here, pretty heavily sedated. He's going to need to be kept very still for at least the next three or four days, and I really wouldn't want him to be left alone during that time."

"He wouldn't be, Doc. I'm on paid leave for at least a week," Ned said.

"Well, why don't you call me late tomorrow morning and we'll see if he's well enough to be cared for at home."

"Great. I can do that. What happens after four days? How long before he's healed up enough to run around and be a dog again?"

"Several more weeks at least before that," she said. "But you won't have to wonder when he's ready. He'll let you know." She smiled. "Well, I better get in there and tidy up some loose ends."

"Thanks so much, Doc," Kim said. She gave her a big hug.

Before she walked back into the infirmary, she looked down at Russell. "That was a very brave thing you did, young man. And you watch what happens once Parker gets better. He's not going to forget how you carried him all that way and took care of him until you got here."

Russell smiled. "I'm just so glad he's going to be okay."

The Doc slipped behind the Infirmary door. Kim turned to Ned. "Do you think you could bring Russell home? I've got to finish up a few things in there and shut down my office for the weekend."

"Yeah, I can do that." He looked at Russell. "You ready to go?"

"Yes. Totally."

"Thanks so much, Kim. Really, for everything you did here tonight." They started walking down the hallway.

"Wait Ned," Kim said.

Ned stopped and turned.

"Can I talk to you for just a minute? Alone?"

"Sure. Why don't you wait for me by the car, Russell? I'll be there in a second."

After Russell left, Kim walked up and stood close to Ned. "I was just wondering, after you drop Russell back home, could we meet somewhere and talk. Just for a few minutes?"

"Sure, Kim. Where do you want to meet?"

She thought a minute. "How about that same bench at the lake by the city center?"

"You mean the one where you..." He decided not to say *dumped me*?

"Yeah, that one."

"See you there in about twenty minutes."

56

K im got there a few minutes before Ned but, for safety's sake, waited in her car, parked under a streetlight. The city center park was well lit and not considered a crime area. If anything, just the opposite. In fact, for the most part Summerville was ranked as one of the safest small towns in Florida.

Still though, she felt better getting out of her car when she saw Ned walking toward the bench. When she got to within fifty yards, she stopped for a moment just to look at him. She watched as he gazed across the lake, looked up at the moon and took in the stars, then sat in the same spot he'd sat in a few days ago when she had ended the beginning of their romance.

She realized right then, as she looked at him, that her mother was right. She did love Ned. However it happened, it happened. And she didn't want to be just his dog trainer. She wanted to be more. Much more. She hoped he wasn't too upset at her the way she had ended things and that he'd be willing to give their romance a new start.

She took a deep breath, looked up at the moon, then headed right for Ned. He stood as she arrived. "Hey Ned, thanks so much for meeting with me. I know it's been a long day."

"Are you kidding? I'm not tired. Not anymore. Truth is, I haven't been able to think straight since we left the shelter."

"Why?"

"I've been racking my brain trying to figure out what you want to talk to me about."

He was mostly smiling. "So, you're not mad at me?"

"Mad at you," he repeated, as if the phrase didn't make any sense.

"For the way I ended things between us. I was so confused and upset by what happened. And I wasn't thinking about you at all, about the horrific thing you'd just been through, the kinds of things you must be dealing with inside. I was totally consumed by my own feelings and fears. That was a horrible thing to do, and I want to apologize."

"Oh, is that why you wanted to meet, to apologize?"

"Well, yes. That's part of it." She looked down, wrestling for the words. She should just say it. She looked up, into his eyes. "Ned, the thing is...I love you. And I was wondering if you might still be willing to...be willing to..."

Ned stepped toward her, gently put his hands on either side of her shoulders, drew her close and kissed her softly on the lips. He paused, to see if she was kissing back. She was, so he wrapped his arms around her, pulled her closer in and kissed her again. Fuller, stronger this time. He pulled back and looked down. "I love you, too, Kim. I have for a while now."

She reached up and kissed him again. This time with more passion. And he eagerly responded.

After a few more tender kisses, he looked at her and said, "I don't have to be a cop, Kim. If I can't have you, I don't want to be."

"Oh Ned." Tears welled up in her eyes. She kissed him some more. Then said, "I don't care if you're a cop or sit at a desk all day. I just want to be with you."

57

One Week Later

Ned was meeting Kim for lunch at the city center park. At what both considered *their* bench now. Today was a big day. It was Parker's first day taking a walk of any length since his injury. And it was the last day of Ned's suspension-with-pay. The investigation had completely cleared him, and his normal duties would resume once again in the morning.

Ned looked down at Parker walking beside him. All the stitches, pins and wires had been removed a few days ago, so his coat which had actually been making a comeback, once again looked pretty horrendous. Happily, Parker was oblivious to his appearance. Although he walked a little less steady and quite a bit slower, he held his head up high as they walked together down the sidewalk.

Ned was quite sure that at least part of Parker's enthusiasm was the smells coming from the bag Ned carried in his other hand. Chick-fil-A sandwiches for him and Kim, and a grilled chicken breast, cut up in pieces for Parker.

"Ned!"

Ned looked up. It was Kim, waving and smiling. When he reached her, they kissed and took a seat. "I come bearing gifts."

"I was hoping it was gonna be Chick-fil-A," she said.

"Parker was, too."

He was wagging his tail furiously and doing his best to greet Kim fully, but you could tell it caused him some pain. She bent down and patted him softly on the head. "You poor thing. Are you feeling any better? It's so good to see you outside."

He loved it when she talked to him like that.

"He's really doing very well, considering," Ned said. "And this time off together has really made us Best Buds. He's next to me every moment except the bathroom and the shower, and he wants to be next to me in there, too."

Kim laughed. "How are things going with Russell? Have you seen him much the last few days?"

"Well yeah, pretty much. He's a celebrity now at that school, since that video got out of him creaming those two bullies. And he and I are still going to those self-defense classes on Tuesdays and Thursdays. He's been coming over quite a bit to check on Parker. And of course, Parker goes nuts when he sees him. I think they're going to be best friends for life. Starting tomorrow, since I go back to work like normal, Russell's going to start looking in on Parker for me after school."

"That's right," Kim said. "Today's the last day of your leave."

"You know, Kim, I wasn't kidding last week when I said I don't have to be a cop."

"I know, but we don't have to talk about that now. Whether you do that, or something else, I'm not going anywhere." She leaned over and kissed him on the cheek. "Now do I get my chicken sandwich?"

He smiled and handed it to her. "Found out yesterday what's gonna happen to those two boys who hurt Parker. Couldn't really file assault charges, since they didn't actually hurt Russell. But they will be charged with a first-degree misdemeanor for animal cruelty. No jail time, because it's a first offense, but they've been ordered to pay back the Humane Society for all of Parker's vet bills, in lieu of a fine."

"Wow, our CEO will be glad to hear that. And I'm glad they're not getting away with it scot-free. They need to feel some consequences."

"Yep, although I'm sure they've been feeling them all week, if you know what I mean. Not just from the whupping Russell gave them, but from the humiliation of that video."

"Yeah, I can see that," she said. She took a bite of her chicken sandwich.

Ned was about to eat his, but he noticed Parker sitting there so politely, staring at the bag. "Do you want this?"

Parker's tale started to wag.

"What...this?" Ned pointed inside the bag.

Parker's front feet were prancing now.

"I think you do. I think you want some of this."

"Oh Ned," Kim said. "Give him some."

"I am." He looked back at Parker. "Who's a good boy? Who's a good boy?"

Parker stood, came closer and nudged the bottom of the bag with his nose.

"Okay, you sit back down, and I'll get you some."

Parker instantly obeyed, but he couldn't stop his tail or his front feet from moving. Ned got out the container holding the chunks of grilled chicken breast, opened the lid and waved it front of Parker's nose. Parker licked his lips.

"Ned!"

"I'm giving it to him. I'm just making it special." He looked down at Parker, while holding three pieces of chicken in the palm of his hand. "Who's a good boy?"

WANT TO READ MORE?

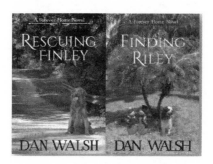

Saving Parker is actually the 3rd book in the *Forever Home Series*. If you've read it first, no harm done. Dan wrote each book in the series to be easily read as stand-alone novels. But we think you'd really enjoy reading the first two books, *Rescuing Finley* and *Finding Riley*. You'll recognize many of the same characters and even some of the same places.

Here are the links for *Rescuing Finley* and *Finding Riley*. You can download either one now and start reading it in minutes:

Rescuing Finley: amzn.to/1Hn0vrg
Finding Riley: amzn.to/2c7xdWY

If Dan is a new author to you and you haven't yet read any of his other novels (there are 18 others in print) you'll be happy to learn most are written in a similar genre and style, although in 2014 Dan also began to write the *Jack Turner Suspense* series. His novels have won multiple national awards and received rave reviews from USA Today and magazines like Publisher's Weekly, Library Journal and RT Book Reviews.

His newer suspense novels have been so well received, Dan has decided to write both kinds of books from now on. As of this writing, his novels have received over 6,000 Amazon reviews (maintaining a 4.6 Star average).

WANT TO HELP THE AUTHOR?

If you enjoyed reading *Saving Parker*, the best thing you can do to help Dan is very simple—***tell others about it***. Word-of-mouth "advertising" is the most powerful marketing tool there is. Better than expensive TV commercials or full-page magazine ads.

Leaving good reviews is the best way to insure Dan will be able to keep writing novels fulltime. So, he'd greatly appreciate it if you'd consider leaving a rating for the book and writing a brief review. Doesn't have to be long (even a sentence or two will help).

Here's the Amazon link for *Saving Parker*. Scroll down a little to the area that says "**Customer Reviews.**" Right beside the graphic that shows the number of stars is a box that says: "**Write a Customer Review.**"

http://amzn.to/2g9vKkA

SIGN UP TO RECEIVE DAN'S NEWSLETTER

If you'd like to get an email alert whenever Dan has a new book coming out or when a special deal is being offered on any of Dan's books, go to his website link below and sign up for his newsletter (it's right below the Welcome paragraph).

From his homepage, you can also contact Dan or follow him on Facebook, Twitter or Goodreads.

www.danwalshbooks.com

Want to Read Some of Dan's Other Novels?

You can check out all of Dan's novels by going to his Author Page on Amazon. Here's the link:

http://amzn.to/2cG5I9o

If you'd like to write Dan, feel free to email him at

dwalsh@danwalshbooks.com. He loves to get reader emails and reads all of them himself.

ACKNOWLEDGMENTS

There are a few people I absolutely must thank for helping to get *Finding Riley* into print. Starting with my wife, Cindi. Not just for her encouragement and support. Over the years, Cindi has become a first-rate editor. She's provided vital editorial help not just with the storyline and characters in this book, but all my novels. I want to also thank my great team of proof-readers, who caught many of the typos Cindi and I missed. Thank you Terry Giordano, Jann W. Martin, Kimberly Spina, Delores Kight, Patricia Keough-Wilson, Debbie Mahle and Rachel Savage.

Dan Walsh

ABOUT THE AUTHOR

Dan was born in Philadelphia in 1957. His family moved down to Daytona Beach, Florida in 1965, when his father began to work with GE on the Apollo space program. That's where Dan grew up.

He married Cindi, the love of his life in 1976. They have two grown children and three grandchildren. Dan served as a pastor for 25 years, then began writing fiction full-time in 2010. His bestselling novels have won numerous awards, including 3 ACFW Carol Awards (he was a finalist 6 times) and 3 Selah Awards. Four of Dan's novels were finalists for RT Reviews' Inspirational Book of the Year.